URWIND

COIMBRA GROUP

Annual Conference 30.5. – 2.6.2007

University of Turku | Åbo Akademi University

BO CARPELAN

....

Urwind

TRANSLATED FROM THE
FINLAND-SWEDISH BY
DAVID MCDUFF

CARCANET

First published in Great Britain in 1996 by
Carcanet Press Limited
402–406 Corn Exchange Buildings
Manchester M4 3BY

Translation copyright © 1996 David McDuff

Translated from the Finland-Swedish, *Unwind*
© 1993 Schildts, Helsinki, Finland

A CIP catalogue record for this book
is available from the British Library.
ISBN 1 85754 250 9

The publisher acknowledges financial assistance
from the Arts Council of England, and warmly thanks
the Finnish Literature Centre for a translation grant

Set in 10.5/12pt Bembo by Posthouse Printing, Findhorn, Forres
Printed and bound in England by SRP Ltd, Exeter

I want
cars, breasts to split apart,
houses to stand on their roofs and the ground to hover in the air
all the lines, the forms be hurled up in the air
like a topsy-turviness,
the colours to scream kaleidoscopically
sounds to split apart, the rapids' boom become the play of strings
and the horn burst in a clap of thunder,
and all be as it is,
from the inside's out. That we stand in balance
on opened street's abyss's walls
and hold house and eyes together.

Gunnar Björling, Sungreen

1 The Name Urwind

On the way in from the airport I saw a lonely man in a deserted parking lot. The snow lay in dirty patches, a January pelt for a slumbering beast of prey. The big supermarket lay there, a rock made of sheet metal, and behind it the sun was setting in a blood-red streak. It was mingled with the heavy odour of scent from the woman in front of me in the bus. The twilight fell quickly. Suddenly the man flared, a torch, stretched up his arms, burned inside my eyes like a choked scream, I would have liked to smash the bus window, but everyone sat motionless, did not see it, the bus went gliding on in its own reflections, from the radio came a droning, incomprehensible voice. Clouds glided swiftly across the sky, pregnant with snow. When I opened my eyes, wet with sweat, the man was gone, all that remained was an empty plain, marshy meadows, clustered suburbs drowning in darkness. The bus glided into an endless tunnel, illumined by lamps with an orange glow. My lips tasted of metal, my clothes were a thin membrane against the world around me, where a violent wind was blowing. We are hurled forward, you in your aeroplane, I in my airport bus, glistening farewells, merely. Each weekday contains its hidden vertigo, it breaks out like a sudden fire, a text that must be interpreted. Perhaps it will illumine my own face, so I will manage to interpret it before it returns to its darkness?

I remember the image of the burning man because I cannot explain it. I am writing a diary for you, you will receive it as a part of me when you come back. You looked at me with your quiet grey eyes and said: It will do us both good to be separated from each other. Perhaps in a year's time we will see each other more clearly. I don't reply, kiss you, you are going among other people, I stand in an empty field and can no longer see you. I came back, washed up the two coffee cups; furniture, room stood empty and lifeless. I could not endure them, went down to the secondhand bookshop, opened up and am now sitting in the study facing the courtyard and writing to you, at long range. Or is to myself that I write, this unfamiliar I that dodges off round each windy corner, letting the wet snow lash me in the face? Fire, water and wind, and that heavy smell from the sea. But I protect myself, I surround myself with books, their silence does not demand anything, they exist, they are alive, they are for anyone to open, unlike us human beings. The green lamp burns, images penetrate behind my eyes, the narrow fanlight that faces the courtyard looks as though it were covered in black paint. I get up and draw the curtain so that no one can spy on me in secret. You will be gone for a year, and I will write reports to you, one for each week. You know me? I bury myself in silence and solitude, I am fifty-three years heavy, no clothes can hide an empty face, a façade. My memory hurls me forward, grows ever more mysterious and contains so many dead people. What cannot be said must be said, by the stranger who sits here with his hands threaded in mine. Blue veins, red knuckles, two sprawling fingers, a text stained by patches of snow. As though I were standing alone in a parking lot, being observed by someone.

You have left silence behind you. The greater the silence around me, the more attention it demands. That is why we drown ourselves in background music, in the droning from the TV, in hundreds of decibels, in iron filings that lie like a thick lump over cities and squares. How frightening they are, a silent, empty street, a gloomy park, a graveyard that creates its own silence, a great, calm sea. We yearn for them and flee from them, now the wind blows towards us, now it hurls us forward, gravel forces its way into our eyes, our breath stands like smoke beneath cold days, then we notice that we have our own wind, our breath. When it stops, the uttermost silence is there. Listen!

I listen. Papa is talking there in the room that faces the street, he has been dead for many years, of course, but I can hear him, the customer leaves, the doorbell tinkles, it is silent. I used to sit here looking out through the fanlight at a pale narrow strip of rear courtyard, it was there in my eye even when I was a child. The room was much bigger then, the table higher, but the light was the same. What bound us together, then? The name? Papa used to say that water, not wind, was our true element. At an exhibition of silver from the Hanseatic era, do you remember, there was a large, glittering goblet with fishes and dolphins, wonderfully dreamt-up and engraved, by the silversmith Heinrich Urwäder. Perhaps he and our progenitor had once met in a Danzig beer cellar, spoken silver and unspoken gold. Wind and weather moved through the two men, Heinrich fair, David dark. From the lane outside comes a howling roar, and the sea swells with beer foam. Both speak within me, the one coarser, the other more absent-minded, more of a dreamer. He must have been, it passes like a brush-stroke through the family and unites, as two watercourses unite, with mother's Cedermark.

I play with the interpretations of Urwind. It is the original primor-dial wind from the universe, the one that blows out of nothing into nothing, hurling stars into that storm-centre that is called the soul. It has its own compass card, it is the invisible symbol of metamorphosis, it exists in bowed trees and the snowy twilight out there. It moves through human beings in love and hatred and hurls them forward, it drives language like a mighty sail before it, it smells of salt and distant lands. It begins from nothing, a gleam of frozen light on the precipice of an ice barrier. It is followed by a rumbling, a landslide of blocks falling down into smoking black water, as if from some unknown continent there might spring a force not yet seen or experienced. It is timeless, it was there before the stars, it is irrational and unpredictable. If you lean forward, you will see through the window of the flight cabin for one giddying moment a part of Greenland's rocky coast falling into the sea, like a cloud in the clear air.

But it is not only silence and mystery, cold from an outer space. It also blows during distant blue voyages, a warm, steady wind, it exists in our dreams, in our happily straying thoughts, in the grass, in the field of grain, in the eye of the child, in the shared movements of two bodies. It has no pattern, it has the blue colour of space. If you capture it, it alters form, becomes the great primordial wind, the room with the shrieking swallows, the rafters, thick as arms, supporting the sky. Constantly it expands, gathers in its dark corners childhood summers, the smell of sun-scorched wood, the dust's golden paths of light laid over floorbeams and sawdust. The *urvind*, the primordial attic, with its forgotten treasures, its yellowed bundles of newspapers, its tattered prams, its dark cupboards of rumbling voices! Towards nightfall it gathers together all the clockwork of human life: sundials, silent now and without shadow, wall clocks with stiffened beards and staring dials, with panting voices, asthmatic breathings and weights heavy with years. There in old wooden chests lie forgotten turnip watches with Roman faces, their time is for ever lost. Does not the child hear a gentle chiming, as though someone had moved there, inside the worn, wooden dress-coat of the grandfather clock? But there is only the second-swift flight and flutter of the swallows. When they are gone, all time comes to a standstill, and the evening rises from the earth out there, slowly approaching the intermediate floor and the dead, grave Junghans clock. It is the *urvind*, the primordial wind, that throws the time this way and that, it exists right at the very top, near the sky. Not that it fares any better in some old manor house out in the country. Perhaps children who still play there turn into birds and come hurtling out, their arms spread like clock-hands, gliding like shadows over the light-flecked, constantly shifting fields of lost summers? In the attic time takes forty winks in an old hammock, it looks like my grandfather and is dressed in a crumpled summer shirt of the sky's colour, it is the prisoner of the attic.

But when the wind that blows there pulls open the attic door, time whirls with passion out of the room, the air is filled with bell-sounds and grinding clockwork. There metal-rattling alarm clocks fly with their furious umbrellas, there the old turnip watches throng in a romping dance with water-clocks and swinging weights, there are corpse-pale clock dials and booming tower clocks that collide with the roofbeams and come falling down in a rain of feathers, cogwheels and clock-hands. It is the rattling cacophony of metallic time we live in, each one of us with our clock dial like a blow in the face, our hands and chains, our dangling weights, our frenzied, incorrigible clocks. The primordial wind cuts deep tracks in our faces, with our wound-up clockwork we fly like birds of prey in the tailwind of time. Daniel! Now your name sweeps you in towards the abysses, and you feel their cold breath. Urwind and Urwäder stand there leaning over you, two giant-like shadows. Wake up, they say with a dark, shared voice, take you by the arm, shake you. You wake up, you see that the green lamp is burning quietly, that the simple things have formed up around you: the coffee cup, the pad, the pen, the table, the sofa-bed. My winter overcoat hangs with weary arms on the hook by the door to the secondhand bookshop. Books stand tightly pressed against books, everything is silent with the unspoken. In two rooms and a cellar thousands of thoughts are waiting to be forgotten or rediscovered, fall as the snow falls out there, in a gentle, crazy whirling.

I know that you think I spend too much time here, in the room facing the rear courtyard. I have a kitchenette, I have had a simple shower room put in, I have my CD player, I have left the TV in our living-room, even if you can scarcely watch it. Do you think I will come back to you from here renewed, like a fiery angel? Can you see my fantastic wings bearing me over the courtyard and up the stairs, am I invisible, perhaps? Is that why I chase my name like a magpie chasing a silver spoon? Forged by the silversmith Urwäder, perhaps, or his colleague Urwind? My first day of solitude is coming to an end, it is late at night, tomorrow I will put out the week's birthday boys, Forster and Salinger, Cicero and Dürrenmatt, by now you will soon be in N.Y. I am falling asleep on the sofa with your gaze so close to me, so hard to capture.

Something has happened, it is morning. I was woken in the middle of the night by the presence of something in the room. I sat up, my heart beating. A faint light behind the curtains revealed a gleam of morning. My feet were dangling over the edge of the sofa, in grandfather's chair sat a child, I could see it, it radiated a peculiar light. It was a little boy, I was seized not only by fear but also by sorrow, as though a whole life had gone past without trace, passed through me as through an empty space and then closed the door. I thought I had experienced all this before, that he came, that he saw me. When he perceived that I was awake, that I was leaning forward, he quickly slid down from the chair and ran in the semi-twilight to the door to the rear courtyard, opened it and was gone. The chill of morning swept in with the smell of waterlogged snow. I sit and write, to whom? The man who burned, the child who disappeared, they are all vague signs, and I try to capture the intangible in words as though I were looking for something, someone, to remember.

Snow has fallen, it is several degrees below zero, and Monday. There are the footprints of the boy who ran from my door. Life is so weightless that it is scarcely perceived before it is over, so heavy that it feels like a torment, a void that is you, and must be filled. Have I any name at all? If I knelt down there in the courtyard and peeped in through my window, what would I see? The unmade sofa-bed, the light falling from the shower room, the chair, the dark bookshelves. I would see the table and the lamp, at the table no one.

2 The Pursuer

The cold strikes, forcing the house's inhabitants into bundles of clothes
and snowy silence. Sounds reverberate like gashes in the bright air. The
silence expands towards evening and the darkness arches with black
starry heavens. Life's pattern seems hammered into my consciousness
with steel nails. Houses interpenetrate, and the dreams that are dreamt
behind closed doors are secret or obliterated by ice-floes. They drift
into black floatways along the quays, where in the mornings the smoke
rises towards a sky fragile as glass. Sparking snow-ploughs churn up
their black tracks in my sleep at night. Everything that happens
happens slowly at this furtive time. People walk in their own blackness,
it is only the children who roll like motley-coloured spools of thread
in and out of the snow of the parks. Each morning the dawn comes
that tiny bit earlier. No one notices it, it stands unheeded in the cold.
Again a week has drifted by, I have stood in the secondhand bookshop
and sold tranquillity to those who need it, erotic ardour to the hungry,
Gustaviana to a remote expert who engaged in an odd, passionate
conversation about the cold behind the burning masks, about those
bloodstains that led from the bedchamber via the tavern to the guillo-
tine, about geniuses who were shovelled unnoticed into paupers'
graves, about the salons' whiff of dirt and excrement. 'Away with time
we hurrying whirl, and that we live we know it not.' Is that so unlike
today's anguish-ridden life, laboriously concealed by social welfare,
flaking away like an icy wall before capricious, merciless winds? Those
tender passions, those powdered wigs, that amorous rapture, those
beer-distended rapes, those courteous heel-clickings, and also: this
pure image of you who stand so clearly before my eye: 'At night, when
gale and tumult burden others' ears, then hope lulls me to sleep: in
dreams I seem to hear a weak, deceptive ice, by storm-wind strained,

and the oar's power on the water quickly reattained.' He goes, the Gustavian, with a little volume of Nordenflycht, and I return to my absent-mindedness. What is the present? A moment, merely, which we don't have time to capture. Newspaper headlines, rules of conduct, party programmes, white paper and printer's ink float above a frozen city, and curiosity, life-giving, colour-imparting curiosity becomes a bleary eye at a keyhole. If we could see as children do, then houses, staircases, rooms and the human beings in them with their stunted shadows would acquire their true proportions. Colours would glow, surprises fill our days, warmth stream out of dammed-up forms.

I have read your letter, you have arrived, everything is new and strange, you are burning with eagerness to get started. What have I to offer apart from weather and wind? Like a woodworm I try to bore my way further. Mask and *mask* [worm]: how strange the coincidences and ambiguities of language are, and the images they conjure up from the underworld: quick changes of face, figures that find their way up from cold-saturated ground, death-screens white as chalk in a darkness where the cold rows of lights from the motorways gleam with their exhausted, empty distance. Masks, masks, and behind them, inside them, the same suffering human beings, the same longing.

Bernt dropped by with his blinking eyes, his pin-shaped body that twines itself round every thought he spins out of himself, suddenly he stopped and looked at the window: who is that person? I turned round but saw nothing. He insisted that the figure had burning eyes, moved sideways and blew sulphur at the windowpane, that disaster and ruin were nigh and could be detected in the slightest and most insignificant changes: a knife that fell from the table and landed with its end stuck in the floor, a magpie that chattered all night, strange explosions from the sea to the south, a luminous cloud with the features of Hitler. His eyes gleamed with happy excitement, and I too grew animated, brought out two glasses. When he had gone, I hung up the Closed For The Occasion sign – what occasion? – and went out the back way. The masonry, the house-wall, everything seemed familiar, and a boy stood, indistinct as a shadow, in the entrance, and then disappeared. I saw that my door was peeling, that the cold had left white frost-marks on the house-fronts. Windows reflected moving clouds, in the clear air there was much disturbance, it blew out of me like smoke. A few frozen pigeons clung firmly to the metal windowsills or flew up with rattling wing-beats: so ugly.

There, suddenly, stands the lad with in the black leather jacket and blood-red-gleaming motor-cycle helmet. I carry my childish heart on the outside of my winter sweater, it throbs with the wing-beats of the pigeons. In the black perspex in front of his face you see a mirror-image of yourself, your round face with its wide open eyes. In a flash he seizes you under the arms and raises you up against the fire wall, his chewing jaw is right up against you, your knitted sweater rides up, he breathes with tortured breaths, raising you higher and higher, holding you over the wall. Parts of you fly like sparks of terror down into the abyss below you, you lean backwards, you are rigid, already dead and yet a stifled scream, your eyes see black house-roofs and a white sky, you have already fallen, all is silent, you are a living, burning body, blood and bones being transformed into death, your mouth is open, you see it all, you are lost, refuse being thrown away.

He puts you down as suddenly as he grabbed hold of you. Fuck off, scram, his voice is indifferent, he turns and goes, strolls away, I lie in the snow and am merely eye, snow, sparkling light, breathing, my body's sweat. A window is thrown open, a familiar voice calls: Daniel! What are you doing? Come upstairs! I crawl upstairs, so small am I, my knees almost sewn to my chin, there is no one in the neighbourhood, no one has seen my shame, my fear. Violence and walls, streets and ravines divide people from one another, and the great silence in the entrance sucks me into it as though I were a lost mitten. I cover my face with it, it is cold and damp with frozen snow, that is what it was like, the burning skin, the smell of melting wool, the cries of the playing children blending with those of the birds. Round every corner, outside closed doors, on unfamiliar staircases, waits the pursuer, he is invisible and smells of garlic, sweat and metal, he carries a stiletto, he is a shiny metal nail hammered into your heart. Turn round, and you see a magpie on the coping of the wall; it is scornfully measuring the silence with its tailfeathers.

. The heavy door to the staircase is like a block of stone, I struggle and pull, it opens soundlessly into the entrance, where all the dead are gathered to look at me, for I am quite small and Mamma has just knitted for me, with effort, pointed cap, sweater and mittens, she has made them all and padded them, and I struggle and pull. Now I need you, Maria, but you aren't there, you can't see my runny nose and my heart blinking like a lamp in the snow. Calm down, I say to myself, there is no one here, no one means you any harm, no one is waiting for you on the stairs, tranquil sounds are coming from behind closed doors, there are the Laaksonens and the Bergströms, your home is somewhere here, and someone called out to you, recognized you, it was Aunt Viktoria, who sees and hears everything. And the traffic, calmly and silently flowing on! The crosses of the windows stand silent. The war will soon be over, says Papa. Viktoria says we shall be married in the autumn, she will give up everything and go with me to Madagascar, that is what she has told me, but it is not always to be relied on. In to the staircase comes Mrs Rosendal, she sees me, I am sitting on a cold step, like a blind man. What are you doing? she asks silently, are you going to see your aunt? I nod, she pulls me into the lift, her warmth surrounds me, the winter cap is a mighty bird's nest on top of her head, she pants and gives off steam, we are hoisted aloft, if I close my eyes I can hear the faint creaking of the lift, walls and staircases fall away and a cold wind carries us, it is still there inside me, it is perspicacity's heart.

Mrs Rosendal rolls out of the lift and is about to close the door, but I follow. I don't want to ride alone. I would rather walk. She nods to me. There is a smell of friendly solitude about her. She is one of those people you walk past, one of those whom no one stops in order to exchange a few words, she is fat, she has lived in the house for a long time, she was here before she was born, she closes her door as silently as she follows her life, she expects nothing of existence other than shopping, cleaning, keeping the memory of her dead husband alive, cemeteries do not frighten her, she smiles at me. Greet your Papa, she says surprisingly, tell him that Roald is coming on a visit soon, your Papa's cousin Roald, can you remember? That's what he writes. How old do you think I am? She looks at me with her clear blue eyes, I don't know what to answer, I whisper: Fifty. She begins to laugh, her whole body shakes, she shuts the lift door with a determined slam, she looks back, say thirty, she says, she opens the door and vanishes. For a moment in eternity we will ring at her door, Maria, one hot day in July, but I do not know it yet, my life is that of a child in its beginning, the city has not frozen yet, grown-ups have not yet become grown-up, the dead are still alive and will only be forgotten when no one can hear their voices any more in the wind-tormented house.

3 Snow Letter

I have written you a snow letter. The day was clear, with clouds like
drifting mist, woolly and small. In January the wind's paintbrush is
allusive and creates distance. But the darkness rises from the forests
around the city; a pregnant bank of cloud, blue-violet, is suddenly
there, and it gets dark in the middle of the day. Then it reaches my
room, too, and the silence thickens. The first snow falls, gleams like dust
and down in the light from the setting sun. Then the snowstorm is
there, whirls through gateways and along streets, stops, rises, turns,
rushes onwards again beneath the courtyard's swaying lamps. How
long did I sit there, on the staircase, after Mrs Rosendal slammed her
door shut, as I watched the darkness rising, stair by stair? Each year is a
snowflake, it blows around between now and the past. A door crashes
shut, a door crashes open, out flies a grey soldier's uniform and is
followed, mumbling and swaying, by a man in long johns while a
woman screams: Swine! And again the staircase booms with a door
being slammed shut. People trudge through one another, leaving traces
of blood. Groaning, he puts his clothes on there on the staircase, sees
me, leans forward as though he were examining a rare insect, his breath
smells of spirits, he says: Goddammit, one of these days I'll shoot that
woman, it's a damn sight better to be at the front! Do you understand?
He takes me with a large, hot hand under the chin, the frost wells up
like a mighty breath from the underworld, the whole house breathes
under an immense pressure, ice-floes slam shut, I look into his eyes,
they expire, are dead, he gets up and totters down the staircase, in the
whirling snow he makes his way across the courtyard, trailing the
jacket of his uniform behind him, here on the staircase all is quiet, pale
and shabby. If the door slams down at the bottom I hold my breath. As
I pass my hand over my face the mitten is still wet, how invisible and

lovely it feels, the coolness over my forehead, over my cheeks, around my neck. I feel it now, I stand in the shower room and slowly lift my face, take in my gaze, it watches without curiosity the man taking his shower, then turns away, a light goes on in the room behind him, it grows dark, the door is closed.

A tremor passes through the air, the wind increases, the stairwell shakes, I begin to crawl up the stairs to Viktoria on all fours, I am a purposeful steambath, driven by fear, my sweater is too tight. If now I were to slip and fall I would curl up like a hedgehog, a ball of wool. It would roll down each step with soft thuds, no one would see me, I would fall like a dark ball out through the door, roll out through the gateway into the back yard. There an old woman in an apron would catch me in her wide skirt, she would carry me home to her one-room flat on D staircase, sighing she would put me on her kitchen table, shake the snow from the grey shawl around her shoulders, take out two thick knitting needles of fragrant wood and begin her spectacle-squinting, humming, quivering labour of creating a sweater, one of the many sweaters in her life. Everyone knitted during the war. I rest in her lap, gradually unravel, roll around in her coarse hand. I give a squeak in there, oh-ing and ah-ing she frees me from the yarn, I am smaller than a clenched fist, that is how small I am. I feel it hurt me in every limb, this soft fall from stair to stair. She opens her door, shows me the way back, now I sit here and write, she could have no inkling of that, she is long since dead.

How heavy it feels to struggle up this cold and vertiginous stairwell while the snowstorm quietly rages out there. It is as though I had been making my way up here for decades and had slowly grown, become heavier, acquired eyes ever more hesitant, ever more difficult to find the way with. But Viktoria is surely waiting for me, why, we shall get married this autumn, she says. I sniff the air. At the Bengtssons' they are frying herring, where did they get it? Out under the door it streams, bones, spines, dead heads, dead eyes. At the Pietinens' they are listening to the news, there is the sound of Sibelius, a woman is screaming: 'If you touch me, I'll leave!' Hot lava penetrates across the thresholds, here anyone at all may give up the ghost without anyone hearing, snow whirls in through the windows and covers all those who are asleep, they lie in rows as along wintry roads near the front. Each window is a darkness, each stair a year of my life – how many years do I have left?

I no longer count my years. But I still feel as though someone were following me up the staircase, and everyone who goes there stops and listens: no, that was an error, you are alone. Who is listening behind the doors you do not know. Bengtsson, Pietinen, Rista, Peterzen, Kivinen, Berg, and Cedermark. No, Viktoria is not listening at the door, she hears me inside herself, she is writing me a long snow letter, I hold it like an icetray on my splayed fingers, it melts and leaves only a wet hand behind it. I remember that there on the staircase I would have gone into anyone's apartment, slipped like an invisible letter through the letterboxes, I saw the hallways, the dark clothes, the pocket torch with its blackened eye, its white crack of light, I move about in the living room, the radio glows, the tap in the kitchen leaks, the lower part of the blackout curtains are covered by a grey woollen blanket against the cold and the draught. I am the speck of dust or the snowflake in the filtering light.

Suddenly the memory and the silence are always dispersed, a door opens with a crash, out tumbles a shouting, shrieking, many-coloured flock of padded small children, and I stand, as then, pressed against the wall. There are small, round faces, windproof jerkins, boots, knitted caps, rucksacks with English slogans, some flow down the handrail, others shout for joy, pull at the lift door, gleam a thousandfold in the mirrors, a boy whom I think I recognize runs past, he is the mirror image of my eyes, he looks at me, yes, without curiosity his gaze lifts and meets mine in the mirror, now the entire flock streams out across the back courtyard and scatters like sand in the snow, the door to the beating-balcony is open. A magpie flies twittering up and writes with its long tailfeathers an invisible text in the clear January air. Now I can see Viktoria's blue door. On it hangs a fragrant Christmas wreath, it is small, soon it will wither, like one from a child's funeral. How raw and cold it is, and near the stars. And the wind can be heard, in the distance. Old grandfather Berg opens his door and peeps out, he has the beard of a Santa Claus and follows with his eyes everything that moves on the staircase, lets in children he does not like and hides them under his bed, Stina told me that, she is in my class and is top of it, she knows. Be careful of him, Daniel! But he smiles at me toothlessly and shuts his door, soundlessly. I reach up for Viktoria's bell, I see myself already in her room, I see everything a little before it happens, it feels like an emptiness in my stomach.

4 In Viktoria's Room

In the hallway there is a smell of warmth, and Viktoria squints at me and asks how old I am now, I have grown since last time, I am a big rascal, soon we will be able to stand before the altar together, she laughs hoarsely, and the birthmarks in her face darken. She goes ahead of me down the corridor to her room, all the other rooms she has ever had have been rented, only the most necessary things are left, but all brilliance comes from within, Daniel. And she looks at me with her large, pale eyes. They were dark as Andalusian nights once, says Viktoria, they saw so much that was foreign, then one grows dark, but perhaps you won't understand that, even though you say you are fifty. And Maria, your little playmate, is she fifty, too? They all go rushing around with their years and experience, but I sit here and look at clouds in the sky, and sometimes they are just steam on my windows, or my eyes, what do you think? Viktoria lights her fourth cigarette of the day, she rations them strictly, but the ration is a generous one, what other enjoyment is there in life? In Cairo I nearly burned down the whole hotel, that was when I went to sleep with a cigarette in my mouth, that was when David was alive.

She looks at me from under deep, violet eyelids. Suddenly she can sink into silence, she sits motionless and travels far away, you must learn that art, it is the only way to survive. Papa used to say that she had travelled her whole life away. Once she had had a lot of money, she accepted gladly what David gave her, she was beautiful and still is, she was merely broken accidentally by sorrow and death, David, the children. One daughter is left, lives in Australia, Mamma knows everything but tells very little, they sit together, she and Aunt Viktoria, and remember and experience. There are so many colours, sparkling and corroding, their effect can be seen on Victoria's skin, as though she had spent her life on the oceans, sailed like an albatross on upward-moving windcurrents. How do you live that secondhand bookshop life of yours, she asks me. Do you sit like me, listening to the future, in which many dead voices can be heard? Do you want coffee or fruit-juice, one always supposes that children want fruit-juice, but you are no child, or are you? Dani still looks out from your adult face. Today my hands are trembling more than usual; people with their firmly-rooted, sordid outlook on things think I'm an alcoholic, and they are not entirely wrong.

She falls silent and sinks into wandering, absent-mindedness; we have learned how to sit silent together. Then she studies me: Anna and Fredrike waited a long time for you, do you know that? But you were abroad, travelling, in their dreams I suppose, and I used to tell them: he'll come. As vividly as you've dreamt of him. From the wind he'll come, like a snowflake, and here you are now, name and all. She laughs, she has a lot of gold fillings, her hair is always a little wild around her face, catching the last light outside, she always smells old-fashioned, lavender, you also smelled like that, when I met you at any rate: a pure, unornamented smell.

I sit at Viktoria's table, a stained disc of wood, I help her to drink, bring the cup to her mouth, light her trembling cigarette, there are wrinkles around her mouth and eyes as though she had been squinting at the sun for a long time and been burned by it. She tells of people who fly around her rooms, of birds that pop up between the books in Papa's bookcase, exotic, magnificent, how their singing fills the nights with its ecstasy, only to fade and vanish towards morning when the sea resumes its song. She tells of shipwrecks in completely calm seas, the silent sinking, the dark eddies. She tells of what she saw when the Egyptian graves were opened and a cold shadow from a dead Pharaoh passed through her, of cities where one can live without ever knowing debt, of when Mamma and she were small and hid behind a rhubarb leaf when the Dragon was looking for them. She says: human beings are riddles, you try to read them but don't understand them, and you yourself are impalpable and will fall into the grave, wondering, confused, grateful, too. Perhaps our wandering thoughts turn into birds when we are gone? Who thinks about mortality when he is young? We are immortal far beyond thirty, then some black moment eventually stops us, some give up, they don't show it but they have resigned themselves, there are quite young people who do so, are forced to do so. If I don't understand my life, who will understand it ? And it is so strange, stranger than the table in here or the tree out there, they will be there when I am dead, you shall have them both, Daniel, I will give you them. The blue table is perhaps easier to own, the tree is harder, but public property it is not, it is yours when you see it, it stands with arms of snow, as fine as nerves. To live one's life, what else is there to do here? Eat your sandwich, it's a miracle. Whole and pure I have tried to be, that was always what your grandmother preached, you remember her, she lives so near us after all, every day we have something to tell each other, even if I have to compose her side of the conversation. That way I am always learning something. Whole – do I look completely whole? Used up – but whole. What's your opinion, little Daniel? I know what your Papa usually says about me: that I am absent a little too often. Like hiding under a table and listening to what the big, grown-up people come out with in their arrogance, or wisdom, or both, simultaneously. It's so dark in January, oughtn't we to turn it into June? Have another sandwich. I like to watch your legs, they're like the pendulum of a chiming clock. You have all the time in the world, Daniel, but mine is starting to be on the wane. I don't think we shall get married. I think we shall be good friends.

Those are words she managed to remember and whispered to me before she died. I am looking at my legs. Indeed, they sway to and fro, they don't touch the floor. The room is silent, Viktoria dark against all the snow light out there, where the wind whirls up like mist towards the edge of the roof. Viktoria's hands are long, narrow and sinewy, all unease is in them, but now they rest on the table, drum impatiently sometimes, her gaze is the gaze of a young girl. The few items of furniture she has left from her long life, an old secretaire, three white chairs from grandmother's house, the table, the old mahogany bed where she lay when she was still young and her lovers called her Olympia, the conch shells, an old Inca statue, three of Mamma's watercolours, they all surround her with great trust. Something about her is always inexplicable, as around people who walk alone and do not show their sorrow. From her room one can see the city where it lies with its raw winds, see the sea, see the open streets, see the rear courtyard's black footprints in white snow. She strokes her face, leans forward and looks at me as though she were clothing herself in my body, it is like a pain in some part of me.

Then suddenly a ring is heard at the door. Viktoria stiffens, she whispers to me: go and see who it is, look through the peephole! I'll move up a chair. And I climb up, put my eye to the small glass pupil, there is the young lad in his black leather jacket, he has taken off his helmet, he brings his plum-shaped head to the door, opens his mouth, then slowly withdraws, vanishes. I tell her in a whisper who it was. He thinks he's my son, says Viktoria. Perhaps he is?

She is so pale, her voice thin, like the paper in front of me, God knows what has been tormenting her these last years, here in the study she has sat, nervously smoking her Gauloises until one could cut the air with a knife, what she and you talked about remained a secret, I sat and read, listened to you, all those sharp, brilliant moments in eternity. But now she beckons to me to follow. Wait a moment! Is the door to the street closed? The till locked? Life tidied up for new events? It is all happening here and now, the past is waiting for me, it has the blue colour of her eyes.

5 Pay Attention

Viktoria goes ahead of me, her secrets screw themselves into the raw, cold air down the kitchen staircase that leads straight into the bowels of the earth and comes out in Japan – Papa told me that. There all traffic stops in astonishment, and all you have to do is to calmly turn round and close the door, then no one can get at you. Viktoria's face is pale in the light from the courtyard window. People who walk downstairs age quickly, their feet look as though they were constantly afraid of falling. I let my hand slide along the cold, sweaty iron banister, in the wall of the staircase sullen cold cupboards are concealed, there war vegetables and war potatoes spread their revolting smell, there stand secret bottles of fruit-juice with unreadable labels, there are ventilation holes for those who are locked in, and there rusty padlocks hang. Outside the inner courtyard flies with walls pressed together in the echo of booming dustbin lids. Everything is so old, even the rats that fatly flee into their own darkness. On a wire rope stretched between the blotchy walls sits a blackbird, attentively following the invisible events in the air, turning its yellow beak as though pulled by a jerky hand. Come on! Victoria hisses, pulls me downstairs, I am not a child any longer after all, I realize that she has secrets, grown-ups flee at once when someone rings at the door, dragons stand there, hissing. All grown-ups look so peculiar, I will grow up and hide, and then they will not get hold of me. The city's streets stretch like tensed wires out towards fields and forests, they stand like steel-plate shields against the enemy. January is moving towards its close and all is tottering, the people on the slippery pavements, the birds in their ice-channels, stone is laid upon stone, and mighty hoisting cranes rise above razed fields in the winter mist. The mist has lain there since the war. On the winding staircase there are no names on the doors, they stand utterly silent and show their backs. Viktoria stops and knocks at the door with a bony and mottled fist, a man in a white coat opens it, he nods and we pass a dark kitchen with washing-up, pots, a gas stove, into a studio where the light is streaming from high, misted windows down on to easels and canvases, the floor is made of broad boards, it smells of turpentine and paint. Viktoria and Hannes, who is a painter, talk quietly to each other while I look at a canvas of black beams falling on to a white field.

Go now, says Viktoria to me. Hannes will see you to the door, then you'll be on your right staircase. What is my right staircase? Hannes grunts into his beard, he has very small eyes that glitter like tinfoil, he opens the door and says: Come back when you want to! He smiles and closes the door, accept it as it is, as always. The staircase gleams with dead steel and polish, everything that happens here happens quickly. The lift is silent on the bottom floor, it has cables and rubbish on its head. I go down the stairs and see a passage and a door leading to a grey-white courtyard. It suddenly opens and a big old man with long, unkempt hair pushes in, carrying a bare lady with wings, she is completely white, even whiter than Viktoria. He shuffles over to the lift, his eyes are watery and his voice thin and squeaky, he is dressed in old army clothes, women! he shouts, women! his mouth reeks garlic and sulphur, he steps back. Panting, he puts the white lady down on the floor, presses the button, the lift is already there, though, he grows furious as he opens the iron gate and I hold on to the door he groans, Heaven! Hell! The four elements! Come along! No pardon! Children must do what they're told! As he hauls me inside, three witches appear, walk with rattling heels along the hallway, they are dressed the same, they have fur coats and blonde, sleeked-back hair, headbands made from the tails of wild animals, blood-red fingernails, each one is wrapped in her own cloud of scent, their unkempt hair cries: More women! Room for more women! And they all squeeze themselves into the lift, glittering and gleaming with suppressed laughter, they look askance at the white statue but the unkempt old man shows them his teeth in terrible grimaces, I stand pressed in a corner, there is a mirror with a picture of us, that makes everything twice as crowded so I have to get down and crawl between their legs, they squeal and laugh. The whole lift shakes with something suppressed and unspoken, it struggles up and stops, it is emptied of everything, of the three witches, of the old man with the wild hair, of the white statue, they do not look back, I am both large and small, I have seen everything, doors bang, it goes quiet. Every time I enter a staircase I hear it, the silence.

I must choose. If I go downstairs, it will all begin again. If I go upstairs, perhaps Viktoria will still be there, and the Painter. I go upstairs, the staircase goes reluctantly up inside me, each step is a breath, but through the window the courtyard lies white as a sheet. I sit on the stairs, listening. There is a very faint music, there are flecks of light and faint echoes, it constructs corridors in me, it is lonely as I am and smells of February. If I listen carefully, time really does move backwards, the morning comes, it is night and evening and day. What's your name, asks a friendly voice, why are you sitting here, where do you live? She sits beside me, she is the angel with the white wings, she is wearing a large knitted cardigan. Daniel, I whisper, Daniel, she says, have you got lost? I shake my head, I want to go back to Viktoria, the angel smiles and takes me by the hand. Come!

I try to look at her attentively. She has a narrow face and a large mouth. One eye squints slightly, it is looking for something outside the staircase. Her cardigan smells cleanly of soap. I lean forward, it is as though a great sleep were falling over me, as though all my protection were there, with the girl who is an angel and will soon fly away. Come! she says again, take my hand, and like a bridal couple we climb the stairs, hover like snowflakes in the silence. Do you recognize yourself? she asks, do you know what door you must ring at, are you from here at all? I hesitate, am I from here at all, do I come from the other side of the globe, perhaps I am in Japan, she looks Japanese, she has dark hair with a fringe, slanting eyes, red mouth, she is no angel at all! I tear myself away from her hand, there is Hanne's door, I recognize it, it has moved here in order to save me, I ring and ring, the door opens and Hannes sticks out his beard, and I cry. I think your boy's got lost, says the Japanese woman, smiling, and Hannes smiles at her, he nods and thanks her and hauls me inside. I wipe my tears with the arm of my pullover, Viktoria sits on a stool watching me, I am a grown man after all, an experienced secondhand bookshop owner, a heavy and stubborn bookworm, what am I doing here, in what room of memory do I find myself now, what time is being slowly torn open, like a ripped web? It is all turning into rags and tatters. I want back to the origin, the starting point, the innermost despair in me, I walk through the studio, it has a colder light now, Viktoria follows me, she has grown older, soon she will be dead and gone. We struggle heavily up the kitchen stairs we left an eternal moment ago, we are back in her kitchen. I lift my head from the table, we listen. But no one rings, no one stands outside the door, it is too early, what we are experiencing is set in the future. I will meet you, Maria, I will share my life with you, I am in my beginning and hear Viktoria's voice: Daniel! Listen! Pay attention! One day all the confusion will be over, all the torment and the unexplained, you will learn to live in the great absent-mindedness, that opens all doors and windows, so that the light can flow in and lead you away. Where? Do not ask where. Live your life, that is the answer. Don't forget to remember, it leads you forward. Oh, Daniel, you are still a child, you have such happy, attentive eyes. Don't lose them, Daniel! Be inquisitive! Pay attention! Do you promise?

She held her hands so tenderly around my head. It was long ago, in a dark, friendly corner of paradise.

6 The Restaurant Kitchen and the Stilén Family

I realize that you are working hard and that the demands over there are different from what we are accustomed to here. I run over to check the post every day, and at home it is empty and silent. When – if – you read this you will notice that I have not been idle, either. When I returned from Viktoria's just now nearly all the doors on the staircase were ajar, and pale faces peeped out, some stood outside their doors, as though they were homeless. It seemed to me as if they were all dead, only their clothes remained, and a mask before a crumbled face. I was inside them all, in the accountant and the engineer, in the charwoman and the schoolchild, I saw with my eyes into their bodies, it felt so strange and frightening, and I rushed down the stairs and in the gateway was immediately sucked into the restaurant kitchen that moved in last year and now seems to be expanding in all directions. I stood in a gigantic glittering room with steel tables like mirroring ponds beneath powerful, spiralling fluorescent tubes that spread their icy torrent of light over the big room. On pulleys along the far wall animals' carcases hung on hooks like swollen overcoats, and beside a meat grinder, lonely with its bald, red snout, lay the head of a pig. Control panels blink rhythmically, and the gigantic boiling vats quiver with dammed-up energy. Against the black background of the kitchen ranges the copper cauldrons flash with white steam that is sucked up by air-conditioning ducts with a faint but distinct hum. On the floor beside the meat grinder lie two tomatoes, rolling in an invisible draught. Beneath the windows that display a white sky lie the great aquariums with their listless fish and slowly crawling crustaceans; mouths open like kisses and blow out air-bubbles, claws are raised in helpless greeting; then the swing door opens and in rushes a thin man in a tall, white chef's hat, the empty kitchen is filled with his raging, it ferments, it bubbles, it seethes, invisible substances are ground in steel-gleaming vessels, fed into the automats, boiled, fried and consumed. Here there is a smell of human flesh. But only the chef is in view, he jerks a frying pan towards him and throws a pancake up in the air as he hisses at me: Go away! Out of here! And the pancake falls like an enormous, rigidly gleaming coin with a terrible crash, down into the pan. It sounds like a thunderstorm, the lighting atrophies and flares up again.

This is the world's kitchen, here people will come gushing in, groaning with hunger they will throw themselves over shining steel, white tiles, freezers with reinforced glass, with their hands in boiling water they will scoop from white foam the red meat, the steaming potatoes, dead fish will be ripped open, rivers of sauces will flow between those that crawl on the floor, the alarm bell will rustle up a horde of waiters and stewards, and while in a corner the head chef distributes the truffles in the ready-prepared dishes with two crossed beans, a slice of carrot cut like a deathshead and the gleaming pepper steak, the supplicants, the beggars and the mute, gaping children are driven outside. Curt shouts of command are heard in there, white napkins flash by like lightning, steam wraps the combatants in an odour of fat and cabbage.

Then Beda Stilén catches sight of me, her sleeves are rolled up, she is blotchy with heat, her arms pale as pork sausages, she pulls me along with her, she shouts in my ear, that Stig has been looking for me all day, and then Daniel comes and hides here, she drags me over wet floors and wilting lettuce, into the narrow hallway of the Stilén household, where there is always a smell of dead mice, and where the clothes hang in constant darkness, as though they were trying to hide. And it is silent, warm, blessedly silent. In the living room stands a large, unwieldy cupboard, into which the whole family can get and hide if necessary, they may have done that during the war, when Stig and I were born, there are the marks of bullets and sharp nails, the cupboard is a big coffin, painted black. In his padded chair sits Mr Stilén, small and ominously silent, he has shiny, side-combed hair with a white parting, once upon a time he was the house concierge, now he has been promoted to supervisor by Manager Jansson who only has one eye, but a giantlike one, says Papa.

Herman Stilén is in his shirtsleeves, he has a black waistcoat and an old-fashioned watch on a chain. He usually takes care of the simpler electrical tasks, with a mini-screwdriver he sets to work on connections and plugs as though he were trepanning the house's skull. He is full of suppressed energy, he charges himself up and explodes in controlled snortings: Watch this! Mongsewer Daniel! In yer own! Exalted! Person! Stig sits with his carrot-red hair and grins at me, he swings his legs while he gives his Papa anxious glances, and in between he grimaces as though he secretly wanted order me around. So it has always been, cramped, shut-in, unspoken. Beda circles around Herman but he hisses: into the kitchen with you, woman, and she sails out in her stained apron after giving me a caress that feels like a box on the ear. It is silent in the room with the heavy dark-painted chairs, the mighty table with bevelled legs, silent as on the wall tapestry with the shore, the birch, the elk and the water-mirror of the bay. A grey, stable light always falls into this room, from which the family can follow everything that happens down in the courtyard.

We used to play Old Maid here, Stig and I, and test each other on our homework. At its best, it was work, effort, assertion, stubbornness, weight and influence. All the rest is hidden madness. I could sometimes see it in Stig, how behind his eyes a wild look set in, it drew him with an iron hand out of his lumbering body and made him restless, constantly talking, manic. In between, he would sink into the same rigidly gazing silence as his pater's. Yes, pater is the right expression, a stern little pater with a waistcoat, watch-chain, mouse-grey belly, a silence stitched firmly to one and the same table through his whole life, with those red, blunt hands tightly gripping the worn armrests, patched with leather by the loud-voiced Beda, clattering in the kitchen next door, clattering and clattering: the kitchen is her life, her realm and curse. Sometimes she has fits of crying, and then Herman says to her sharply: Mamma! Control yourself!

She pinches her mouth together, flames rise into her face, with her sleeve she wipes dust from the family photograph on the cupboard, from Granny's room there comes a shrill What? What? but no one hears, we are all four silent as a Sunday. In spite of violent daily cleaning there is a smell of cloth and cooking fumes, and something heavier: a mild contempt, I know it, I am the bookworm's boy and books are something one can do without except when it's a matter of struggling grimly forward. Herman sits and observes, and there in the stillness it is as though I might suddenly ride switchback into his motionless head with its white parting, as though with his heavy eyelids I saw the world as a narrow strip of light under a door, I sit with his arms and hands, they are clenched, they look at the strange boy as though he were a threat to this very limited, precisely planned life. He sits and observes. He concentrates in himself all supervision, not only of the house but also of the people who live there. Those impractical numbskulls. In his thoughts he flicks invisible crumbs off his waistcoat with his fingers, he sits with his feet in their black shoes slightly turned inwards. Suddenly he gets up, beckons to me, goes over to the window, I follow. I don't suppose you've ever had a car? There. Look there. My car. Not used yet. When it gets warmer. If you have connections you get things more cheaply. Isn't that so, Stig? He pulls him gently by the hair, says: Top of the class! What do you say? Will you pass your driving test in a few years' time? Take Daniel for a trip through the town. It will do him good to get away for a bit, away from the dark and the dust. Isn't that so, Daniel. No, no one can lead Herman Stilén up the garden path. He laughs, shortly. Something dark and pompous permeates everything here, the wedding bouquet that stands like a mummy on the top shelf of the cupboard, the window with its pale cross turned out towards the sky with its flying clouds, the heavy brown curtains that hang motionless, everything holds its breath and yet fills the room to bursting-point, and life runs along the walls and is gone. It has all been accumulated with dry passion. The devil, he says, the devil drives us to sloth, mark my words. He marks them, one by one. You are a remarkable man, Bergsrådinna Petri said to me yesterday. I mended their crystal chandelier. If I'm needed, I'm there. He shows his bunch of keys: the key to the gateway, to the stairs, to the parking barrier, to the three shop premises that face the street. No one jumps on me so easily!

He goes and sits down. Stig gives me an uncertain look. On the television set lies a lace cloth and on the cloth stands a vase of plastic tulips. There is a violent clattering in the kitchen, and Herman Stilén shouts at us in a shrill voice: Silence! Silence! Stig and I move towards the door but the Father comes up to us, looks at me with his narrow eyes and says: You have come to lure Stig away from his lessons. Do not attempt to deny it! The gentlemen have their own plans for Sunday, oh yes! Then Beda stands in the doorway and hoots as through a fog: Herman! Calm down! Remember what happened last time!

He stands there, like a black bird, stripped of all glory, only his breast feathers are ruffled, the small, clawlike feet scrape against the shiny linoleum floor. Beda says: if you start shouting you know what will happen. Let the boys go. They rely on you. Everyone relies on you. Stig relies on you. Daniel is here because he relies on you.

Beda leans over him, she covers him with her body. Away in the corner, in the dimness, in the large mirror, I see a glimpse of a child, or a doll. Stig pulls me out through the door. The light is so faint that a gust of wind could blow it out. Herman sobs. Beda comforts.

7 Granny In Bed

Stig leans against the living-room door as though he were having to struggle against an immense pressure, slowly the door closes, and we stand in Granny's room with its smell of protracted illness, twilight and isolation. You remember, Maria, those long years by Mamma's bed. Granny sits up in her big iron bed with the brass knobs, they can be unscrewed, and secret documents, hair-raising testaments, rolled-up banknotes and mouldering love letters can be rolled and stuffed down into the legs: Heh! My cash boxes, the old woman wheezes, looking around her, her onion-head jerky, the way an owl does. Stig whispers in my ear: Did you see any car? No, not me. Papa imagines things, he's a bit —: and Stig taps his temple, he smells of garlic. But Granny is beginning one of her shrill, uninterruptable monologues, it flows out into the room, finds its way towards the high window giving on to the courtyard well, the sky is not visible, only its February twilight. Ah, Daniel, Daniel, come over here so I can touch you. Have you struggled your way up from the lions' den, have you done battle with the incunabulae, have you from the darkness of the spirit attained the light of my transfigured room? When you were very small you sat in a corner, and when I came to do the cleaning you ran away as though you had seen a ghost, I wasn't one yet then. Fredrik put you on the shelf beside the other books, he blew on you so the dust flew, and he taught me foreign words. He tried with Herman but nothing came of it. Herman, he said, Herman was born with a waistcoat and turnip watch. Go over to the window so I can see you better. You're thin and you'd like to cut and run, wouldn't you, Stig? Stig! You have a strange bird beside you, have you the sense to look after him? If he's like his Papa he'll suddenly fly on his way, brood for a long time and then stretch out his arms, like this! and like this! But your backside is far too heavy, Stig, that's probably why you dream of being an airman, you read and read but don't really understand any of it, it's all stirred up inside your head, but you like to come creeping over here and have Granny read to you, don't you, Stig? Stories! About witches and the princesses they slowly devour, and kings who cut off heads and farmhands who eat crows and get drowned and dragons that guard gold, like me, I keep it under my bed, no one will get it. Dragons, bats and snakes. Ah! Spiders. Don't like them. Tired. Always. No light. Gone.

In the wardrobe mirror I can barely make out her voice, it is so thin, only an elevation in the bedcover and an indistinct, lowered face. Stig pulls and heaves at the bed as he hisses: damned old woman, damned old woman, I'll show you I can fly, the bed is on wheels, it moves over to the window where Granny can observe the changes out there, the light that comes and goes on the fire wall, the dirty pigeons that fly as if being thrown to and fro, the clouds that go on drifting by, the sound of the dustbin lid, children shouting, a sprig of birch that has forced its way out of a crack between the bricks, what she sees she rearranges in her head, in her bony limbs, in her sinews and leathery skin, in the chewing of her jaws, and inside her eyes which, over by the window, are like black pins. Hah, she says, a great disorder will certainly come, but I have my things, I have a bed, a wardrobe, a bedside table, a stick, and claws, look!

She holds up her thin arm, it is like twisted rope, yes, there are claws there. She nods, satisfied. Observe, she says, observe, now it is light, now it is dark, now there is a smell of cabbage soup, now of jasmine. If I want to I can hang up another window, in it there are forest and meadows, barns, cows in the meadow, a horse, the bay, the pier I walk down on to, down to Jansson's pier where it smells of herring, and I climb on board and I can hear the threshing machine and there are soldiers, shouting, but I put off from land, I have had enough, I'm going away, Herman is big enough to look after himself, isn't he? But he just goes on crying, the cry-baby, and Beda will have to comfort him, I couldn't do it. We must go, says Stig, do you hear what I say? Go go says Granny. I'm cold, I'm shrinking, in the grave I'll be no bigger than a nutmeg, it doesn't matter, people are strange, they are what they are, that is what one learns from life. Pfiu, then it's all gone.

She begins to cough. Stig hauls out the basin and supports her, she leans forward but nothing comes up, she falls back on the cushion, Stig wipes her forehead with a wet handkerchief that is lying on the table, we push the bed back into place, I can still hear the screeching. The cupboard door has slid open, reflecting the window, the wall, the window in the wall, it slides slowly past, the light only a streak, I look at the darkness in the cupboard bur no one rises out of it, with raised arms, with bared teeth, no, no one.

8 Day Nursery

A wind, as from an abyss, rises up around us. The air is instantly filled
with vertigo. The foot hesitates in the air, finds no support. It is just
before darkness falls, and the city hovers below us with its blind lights.
The whole of my life is pressed into my hand that holds the ice-cold
doorknob. As if a bomb had destroyed a part of the building, an iron
girder stretches before us from the wall to another part of the building.
Above us in invisible convulsions electric cables and steel construc-
tions, some of them stairways, some of them baskets that sway in the
wind. We stand on a narrow platform above the chasm of the courtyard, half-blind I press myself against the house wall and feel the
sucking from the depths below me. Along the girder one glimpses wire
ropes to take hold of, the wind is heavy with the smell of salt from the
sea and with ash. Stig is already standing out there, he reaches out a
hand, he shouts something to me, there are only a few steps to go and
then we are in safety, but I cling tight, the door behind me is locked,
and above me there is a gigantic illuminated clock face with black
stains on it, a great mechanical moon, a face that will fall on top of me
and wipe me out, and we will fall together, I catch hold of the rusty
minute hand, it cuts into my hands, bends outwards but does not
break, it moves slowly forward with my half-dead weight and overtakes the hour hand. Someone calls out far away, now I begin to lose
my cramp-like grip, twelve booming chimes penetrate through me,
through rasping breaths, through heartbeats, time triumphs as I fall, I
hold on tight with bleeding hands, slowly I swing outwards and see for
one last time the city and the harbour, the dark, sharp house-roofs and
the cheerfully turning weathervanes, hear the roar of the traffic, I am
no one, just a frozen eye, I release my grip, let my breath out, can
manage no longer, fall.

Oops! My ear goes all red and hot where I lie with my head on the play table. Aunt Inna shakes me cautiously and Lena and Tommy shout: Danni's asleep! Danni's asleep! So terrible to have such a little-developed body and grown-up thoughts but not be able to express them. My trousers are also too tight, and my feet don't touch the floor. When I am there I am much more secure, then I can sit under the table. What an awful dream I had. Now I lie down flat on the floor, it carries me, out through my eyes a child looks candidly, Lisa knocks on the floor with a wooden boat and laughs, she has pointed teeth, like some creature I saw at the zoo. How ugly she is. She doesn't know anything. Danni Danni Danni she cries, but I sit in my corner, I have stools around me. I have a big box full of bricks. They are spheres, pyramids and spaces, and there is room for them all. I have a cloth and I lay it over chairs, and no one sees me and does not know that I am no child, that someone else looks out here, it isn't me, that sooner or later they will get a look at the Devil. So says Papa, who has read it in a book. Outside there is dirty snow and Mamma brought me here and had holes in her boots so all the water got in. On the square stood an old woman who could fly, while she talked she flew away out over the harbour, her dress was wet at the hem. Peter stands on a stool and beats a drum, and Anja pulls and heaves to get the drum but doesn't get it. Ylva draws big farting horses, but Aunt Inna sweeps us all together around a table, and we play the finger-game that is stupid, but Lena keeps shouting Boom! Boom! and we colour that. There is a smell of oatmeal porridge, it streams all over the place. They all go rushing out, and only a bit of me remains there in the corner. Then there is lots of snow and we shout and then we have to sleep, but I draw a bird with so many colours that it gets really wild. It is red and has big black eyes and sits quite still on my roof. I draw a clock and a bridge and eat porridge, the spoon is too big, it won't go in, but Aunt Inna says that it isn't, and now Daniel must be good. Which Daniel, the one who is sitting here or the one who is sitting there under the table though nobody knows it? When you pour milk around the porridge it turns into an island and swims away.

Now Aunt Inna and the other aunt and the aunt from the kitchen go into the other room and shut the door, I think I know what they're talking about, but I don't tell anyone, it's a secret. There are stairs everywhere that boom and echo and my desk is over by the window, and inside it I have a book about a bear, and suddenly it roars and comes leaping out of the desk and takes the teacher in its mouth and runs away with her, though it can't, because it's in a book. Lisa sits knitting a bag made of fishing net and it is full of fish and the bear eats it. Mamma is nervous and doesn't get here on time, I look right and left, first left, then right, and then I begin to run. There are a lot of us in the class but I am alone with Lotta, she asks me home. She has such long hair that she can sit on it, but one day Mona goes and cuts it and Lotta screams, and I don't go home with her. I have a schoolbag that is green, its says Kiss on it, but I tear that off, I'm not a Kiss. Now it is February and it is supposed to be winter, but I melt it all away, water purls and the sun shines and it is summer. I have a tank from the war, only a little one, it rolls up and down the blanket in my bed, but sometimes it flies if I want it to. Because I can make myself invisible and I am only two eyes that see everything, people, cars and trees, and I write them down, so they will stay. The grown-ups talk and I listen. I have also made a string bag, it is so big that I can catch the whole class in it and drag them with me, they kick and shout, but Splash! They disappear down there, only little bubbles of air rise up. I saw it on TV. Robbert has a little uniform, his papa was almost killed in the war. Gun knocks Olle's house down, Olle knocks her house down, it is war and what will be left for the children, what? Singing and circle-games, and then the school comes and gobbles us all up, the last thing that is seen of us is our legs, they stick out of the hole and kick, and then the big crocodile just spits out the bones. When I was eleven Papa bought a TV set, I saw all that, but it had happened before, all that, all the people fighting and shooting, and Stig's grandma was there, firing a sub-machine gun, in her nightgown, and then her bed rolled into the wall with a bang and disappeared, you could only hear her scratching.

What a wind it was, and what a whirling! There were bruises and bloodstains and in between everything so calm and timid. Their marks are everywhere, on floors and walls, in forgotten cots and battered old books I keep beside me when I sleep. That was how the grey days of childhood went, and the light ones, summer-like, and always there was a music there, a calm, low song, as though yearning always had a refuge and a dwelling, a room to itself. A heavenly door opened on to the spaces beneath which we are all tiny, grains of dust, merely.

9 The Haffner

I have grown at least three millimetres. When you come back from the States and your irrational, surprising and exhausting research, you will perhaps discover that I have completely grown up! You say that the weather there changes overnight, from heat to cold, and that the wind can suddenly rise and sweep across Boston Common like steel plate. Here it just blows all the time, as though the city were devoting a large part of its energy to sweeping the streets with greyness and raw sleet from the sea – you know how often we have stood on the ramparts looking southwards, and there has been a brightness there that ought to be able sweep away so much of the hesitation and cowardice that surrounds us... But people are becoming ever more silent and closed up in themselves and ever more violent in their local pubs. The TV over-flows with rubbishy entertainment so that the very screen itself has to be cleaned of filth once a week, and our hidden rulers are the buyers of American serials, and their education is unknown. Everything is uncer-tain except distress, poverty, loneliness and fragile human relationships. Is it better at Harvard? My life alters with the days, sleet today and tomorrow perhaps a sign of spring. Bernt, who looked in a few days ago, says I am reaching that infantile state that is the precondition and foundation of all good fertile soil, and then he shakes his pinlike head and buys some well-thumbed Asterixes in order to relive 'the repulsive Gallic Wars of our school-years when we learned how to pile up corpses in the rivers so as to be able to drive across them in tanks': he mixes up past and present, the way time itself does, everything affects everything else and forms a confusing and wonderful mosaic that resembles the logic of dreams, indeed, surpasses it; Bernt is beginning more and more to resemble a hairy noctuid moth, blinking his eyes the way they flap their wings. The Pietinens' boy crept cautiously in for the first time in his life with his grey old man's face, looking – who would have thought it! – for something about music, 'real' music, Bach, Mozart. He smelled of his papa's tobacco smoke and reminded me of silent Sundays when Papa lit his cigarillo at 3 o'clock in the afternoon. Music, yes: it leads me to a room, not so far away, because with the years it has been built within my inner self and floats there like a crystal in my consciousness and emotions, and the two are one. And on its modest door is written, perhaps, in a childish and uncertain hand, Haffner-Urwind. You know it: every time like Mozart himself I am 'utterly surprised' by this experience in my inner being, by this clear form that is the beauty of the soul and the most extreme nerve-end of longing.

So come with me once more, one windy day last week when time faltered between winter and something that was slightly less winter, to a concert with Anna and me – you remember, we began to call her Anna when we got married and Mamma began to call me Daniel and not Dani any more? It was an evening of empty streets, solitary lamps, and the smell of malt from the brewery down at the docks. As a child I used to call Mamma Marina Miranda de la Cruz, that was what she looked like, and as dark. She knew I had listened to the Haffner, had formed a secret society of which I was the only member, she wanted to gain entrance to it, and she discovered that the Haffner was on the programme at the Hall of Solemnity. We sit in the big, beautiful hall, there are pillars and lights, expectancy and all that I have already listened to and know, like a perfectly clear and many-meaninged whirlpool inside me. I had to give it a name, and went to the library, found K385 in D major, first found the serenade between the *Entführung* and Mozart's own marriage, and how, a year later, he turned it into a symphony, he thought it would make a 'good effect', he got 23 gold ducats from the Emperor, I can feel their weight in my hand. I curl up, do not want to be seen, the lights go down, it is as though all our people there, Bernt, Mrs Rosendal, Viktoria, the witches, they are all waiting for a miracle to happen in their lives, for the solitary to become the shared, for the silence to reply to them with a soft: you're alive! Like a flower-scent in existence.

There is the conductor, a large-built man going uncertainly up on to the podium, half-sitting on the surround, most peculiar. Then he collects himself. The thievish magpie strikes, flaps its soot-grey wings, feathers and blood fly there, someone gets up and sits down again, and everything falls apart and suddenly stops: the conductor turns towards us, he has large yellow horsey teeth, he neighs and shows his tongue and then staggers out, pushes his way between the instruments as though he were hoofing his way along in flowing water, among stones, the orchestra sits as if crushed, there are horrible vibrations everywhere, and a little smooth-slicked man comes hurriedly forward and talks of an unforeseen mishap, a sudden attack of illness, he talks of patience, his gaze slides over ceiling and people in gentle despair. He asks if, possibly. My heart is beating so hard that the ceiling acquires cracks. He wonders if. Mamma leans towards me, I sense her pure fragrance as in the summers, the fragrance of the night violet, she whispers in my ear: Dani, you know it! I see with blind eyes, I balance like a mountain, there are the allegro moderato, the andante, the minuet and the presto, all squeezed together into a single note that blows through me: now, or never! Never! Never!

But my arm glows like a beacon, it is not me conducting, I struggle out of my inner self and move as Mozart moves, without an I, completely alone, and see the comical seat of my trousers and feel the gaze of the audience like an impelling torment. At the same time I am swept on my way as by a great wind. Isn't that burgomaster Sigmund Haffner sitting there in his saffron-yellow waistcoat, isn't my heart at once burning and icy cold, aren't my eyes the eyes of an old man, it all passes through me with furious rapidity, their surprise, my coldness, their ignorance, my sorrow. When with the manager's help I climb up on to the podium as though I had attained a giddying mountain top, I am all of a sudden completely empty, completely free, without one memory of a single note, my pullover with the hole in the sleeve is no less comical than Mozart's smile, the innermost joy of being alone and not knowing it; and it seems to me as though the lighting in the hall were a great, dark breath, sucking me into an interior I have never seen but have always known was there: death, effacement, triumph. Is not D major a triumph, the joy of trumpets and drums, a burning mask for that which is most concealed, least known, for loneliness? What sorrow to be happy, what happiness in the effaced, the I-less. Cold, cold! I whisper, and raise the baton, Maria you are with me, here is the Haffner, not one of the greatest but one of the most formally perfect, the beauty in that which is naturally formed, like the leaves of trees and their mighty crowns, like morning dew and the open sea, like the innermost joy in love. 'My new Haffner Symphony has quite astonished me, for I had forgotten every note.'

It begins. It has begun. The orchestra sees me, for a moment I hear the music before the allegro moderato, before the preparations for triumph. I alone am responsible, alone have the power to move the stars about the sky and make stones dance. The silence is so taut that it immediately answers. I am no one. Three blows against the rock, a clear, proud stream of water flows out. Joy! The inexplicable reveals itself, formed to a single body, a hovering building, an innermost room. I attain it, I have no age, I am primordially ancient, I am time condensed and wiped away, the wordless, I am the power and the metamorphoses. I cannot read the text of the score, it is the song of a bird, I know it. I know the allegro, I walk its steps in a sun-bright park with heavenly clouds, in its expectancy, I live in the andante's melancholy and move in its dance. I raise romantic hands, I walk on classical feet, the purest sorrow falls like snow and covers my face, it is inexplicable.

Now for a moment it is quiet in the world, the sorrow fell imperceptibly into the andante, the presto too is now over, ice and fire have given way to emptiness, I am no longer here, I am guided away. Then comes the applause, it rises and rises, I stumble down and see Mamma in tears, why is she crying, I am not dead, am I? The world is open in all directions, it flows into me. Did I take the last movement fast enough, as Wolfgang wanted it? 'I, who must always compose, need a clear mind and a silent heart.' We walk home in clarity and silence, Marina Miranda and I, it takes place as in a dream, as though I were passing through one door after the other in an old house in the country, the curtains billow inwards before the wind, Haffner-Urwind has come home, an old servant walks before me, one room for each year, one farewell for each room, and over there, far away, gleams a white door, when it will open I do not know, I am a child confronted by a great mystery.

It is now the end of February and the days pass with black trees and indifferent clouds, towards evening they begin to glow with the lights from the motorways. No one ever wrote about the concert, about my performance, and Mamma said nothing about it, either. It still remains in my heart. I am sitting at your work table and writing, it is evening. I am going to write you a letter, full of the everyday. As Dr Williams, from the part of the country you are in now, put it: 'No ideas but in things'. Those neglected objects that surround us so faithfully and which we go sailing past, blinded by our soulless habits. I have not heard anything from Lena and Jan for a long time, am trying to restrain my unease. A clear mind, a silent heart, a sorrow, that everything disperses so quickly.

10 The Arnolfini Couple

Sooner or later you sit on the edge of your bed and see that your sock
has a hole. Your big toe peeps out, it moves almost completely without
your will, it waves to you, perhaps it wants to tell you something? It is
one of those days that passes aimlessly, with its icy chill in a worn
leather briefcase in which there are some books you have not read and
will never read. You are here, you are there, you are nowhere in the
tangible world, and must sharpen your awareness in order to see yourself. In the bowl by the window there are oranges I ought to have
thrown out a long time ago. They could join the company of many
mile-high ideas, daydreams, plans for travel, retreats, departures,
purchases. The city around you takes no notice of you. I see an enormous expanse of sea, it separates me from you, from the children, from
myself. I have abandoned the secondhand bookshop and have lived at
home for a few days, but it is empty here, I long to be back in a
narrower, warmer space; here the silence is too thin. A cramped chill of
the heart has touched me, as though I had reached some conclusion
without understanding it. As though I had given up on some important point, and have every right to it. I am what I am, only perhaps a
bit less than I had supposed. Clouds pass, waves break as they have
always done, trees stand in their parks and will do so after I have been
consigned to the earth, it feels so strange and completely natural at the
same time. You no longer wonder why you exist, you exist, quite
simply, that is the meaning of it all, that you sit on the edge of a bed
and look at the hole in your sock and your toe in the hole, and you
change your socks so right sock is on left foot and left sock is on right:
thus is the day's first problem solved. You feel free and empty. Perhaps
there is another life you ought to change to, but why? Perhaps what
you have has been marked out for you, it is merely a matter of a little

adjustment. You look at your hand, it is your hand, after all, and you wake early in the mornings and lie quiet and look at the ceiling, it is not a very inspiring ceiling. You wonder about the 'fashion salon' across the street which has not changed its dusty window display in the last year. Perhaps the proprietress is sitting in there, behind her counter, already mouldered away, in eternal semi-twilight? Dust and silence. And high above her the eternal constellations of the stars that Papa taught me, and before me a vague expectancy. For what? That you will come back, that a door will open before that, that I will be transformed, that a wind will rage in through the entrance, that someone will shout: Daniel! From an open window the murmur of water can be heard, in the morning the city is new and sea-bright, and before I go to school I look into the room where Papa sits, his back to me, he is very old, on the window-ledge behind him there is a bowl of oranges, and on the table beside him a vase of irises. The room is an old man's refuge, that is what they look like, I see with the eyes of a child. The sounds that force their way in through the window are meagre: the chattering of a magpie, the chiming from a distant church, vague traffic. In the only mirror on the wall behind the old man I see a picture of you and me, of the light from the window and a burning candle.

You have recognized the picture, it is Jan van Eyck's painting of the Arnolfini couple, of Giovanna and Giovanni, I have held your hand the way he is holding hers, he is not touching it, protecting it only, close against the back of his hand with its warmth, they are not looking at each other. He keeps his other hand raised, as though he were reproaching her for something, or pointing out rules of life to her. But she has her own life, she keeps it hidden, in the folds of her magnificent green gown. In his large black hat he is an earnest reminder of their union, it makes her pale but determined, his cloak with its fur trimming falling in quiet folds, but even more beautiful Giovanna's, from beneath which a blue dress peeps forth. Visible behind them is the large red bed for their courtly love, on the floor there is a pair of wooden sandals, so oddly shaped, with pointed toes and black straps, on the ceiling a branched chandelier with one burning candle.

The dog on the floor, the fruits on the chest by the window, the mirror on the wall, the silence, it is all full of significance, of a strange sensuality, much more powerful than all that open nakedness that impoverishes our own time. The room embraces the two of them with calm and open seriousness. On the wall above the mirror is written *Johannes Eyck fuit hic*, and far away in the mirror we see, from a perspective that the room does not give, a landscape, canal and boats. The buzz of movement reaches me as it is reflected in the mirror. In there one glimpses the artist and someone else, unknown, the mysterious element that is needed so that everything shall be exact, in its place. The frame round the mirror contains ten small paintings on religious themes, there are stains on the wall above the mirror, it is the year 1434, the candle is burning for Christ, the fruits remind us of paradise lost, the dog of faithfulness, the mirror of innocence. The mirror is an eye, it captures the moment that stops and is eternity. Some invisible thing is breaking into the picture, the wind through the window that makes the heavy bed-curtains move imperceptibly, something is taking place and is unsaid. I have to lean forward in order to examine the strange mirror, that blue and red figure in front of Giovanna Cenami and Giovanni Arnolfini, see that the solitary fruit on the window-ledge is still there, that the room is not yet empty, gone, demolished, and each object in the room mouldered, splintered, the dead long dead and living, here, in front of us.

How long you stood in silence in front of Eyck's painting when we were last in London. Don't you think he looks a bit nasty, Giovanni, and she, submissive? He is looking past us with a smile, only hinted at, it is reflected in her. How empty the room would be without the smell of oranges. I can see them glowing. And right at the front, near the floor, light streams in from an invisible, open door outside the picture.

11 The Library

The world-tree murmurs in the children's section of the library. Children sit on its branches, immersed in foliage and books. Karin Lind stands behind the issuing desk, acquiring a wrinkle for each child she captures in her gleaming spectacles. She points to the top of the tree, it stretches its branches through the entire room. We lower our voices, we each walk in our own silence. The magic is quite natural, it streams out of the books, it has a fragrance of the creatures and flowers of distant lands, smells of wet clothes, paper, twilight, noses run, heads incline into their own enchanted labyrinths, mouths spell slowly, fingers follow foreign rivers, I am lost, captured, safe. I grow quickly volume by volume, never again later on will words enter me like this, they are not words, they are living life and transformation. I am there and not there. Right from the first time Mamma brought me here and left me for an hour while she went to do her errands I was at once hunted rabbit and wicked gardener, all the books in the infants' corner stood so happily around me with their red and green spines, there was a sea of pictures to plunge into. I slowly expanded the limits of my world. The library stretched out towards the world of the grown-ups, I was prepared. Oh, those paradisal labyrinths that I learned to explore! I left behind me the winds, the slush, the scraggy trees, the shrieking gulls, the city's unease. In the library silence reigned, dense with thousands of landscapes, it was like climbing mountains. I plunged into the world-tree's shadow, into the world of daydreams with its smell of dry paper, leather, dust, and the moisture from woollen sweaters and rubber boots. There were small books and big atlases that covered a whole table, heavy books that fell to the floor with a crash and scattered their letters like gravel in the gently darkening air. Everyone looked up, then went back again to their reading, page-turning, their painful choices, their hands' sense that here! here! was the right book, the most beautiful pictures, a part of oneself between the covers.

The days pass, room by room, and we are now a good way into March. Right next to the sofa I keep – you have seen them – those children's classics with their red spines, and on the shelf behind my head the row of children's books, I seldom touch it, but it is there. Tattered volumes, childishly scrawled names, the book's number jotted down by me in a blue notebook. So much hard work of the imagination, so many pictures that have travelled through me! Sometimes they fell out of their covers, there were landscapes that faintly glowed, words that had grown weary of a life of silence and now echoed within me, there were the Mississippi River and the Sahara Desert, there were the frigate Delaware and David Balfour, desert islands I roamed, mysterious caves that took me prisoner, a world as inescapable as the world outside the tall windows of the library. Would anyone discover them, see them and live them for the first time, be gripped by them and lie in the dark with happy eyes when Sunday arrived and with them journey back to a reality more tangible than those pallid days at school, those endless hours? Was it I who evoked them? Over the issuing desk I looked at Emerentia Busch, who was on evening duty, she stamped my books as though she had imprinted a glowing seal on their foreheads. Papa used to tell stories about what the library had been like in the old days, about the rules, the old ladies, the snuff-brown books, the silent fear and delight in the dark issuing room, in nooks and crannies where children sat on stools and book-ladders, children who looked out between the books or climbed on top of them, they were sometimes placed back to back, they were dusted down, they were placed on the shelf for new acquisitions or newly-returned books, stood there with their knitted scarves and runny noses, their joy-stained books. There Mamma found me once as she was passing on her way to the adult section, and took me with her. Oh, what animation, what menacing cries among the flock of assistant librarians! Pale hands were raised in agitated whispers, Mamma hisses: he's not reserved! He's not the property of the city! The whole section is listening, mouths gape, Stig's carrot-red hair flames up there beside the sports books, owl-like children blink their eyes, black gaps in white rows of teeth suck in the agitated, compressed air where things unspoken and unwritten sag on the shelves. How can children be used in that way as books like any other? In a shrill voice Emerentia Busch replies that one cannot make mistakes like that with the grown-ups, they do not climb in among the books, they do not hide among text and words, do not lose themselves in the desert of Karakorum or a River of Mercy, they do not leave ham sandwiches between the leaves of *The Lion, the Witch and the Wardrobe*, they do not live like savages or cannibals, drones or dreamers inside the covers that have been purchased with precious municipal resources!

So much the worse for them! shouts Mamma, sparks fly around her, live coals amass in her dark hair. Worse? Emerentia retorts in a bass voice, worse? And what does Mrs Urwind think we do here day in and day out? Every day we clear up books that the children have spread out on the floor, muddy water from Mississippi, beasts of prey from Africa, *buller* [noise] from Bullerby, Fillyjonks and Borrowers, rockets and armour, lock stock and barrel, blood from countless battles, hedgehogs and horses in hordes! There are texts that they swallowed, that are lost for ever! And what do you think we find among the cards in the catalogue? The most peculiar messages to Little My, Karlsson On The Roof, Tarzan and Cruella de Vil! They live here, somewhere, in secret, and compared with their lives your precious Daniel's brief spell as a book is a pipe of snuff! You should see the picture books! Children eat everything, poke their fingers into everything, take a great interest in everything, run up and down behind the book stacks, this how they do it, this is how they spread out their arms, they bring everything toppling down, hurl themselves to the floor, clamber about like monkeys, hide when we have closed, lie here with their pocket torches and read until after midnight, then they start crying, then what they want is to dream themselves back to their nice little beds! Booklearning, I ask you! Urwinds they are, the whole bunch of them, if I may say so, if I may make my voice heard!

Emerentia is burning with indignation and delight. She is a big red cloud, she shakes our dust off us, blows our noses, opens our eyes, what is life in the street compared to life here, tenacious and eternal, here lurk dragons and wolves, human beings fly like bats, everything happens here and now, each book has its secret to reveal, you grow up and get to know many people, remarkable cities, you travel perpetually inside yourself: perhaps what people take for escape is simply being prepared. Yes, strange are the ways of erudition and booklearning. Thoughts and dreams pressed together on white leaves, black ants in an enormous thought-hill wait to be roused from their sleep, go climbing up some beanstalk into the head of an eleven year-old schoolchild with wings. Towards nightfall all is silent between the shelves. The moonlight gleams on the books about astronomy, only a solitary bookworm moves its silver wings inside the beam of light and vanishes up towards the poetry under the roof ridge, it sits there, longing to be outside, all this is contained in my hovering library. A boy sits there, he sees a great tree, he sits with his eyes closed, he draws it on a piece of paper, it grows there in the reading room with black branches, it is only March after all, but there is a shadow of leaves to come, of soughing that makes him silent. He bites his damp mitten so as not to be carried too far away. He has forgotten himself, the darkness does not bother him, he is in his own light world and at last falls asleep with his own text closed tightly beneath his eyes. And the days pass, word is joined to word, week to week. Those who take them in their open hands can hear the heartbeat of the building and the opening of invisible doors.

12 In the Cabin

The April gales have set in and are shaking my sleeping-cabin behind the kitchen. I am trying to keep my ship facing into the wind. The damp hangs like salt mist around me, under the wave-washed deck the forepeak is completely cut off from us. The moon rises and hurls its trail southwards, the waves are rent apart and the whole house quivers at every attack. I sit upright in bed and see the heavy mountain of the water towering up over the bows, we are all sinking, Mamma, Papa and I. The light from the compass transforms our faces into those of the dead: mouths, eye-sockets, black openings. And this quivering that makes the glass of water on my bedside table gleam, this city that, unknowingly, in its immense silence, is in the process of sinking! At the bottom of the wave-trough, in the darkness of the lift-shaft, complete emptiness and forsakenness, the wall of the darkness high above me, the pounding of the engine through my breast: this is the end, the last sleep, a nightmare. Like the rank odour of a great, icy breath.

And then, the scarcely perceptible heave upwards, the slow ascent, as though a hand lifted me, the bed, the cabin, the room, the house, from the black and the moonlit to a dreadful, limitless view of the starry sky, the flying clouds and the crest of the wave on which the vessel is attempting to list, and everything will hurtle overboard, the sleepers, the child who waves on the forepeak and has disappeared, kitchen ranges that are tearing themselves free of their floor clamps. Now a rumbling is heard, and in the rumbling the shrieking of those who are locked in, but there is nothing I can do, only hold the course so that we don't all drown, slowly, slowly the sinking starts again, the journey downwards, the vessel with its stem protruding from the masses of water, its eye rigidly aimed, until my hand fumbles by the bedside table, my green lamp goes on, I sit up and look at the walls, the cupboard by the foot of the bed with the old issues of the National Geographic Magazine; out in the kitchen, in the other room, in the world outside all is silent. Only the distant roaring of the stars, in the miniature radio, where the limitless lives and voices from other planets talk to one another. They don't know that I am listening, that the storm is over, that yet one more terrible catastrophe has been avoided.

The wind in March is capricious. It hurls up waves towards an ever paler sky and makes the washing on the line smack like sails when the courtyard goes about. Sunlit days of hesitant warmth become unease in my dreams, and from the kitchen window I can see the sky's preliminary exercises above black metal-plated roofs. From the library's inner rooms, in my memory tobacco-brown with a faint smell of smoke, I opened the secret door to my bedroom and steered out, not always in night and storm: there were sunlit days, meandering rivers, Mediterranean coasts with dazzling sand, there were all the pictures from distant lands I had stuck up on the walls of my cabin, its name like the word for – The bonnet! Item of female headwear, band under the chin! Away, away, with fluttering cloak, like a sail! There, on the laundry balcony, drawers and underclothes trod their reckless dance in the wind, the one that Granny has invented, with quivering hands has shaped in a secret corner of her magic cave and then not succeeded in holding captive, it has rushed in under her bed and then out again, through doors, down staircases, out to the rear courtyard, no wind that tastes so bitter exists anywhere else, it is blown through and through, and both destitute and lively, it continually rages on the beating-balconies like a desperate ruffian in combat with an invisible enemy, caring nothing for Manager Jansson's curses and Herman Stilén's bustling and gesticulations. The gale, it has been washed, mended, beaten, bleached, so that everything, both outside and in, smells of departure, unease and sea. Long johns recklessly plait themselves around the most minimal of knickers, sheets fly away in nocturnal gales and twine themselves around unsuspecting passers-by, making them flee screaming from their own reflections, or their wet fluttering covers the windows of the house next door in the dawn light with fateful consequences: the residents don't see the day dawn, sleep in, tumble wide-awake from their warm beds at noon and become the laughing-stock of the whole neighbourhood, while the sheets slowly dry and fall like flowerbeds around damp stone bases and over the steps of the rear courtyard, so that people know neither outside nor in about what is outside and in.

I saw it all from my captain's bridge and could contentedly lean back in my bed and with far-seeing gaze enjoy all the sounds and colours that gathered around my bed: Papa's hawking, Mamma's suddenly gently emerging bright voice, the astonishing screams of a sea mew, hurled into the courtyard by the courtyard's own gale: for a moment it hovers motionless, is then thrown out through the window-frame. The daylight that day by day grows ever stronger has its own changing voice, and the silence at home might one day be mute and soundless, to be filled with life on the next. It was only the home-work, which with its muddle and compulsion and the thumbed, underscored lines in the books Papa got hold of cheaply at the second-hand bookshop that stood in the way of the mind's wild wanderings across the sea's expanses. Tough and soggy, formulae and figures wound themselves around my neck and made the air hard to breathe. Then I stretched myself out on the bed and let my gaze follow the cracks in the ceiling, coastlines of far-off continents, where the strange scent of cinnamon and crab-apple mingled with fried Baltic herring in the kitchen. From time to time I could hear an eager voice from the hall and the knock of fate on the kitchen door, and in stormed Klas with his apple-round face and the black gap in his teeth, and the smiling eyes shouted: Get up! Get up! We're going to the pictures! There's a horror film on at the Gloria! Hurry up! I could not tell him about my storm to the south of Greenland, about all the earth's metamorphoses and about my own terror: it was there for all to see and feel. That was the fortune and misfortune of those days, everything existed close to everything else; we ran along evening-deserted streets, Klas had no cap, his black hair glistened with rain, to see a film was a whiff of oxygen, we dived underground, it all took place underground, the terror, the joy, the powerful passions, the terrible, living trees, the invisible beings, the laughing murderer with his Santa Claus mask, the rising water, the space creatures, the slowly growing insects, the vengeful child, the mass-murdering aunts, the popcorn-chewing teenagers with their loud jeering laughter at each endless kiss, the steam from the wide-open eyes, the blissful sinking: there was life, outside only streets with silent house fronts, everything a great, echoing house under an unal-tered sky. The snow had changed to sleet, the sleet to rain, and the rain back to snow again: there was no continuity, only grey sky and days of giddying ether, when the clouds mirrored themselves in the black wet pavements like woolly ice-floes: there were always abysses, and tight, constricting clothes. You should have seen me then, a little rabbit, bounding now this way, now that, an itch, a ticking heart, and those watchful eyes.

But in my room the silence was my own. I sat in the room facing the street and did my homework. The cabin was shrinking and I moved over, got a desk, where I sat with my face propped in my hands and saw the street-lamp swinging in the gale outside, there was distance to everything. Even when I was not there I was there all the same, saw Mamma come in, turn on the lamp by my desk, smooth the bedspread, stand as I did, looking at the house front opposite. I sensed her unease. Perhaps she was thinking of Papa or me, of the future, in the weekdays there was so much that was not said, that was their purpose. What was going to happen to us, to the secondhand book-shop, to the housekeeping money, to the summers, and was the stove in the kitchen going to have to be replaced?

She strokes her hair, she goes out and closes my door, the flat is silent. She sits on a white chair in an almost empty room, light falls in from a window further away, there is a closed door there, then as now.

13 In Our Kitchen

Granny Stilén is not dead at all. Granny has crawled out of her undulating bed and crept up along the water pipes. She has wedged herself in between the teeth of the central heating radiator in the kitchen. I have seen it for myself. When grandfather was still alive she came to the house and looked after Papa. She calls him 'the Master of Arts' and Mamma 'the Master of Arts' wife'. She doesn't let on that we only met quite recently. Her lower jaw projects like a land wharf, and at the top of her thin scalp there is a yellow-grey bun of hair. She has become even more of an owl, her voice more plaintive, as though you had turned on a tap and out flowed groaning sounds and creaking from carts on roads that ceased to be used along ago. Scraggy bushes and ditches follow in her footsteps. There she ran over the meadows when she was a girl and round as an apple, and a terrific crowd of men ran after her. She speaks, now as though she had never left the village, now in words I don't understand, grandfather must have taught her them. Your restless soul, Daniel, where has it gone? Where? Like the gold underneath my bed, everything just flows, and flows away. But they that can climb up on to the shelves, they will escape the deluge. There we turn our backs on our wretchedness and are silent as God is silent when we attack him. Only when the wild beast comes do people have eyes, believe me. Second-sighted, that is what you have to be. Beda and Herman, all they see is the bottom of life's pot. Ah! How the soul aches! And the spirit that has flown up to heaven! Out of the cupboard it flies, with all its goods and chattels. I have packed everything. The money and the hard bread and that which shall be secret, isn't that so, Daniel? You have certainly grown, your shinbones itch, don't they, they nag and nag, both when you're teeny-little, and when you're trudging to the grave. Near the earth all the time. Small as a coffee bean, brown girls the natives have dried so that only the most important bit is left. Look. The beans aren't rationed any more, hallelujah!

Granny chews, Mamma smiles, a pale sun flows in, Granny has hair on her upper lip, red-rimmed eyes as if she had been weeping, but merely snuffles. A winter fly descends into her coffee cup, she quickly places a claw on it, fishes it out, flicks it with thumb and index finger straight into the kitchen sink, she looks like a bird of prey. Her eyes can darken from amber to charcoal, change like the March weather, black tree-branches creep out of her cardigan and stretch towards the flying heavens. She tidies up, puts water on to boil, and tells stories. Her voice is like blowing into a bottle, cobwebs, clay, a voice like a hoarse hen squawking across a muddy road, moss and potato sprouts. She is the Easter witch and the young fair-haired girl who on her path through summer met the pedlar Erik Stilén, everything shimmered then. She has taken part in the most shocking adventures. She has been pursued by horse-traders, fishermen and steel magnates, clodhoppers, smugglers and directors, since Erik died and Herman was born she has been chased by painters and circus artistes, and got out of it all with consternation and wisdom. I once heard Viktoria say to Mamma that Granny Stilén was an abortionist and when I asked what an abortionist was Viktoria said that she spirited away children who had not yet been born, but Mamma got angry and shouted at Viktoria: What are you putting into the ears of an innocent child? Have you no sense? Just think what you're doing! And Viktoria wept, Mamma wept, and the next time Granny turned up she got extra good pastries.

Papa calls her the Gall Rose. She tells the story about the murderer in the laundry room who fled when she chased him out, he fled to Salt Lake, lay down in it, turned completely white and then died. Like an insect she bores into her thoughts, they buzz like bees. Ghosts and trolls give her wings, she glides about with an eagle's gaze and swoops mercilessly down on her prey that bathes in its own blood. Fish-scales fly about her hands when she cleans perch and roach, but best of all she likes to slice cabbage and brown it in the biggest pan. Then her kitchen starts to sing, slowly gushes over the brims, she stirs the cabbage and the fumes drift up to the ceiling and out into the world, seamen sniff the air out in the Gulf of Finland, salty breezes blend with the Gall Rose's cabbage soup, its under-the-earth smell, our land becomes a cabbage-patch in which she runs cutting heads, wearing muddy rubber boots that leave marks in our honest and patriotic hearts; from the pan rises a song at once angry and gentle, a song of eternally boiling and overboiled life, its tenacious fear and crafty power of survival. It is like a passion from the earth and the stones, from mankind's cellar epoch, from the room with the hovering bed where she lies planning the future of the race. We are the same height, she and I, we look each other in the eye, the child and the old woman, we exchange eyes. Mamma asks how Beda and Herman are. Ah! Trash! Mean and bad-tempered, they let her starve. The way all younger people do to old folk. Stick them in an old folks' home, give them medicines so they'll be manageable. But in the war people showed what they were made of. How hath the oppressor ceased! The golden city ceased! Isaiah 14:4. Corruption and worms!

Granny drinks her coffee noisily, Mamma proffers the cake plate. I say Fredrik to the son but the Master of Arts when he's here, I still go down to the bookshop now and then, a well-watered garden in truth! Does the lady remember when the pipes sprang a leak? The work of God, mark my words. He who rescued little Daniel from the lions' den. Well, well, now it's all drunk up. She takes some more, it makes her quite brown, and Papa arrives. After that she addresses herself only to the Master of Arts, she nails him with her gaze, she sees through the walls and right down into the underworld where the drunkards lie in their nylon sacks and where the books hide behind locked doors. The Master of Arts has such a good-natured child. Like the Master of Arts was when the old master was alive. The just man walketh in his integrity; his children are blessed after him. Proverbs 20:7. She talks about her childhood but I do not think that she has ever been a child. From her bright gaze a darkness looks out. She tells about how one fine Sunday the church on the island where she lived was carried away by a tidal wave, higher than Åbo Cathedral and with more ringing of bells, a wave sent by Fate, how the house of the Lord drifted out to sea like a ship with priest, hymn-singing and all, and went aground on Söderskär, it was a miracle wrought by the Lord, and afterwards Söderskär became a place of pilgrimage for all who had lost their dear ones at sea, but the souls of the dead became seabirds, duck and teal, and that is why they cry. And Granny cries.

Then her son Herman rushes in followed by Beda, they shout loudly that Granny has robbed them of their savings in the rose-vase, it is empty, what has Granny done, they shout. Granny scampers like a weasel along the floor, out through the kitchen door, down the winding staircase, Herman and Beda panting after, they are sucked down into their lairs and only a faint belching from the plughole remains behind them, it mingles with my sleep, so that all the sounds are in the wrong place, the sputtering of cabbage from Mamma, the dripping of the tap from Granny, the tenor's aria from Papa, they all strangely mingle, while Fate is a green eye and sees everything. It grows silent, the kitchen shrinks, no one can sit at its table any more, the gas stove stands in its darkness in the corner, the tap drips quietly, we have moved long ago. In the steam from the world's biggest cabbage soup Granny vanishes like a djinn but can always be summoned back. She is indestructible, the bad in the good, the good in the bad, the thing that can always be overlooked and is always there, a little bent old woman still in Lena's and Jan's dreams, a muttering tenacity, a gall-ridden solitude, something inexplicable that remains, like the scent of a gall-rose, a defence against the dark.

There is a gurgling in the radiator, a greeting from Granny. I hear it in my dream, turn over in my bed, you are gone, only the swift image of the boy who looked at me and disappeared, and there in the corner Captain Albert, the bear that Granny gave me once, his eyes gleam with sunlight from distant seas.

14 The Bomb Shelter

Someone carries me me out through the kitchen door. Someone exposes me to cold, to the smell of cement, to darkness. What happened I remember dimly. It was wartime. Searchlights rumbled across the sky, clouds howled, Papa and Mamma lay awake, sprang to their feet, I was carried down into the abyss underneath the house. Now Mamma asks me to go and get a jar of raspberry jam. Someone leans against the cold iron railings that twist through the house past the kitchen doors. Hannes' door is ajar, I stop, open the door cautiously, stand in a kitchen with the smell of turpentine, glue and porridge. From the studio come moans and small, shrill cries. My heart thumps. I peep inside, I am the spy and the exposer, the keyhole and the one who is mute. I see a great powerful woman riding on the sofa, a hairy knee sticks up, a white thigh, closed eyes, undulating black hair, no one sees me, they are in a whimpering world of their own, I see it for the first time, the heat gathers behind eyes, in underbellies, something is ending, something is beginning, a rumbling, explosions, everything totters and is at the same time nailed hard and fast, flesh, blood and death, I take a few steps backwards and creep out, there is lust in every movement, lust in walls, ceiling and floor, the white sky outside is the colour of her thighs, that is what they are doing, that is how they become grown-up, that is how they are blinded, so that they do not see me any more, I am protected, I have my secrets like an overflowing bowl, a filled basin. I open the door to the cellar, it is made of iron, I tug and pull, inside a vapour of darkness hits me, the lighting goes on above aisles and compartments, and I remember dimly how the house held its breath, how black people gathered, how they sat or lay, and the bodies go into one another as with the man with the black beard, with the white woman, I am enveloped, cannot move, am only astonishment and fear, eagerness and horror, the cellar supported by fragile wooden beams, long benches of silent people. Here the world is compressed to mere listening: there are the gun-blasts, the faint quiverings, the whistling that make us bend, the dust that whirls down from the ceiling with its retaining boards. Life goes on in the underworld, in its dark caves and passages, away in the darkness a loving couple entwined in each other's arms, the soldier on leave, the pilot who has a fit, starts screaming, springs to his feet and outside, people who try to hold him back, all of it distant and silent, and filled with the smell of rotting potatoes.

Here now there are only the mere splinters of used-up, wasted time: old rattan furniture, chests, packing cases, chairs that have seen their day, along the passages no longer the silent people, the bundles, the blankets, all those who were then abandoned and huddled close together. From corners then the white sprouts stared from piled-up, tenderly preserved root vegetables, they too lay close together, and the light begins to flicker as then. So close is the air that no other world exists but this, and the heart shrinks to a pulsating stone. Now the wild war rides out over the world and sits astride the soldiers, hair seethes, from inside rises the groan of lust and fear. I am a thousand years older than my limbs, I can scarcely move. Why do I shrink, grow, as though I were a piece of chewing gum in the world's jaws? I unlock our compartment, there on the shelves in the dark coolness the bottles of juice and the jars of sauce and jam. Now and then we got fruit from the country, it was eked out, it was mashed and fed into me, I was a chrysalis, blindly I lived under the ground in those rumbling April nights, I walked on pale sprout-legs and saw the grown-ups slumped against one another or sitting petrified in silence beneath the swaying piercing lamps with their matt brilliance cast over each second of listening. Outside the streets lay black, the sky was criss-crossed by the cones of light from the searchlights, I drew up my knees and sank into the flickering hum beneath my eyelids, Mamma drew me close to her.

Creaking, the wheels of time move backwards, stop, move forwards again. In the dimness under floor upon floor of weight and walls Olof Urwind gets up, he reads aloud 'Now shines the July sun so clear, my memory speaks so wonderfully near upon this morning hour; come youth, if thou wilt now as I, come let us in the thicket breathe some draughts of summer air; today it is a festive day.' I can't remember it, Mamma told me it, the poem was interrupted by a rumble, the earth starts shaking, the light flares, goes out and ignites again, a child weeps and is quickly silent, someone lights a cigarette and is reprimanded, the years trample the world like oxen, there is a rain of sparks against the heel of the boot with which the soldier stamps the fag-end into the floor, which seems to be made of earth, from earth are we come, in a den of earth do we crouch, under all the layers of darkness. Daniel in the lions' den, I destroy all enemies, I screw up my eyes, I live in the arms of the will to life, I am seeing and timeless, I am the rabbit that runs from the master gardener, he wants to kill me, but I live. Opposite me on the bench sit the lovers, he holds his hand under the back of hers, in her hand rests a white stone, the stone of hope and comfort. It is over, it is long since over, the clown who stood up in the silence after the impact of the bomb and makes a scornful bow to superior force, he shouts: here we sit like rats, have you seen the rats in the courtyard, those fat, wonderful rats, they sit on their hindlegs as if they were praying, but they can't stand on their heads, they are not as crazy as us! Crazy! Crazy! And from his wide-open eyes fall tears, he rushes out, no one holds him back. Uncle Olof, he has a noble face, a magnificent profile, a posture like that of a measuring ruler, always equally theatrically and artificially he scans: 'Lock the doors securely on him so he doesn't play the fool anywhere but in his own house', he himself is a fool, no one understands what he says, the gestures too pompous, the stage too dark, the silence too great, the listening passes him by. From the radio comes the electric gravel and a coarse fellow in a rough homespun coat strikes it with his fist and softly swears. In the midst of all this I fall asleep and dream about the faces that froze solid in the ice, they look up with blind eyes at the heavens, and I skate over them, red gashes appear in their white faces. The sky above us is a great drum, plunging the children into deep, black sleep with its booming.

The house shakes, dust trickles down between the rafters, the all-clear sounds protractedly, I stand ten years later with a jam jar in my hand and listen: all quiet, life a gift, the pale April twilight a miracle. Pigeons fly up with clumsy wingbeats and throw themselves tenaciously over black roofs and chimneypots, I contain many 'I's at once, can see them, they go past me like strangers.

15 The Hovering School

With eyes closed, in the warmth of my bed, I can glide like a bird over the city or make my way down into its gaze. But the mornings are already early light, with their cold brilliance that penetrates the sackcloth curtain in front of my room. It is time to drink my cocoa, eat my sandwiches and rush to school. I am late. I move in a flickering house, I run through doors and down stairways, I am the only one who will be punished, all eyes hide behind the indifferent windows in my path, the streets lie like tautened ropes and old autumn leaves quiver in the crowns of the trees in the park that is only a few lost bushes and a statue. Sand blows in the wind and my face feels stiff. Clouds race across the sky, and I across the ground. There is the smell of salt from the sea, the smell of melted snow, the gleaming sunlight caught in the upper rows of the windows of the houses that rush past. Streets, paths between houses, corridors and stairways, open doors banging, squeaking gates opening, tramlines with a leaden glint, dead shop windows. It is five past eight, the minute hand like a bloody arrow between my shoulderblades. I will not be in time for morning prayers, I will be written up, written down, written off, with a chalkmark on my nose, with the rules of grammar like a mound of dried peas rattling inside my clean-blown cranium. I must go in softly, I turn the corner, I stop. There is the enormous, heavy school with its equally heavy door where the little ones from the junior classes pull and heave like ants or whining flies on a flypaper.

But now all is terrifyingly, thunderingly still. Something is happening that is against all reason. The enormous building has torn itself loose from its foundations and is hovering several metres above the ground, it is rising slowly, it is a balloon of stone, a grotesque, angular cloud of bricks and masonry, sheet metal and window-frames. I am there now, there are some other pupils who are late, too, they are running about shouting, windows are opened, from the school comes a humming, a shrill faint din from a thousand throats, there is a glimpse of the gym teacher's goatee and tarred ropes are thrown as from an ocean liner down to us who stand with mouths agape. My heart is beating, it drowns out everything else, and if I look at the luminous basement that has now been shamelessly exposed it forces fire and smoke from its intestines, and when they have dispersed rooms I have never seen are naked and robbed of their secrets. The janitor's wife sits in a white nightgown stretching despairing white arms towards the sky. In a narrow room discarded pointers gush forth like rubbish, some of them have gone mouldy, others are trying with frozen buds to see a new spring, but in vain: fire is licking their yellowed bones. There are storerooms for paper, for chalk, for worn-out desks, there are the urinals with their white, cracked tiles, a pale pupil looks out with fly undone, in the woodwork room the third form are rushing around with with clumsy sailboats, trays and paper knives, all with wide-open eyes and bowed necks: the school's foundations are full of sticks and stones, secret openings, brownish black tar.

And it all coheres, it all hovers, raises itself millimetre by millimetre into the air. The ropes that were hurled out through the windows have been extended with childish knots, how they got them down from the gym hall I do not know, we run and try to anchor the school to the nearest lamp-posts and to the carriage of the old cannon that stands in the school yard. To no purpose! Soon the cannon is dangling with its mouth hanging shamelessly downwards, the lamp-posts are ripped from the ground with a faint hiss, the asphalt cracks and the wind tugs at the school flag on top of the roof, the yellow cloth with its two crossed pointers in blood-red and black, and there stands the headmaster shouting something we cannot hear for the clatter and din from the great stone balloon. Low clouds rage across the sky, and it seems as though it is all taking place in total isolation, as though no one but ourselves can see what is happening. Has the electric wiring already plunged the whole city into rigid despair and darkness? Has the fire brigade arrived? In the basement room, where the old ink bottles are, noble blood flows, and when I see the cannon rise further into the sky I think irreverently: yes! Yes! Scuttle the whole damned football pitch, so that we may at last get some peace! Rise, balloon of stone, towards the sky, vanish like a bad dream from my sight, so that I may at last get some sleep in the mornings!

But we go racing around, see our classmates hanging out of the windows like fresh clusters of grapes, no one dares to take the leap, the distance is already too great. What is it we are trying to save? The eight hundred pupils, the hundred teachers, all that whining wasp-like heat in there behind the creaking walls, in the quivering classrooms, in the gently curving corridors with their tottering plaster busts of Roman emperors and marauders? All those swaying, piercing ceiling lamps! All those dancing plinths! The suddenly agitated asthmatic organ in the great hall! Are they not all getting a cheerful send-off, do they not at last stand before a yearned-for departure, while we on the ground can enjoy a new, free life? Oh, this grotesque pirate ship of stone exposed to the inscrutable playfulness of the elements! Do we not all strive, in sleep and daydream, to overcome the force of gravity, to hover above the heavy fields to the joy and surprise of those nearest us? Ropes break with a sound like that of an immense whiplash, in an inner room behind the kitchen in the janitor's flat sits old deaf Lindroos, reading today's newspaper. Mole-runs, secret archives, broken computers, wooden desks carved right through, old maps fluttering in the whirl-wind beneath this satellite of knowledge and stone!

Now all cherished bonds go asunder. From the north comes a wind that makes the school slowly sway. A unison cry from those who are shut inside is blown like a sail from the open windows. The front door slams to with a bang, like the lid of a gigantic stone coffin. The whole of the mighty building seems to be driven by an inner engine, it quivers, the flag in front of the entrance is drawn down to half-mast and up again, from the prayer hall someone can be heard singing A Safe Stronghold Our God Is Still. And the children join in with shrill voices. No, our dear school will never be itself again. Here a completely new kind of teaching is needed! A shattered, strange curriculum of hovering, adventure, dream! Letters and numerals in a strange and giddying dance! The wingbeats of history surround the mighty school with their all-renewing din. Obsolete facts fly out of crannies in windows and cracks in walls like blind bats. Only the rusty old cannon still keeps the school in place, like an abandoned, scraping drift-anchor. But even the wire rope which the physics teacher with his round spectacles has managed to hurl outside is now tensed to the point of snapping. Everything has become so remarkably, frighteningly quiet: the city, the streets, the school, the sky. The glow from the underworld turns pale and dies away. Only a smell of sweat, chalk and buckwheat porridge now surrounds the great stone balloon. In the pus-yellow light one gust of wind is all that it takes for the school, with a ringing, broken sound from the tensed cable, to teeter and start begin to drift southwards, towards the sea, out over the bay, over proud Sveaborg that still stands on its own ground and does not rely on any foreign help.

And the lycée glides away, as a dream glides away, scrapes across the roofs, tearing off chimneys and television aerials, but continues its resplendent course. It is as though I were there, saw the giddying perspectives, the city with its harbours and churches, the market trade, people like tiny insects rushing from task to task, as though it were all determined and insignificant from the outset: no one sees us, no one follows us, only the indifferent clouds. In the end the enormous building is only a dot in the sky, a flyspeck that is wiped away by the silence.

We who are late stand there for a long time. What can we say to one another? We part as though we had taken part in a conspiracy. Even the few people in the underworld are silent. Majken stands in her night-gown on a stepladder she has found and set up facing the street, she looks as though she is laughing, but nothing is heard. We part without looking at one another, it is as though we stood in the same rear court-yard, craned on the neck of the same amazement, as though it had all happened without being observed by anyone outside. I walk through streets, open the door, the stairs echo as though someone else were walking there, fried Baltic herring, always the same fried Baltic herring turns over in the frying pan behind closed doors. At home it is quiet, Papa at his secondhand bookshop, Mamma at the office, I go into my room and lie down on the bed, pull the old checked blanket over me, sink into a deep, dreamless sleep. Blessed sleep that effaces everything, unease and worry, fear and excitement: crazy life may roll on out there, I am no longer part of it, answer no more questions, see through the cracks of my eyes tables and chairs standing in their places, what they have experienced I do not know, what I have experienced no one knows, we are silent, we sink into sleep, we rest.

Mamma comes home, she places her cool hand on my forehead, I have no fever, I reply evasively to her questions, nothing has happened, I sit at the table in the evening with a sense of triumph like a warmth, yes, almost a fire within me, and at night I find it hard to sleep. Where are they now, how far have they gone? Andrée was forced down, three men go step by step towards their ruin, but the school sailed south after all, perhaps it will land slowly on some Soutb Pacific island, perhaps it stands there crowded round by lianas and naked South Pacific girls, the windows shine as before, from the classrooms come laughter and the teachers' firm voices, a scent of orchids rises along the broad stairway, brightly-coloured parrots take charge of the lessons, the years pass, it all sinks into the jungle of laziness, it all moulders away, walls, blackboards, old teachers, wild pupils, everything collapses, is effaced by green leaves, vanished, invisible, soundless.

When the morning comes I wake up early, sit at the table with pounding heart, no, I don't want to stay at home, I am perfectly well, I take my schoolbag and run along the streets, has it all been found out, has it all been kept quiet, there was nothing in the newspaper. Is that not the noise from the school I hear, as from a swarm of migrating birds, the sky is full of their faint singing. I stop, peep out cautiously from behind a street corner, am merely two large eyes: there it stands, as before, untouched, heavy, with glowing windows. Slowly I approach it, boys stream around in the corridors, the clothes hang on their hangers like men shot dead, there is shouting and unrest, nothing has changed, the late boys from yesterday run past without giving me a glance, each of them carries his own secret as in an invisible rucksack. Now I see it: the cracks in the walls, Augustus's empty pedestal, the fragments of his plaster head, a small fire is lit behind my eyes. Down there, underground, the lighting does not work, in the toilets there is shouting and screaming, high-pitched voices on the point of breaking. And at the gym lesson I discover that all the climbing ropes have vanished. They are old, they have to be renewed, says the teacher, with a rigid face. Everyone is silent. That which changes is a scandal, and is passed over in silence. But behind each closed door a strange light penetrates outwards. Maja, the janitor's wife, looks at me with the same gaze as when she stood on the stepladder from the underworld, a gaze of surprise, suffering and secret understanding. The cannon has gone, it has buried its barrel like a fertile root in the park next door, people have already gathered to admire the new addition to the city's sculptural flora. All the signs are there to be read. Cautiously, I ask Klas what he did yesterday. Yesterday? Why? Where were you? His face burns. He is silent. Behind every word there are hidden events, they force their way into the simplest bits of conversation, people move imperviously and secretively. I am a part of this silent mass. I am alone, I have a thousand eyes.

16 Around Proteus

The events to do with the school have upset me. Breaks in one's daily routine are welcome. But: moderation in all things. I write as though inside me a small welding-flame were driving me onwards. The world hovers in a grain of sand. You write that you have visited the Museum of Modern Art in New York and admired the old American photographs. I remember those wild landscapes, everything so razor-sharp, foreground, background, white flowing watercourses like spilt lead, Yosemite, the trees, a continent still untouched and wild in its silence. What did they experience, the first discoverers, as they stood and observed all that beauty, what were they looking for? A voice of clarity within themselves? With long exposure-times they sought to capture that enormous demand for clarity, purity and solitude within them. They were pieces of gravel, scarcely discernible in the midst of great nature. Were they not seized by a strange, burning unease? That all this was transitory?

Now the April of the soul is here, and I see the walls of the abyss of an opened street, cosmos and chaos like cold gusts of wind, in the window I have set out Cavafy and Blixen, Bang and Hašek, Defoe and of course Shakespeare, yes, I even found some little volumes of Robert Walser, a new edition of Anatole France, a couple of Penguin Henry James, it's the time of spring and departure, and the letters are flying!

But never again as then, in one's teens, when one's contact with things was things themselves. She came walking in the rear courtyard, it was her, Majken, she whispered strange things in my ear, pulled me into the storeroom, it was a sweet initiation and a confirmation: that we both saw what was marvellous about disasters, great and small. We don't learn for school but for life. The self-evident has no shame. It is light, and yet has weight. I felt like a solid body, hovering above the drifting ice-floes, and the loneliness was not so heavy to bear, it was like the air. If it was dark there was always a light. For mornings and evenings became ever lighter, the full moon came out, big and freckled, and through the black crowns of the trees in the courtyard drifted a light violet shadow. Sap rose in each trunk, in each limb. Each labyrinth stood open to the sky, the unease was an itch, an illness, to move about outside was to half-run in someone else's anorak, children were too small, grown-ups too big, every stairway was a ladder from hell to heaven, or at any rate to the primordial attic with its relics, boxes, chests, worn-out bicycles, skis and sticks, and with the faint but clear smell of overripe apples.

When I came home it seemed to me as though all my life I would climb in the same daily rhythm, listen to the same voices, sniff the same cooking smells, fried Baltic herring and fried pork gravy, porridge and cabbage soup, see the same cracks in the walls, the same damp like bruises on beaten skin spreading in stairways and rooms, on walls and people's faces. I tried to be attentive and precise, Papa had talked about that after all, I remembered it, something immensely important was hidden there. But not everything was a pattern, not everything worked out all right, there was a taste of blood and metal in one's mouth, and the growing pains struck up like grass through hard-trodden clay.

Now I had the room that gave on to the street, it faced north, I think you know that the light falls in late, only towards evening. I closed the door behind me as though I wanted to leave it open, I sat on the edge of the bed as though neither past nor present existed, and all the years that have passed since then are like a white cloud that sails across the sky and is gone. I have always seen the light of that green lamp and looked at my dangling legs, sat here and held a letter from you in my hand, a completely weightless contact. Dirty snow was gathering in the rear courtyard, it was no longer the same yard, but the same snow, the same roaming sky. On the stairs I often met the girl with the naked eyes, the family had just moved in, I would have liked to have followed her, take hold of her, but kept away. In the hallway at home I stood in front of the mirror and saw my pale, ugly face, a mocking gleam in my eye, only childishness, gullibility, dark straggling hair, really I had no features at all, everything flowed out like melted snow. After school I dropped in at Papa's secondhand bookshop, slid my finger over the spines of the books, sat here in the room at the back and read or saw through the window the cold light out there, the people talked of the spring, of a brighter time, of all the things that were outside me.

The man down there in the courtyard raises the bottle to his mouth and drinks. It is as though he were seeking my gaze. It was about that time the Petris' son fell from the balcony on the third floor and was killed, he was the same age as me. There was whispering, talking, he had been behaving strangely, we had walked past each other, he slipped along the walls, did not answer when he was spoken to. At the Stiléns' they knew everything, chewed their truths in secret, Papa Herman had rung for an ambulance. Yes, that's all very well, but I know a thing or two! Mockery gathered at the corners of his mouth, I learned a lot there, Granny sometimes came shuffling out and laid a bony hand on my head, but the sideboard, the chairs, the lace covers, the pictures stood rigid and unmoving. The only thing that lent colour to the greyness was Stig's carrot-red hair, a fire from some distant and astonishing side-leap in genes and dreams; the rest was inferiority, a tenacious, smouldering contempt for the better-off, a pride and a mistrust that gave the everyday its worth. Herman's waistcoat stretched with the responsibility of being a family provider, he buttoned it with short, blunt fingers, his eyes were slightly bloodshot. Beneath his gaze Beda was forever active, polishing, dusting, tidying, cooking. The dead boy, Sten, had according to him now come to rest in harbour. Beda went to visit the Bergsrådinna and made the funeral meal. The Bergsråd had locked himself in his room, a dark cave where old books gathered dust and which was haunted. From it stifled sobs were heard. Herman knew that, his voice chanted, but when Stig began to describe what Olof had looked like as he lay there, brain matter and a thin trickle of blood from one ear, his father quickly interrupted him: be silent. Even the house was silent, the doors were silent, the time when people spoke to one another was long past.

It was about that time that Papa told me about King Proteus, about the enormous harbours on the island of Paros, about the massive stone quays that faced the sea, the mysterious light, about the sculpted pattern of pentagons, about a fifth season that was joyfully celebrated on the island, but above all about Proteus' metamorphoses, the stranglehold, how he became lion, snake, panther, wild boar, water, fire and green tree, before he regained his face, how he lived in his cave. And I saw Bergsråd Petri in his cave, metamorphosed, for me he assumed the forms of the stone, the water, the tree and the light, his face was mirrored in the black asphalt of the courtyard, his cry echoed as in mist above the petrified city. The day I saw him he had completely changed, came walking through the gateway, majestic, silent, greeted Papa politely, they exchanged a few words about the weather and the world situation. Death was there, unmentioned, like gusts of wind. It penetrated through the walls, crouched in the cellar, waited to climb out at night, a tall, majestic wave that cascaded through the streets, tearing away all that was loose and fragile, so that only the heaviest façades remained, black in the rumbling moonlight.

I wake up and see another grey day, becalmed. I hear a bright echo: the blackbird is singing.

17 At the Cinema

The days teeter on the slippery tightrope between winter and spring and settle for neither, fly on their way. Time is a clown, performs its somersaults, stumbles and trips over every sorrow, the eye stares wildly, the mouth smiles, the soul weeps: thus I recognize myself. Unease drives me along the streets, I am child and adult, I am gust of wind and silenced eye. When it gets dark, ever more reluctantly do I flee the monotony, the school, Mamma and Papa, my room, the books, walk the eighteen steps down to the cinema ticket counter, the plush-air, the stillness, the expectations. Did you ever experience the same thing? The girls sat there with their chewing gum, did they sink into that fantastic world the same way we boys did, hiding under crude laughter? Everything stopped in expectancy before the closed door to the cinema hall. When it opened, the curtain and the screen were there, the interior with its whisperings, the rustle of bags of sweets in that cavern of dreams, without windows but with giddying views of a white screen, and through it, out to real, tangible, preposterous life. It began with a roaring lion, a naked man beating an enormous gong, a gleaming torch, an inundating music. All that I yearned for was there: the enigma, the mystery, reality made visible, a more generous life.

I ought to have gone alone. I was infatuated, dragged Lena with me into my picture world that wasn't hers. What did we talk about? The important thing lay ahead of us. A glimpse of it was given by the pictures in the foyer, the stars, the posters. Lena's ear was quite small, concealed by her brown hair. She had a pleated tartan skirt, her knees were plump, I wanted to put my hand on them. She talked about the school. She was everywhere, her eyes, her vivacity, her body close to mine as the lights went down. The pale shields of people's faces were all turned up towards the flickering texts, there were Jean Gabin and

Michele Morgan, Vivien Leigh and Clark Gable, Elisabeth Taylor and James Dean, there all was transformed, everydayness wiped out and life converted into image. Resolutely I gripped Lena's hand, it was small and warm, Lena rustled her bag of sweets with her right hand, her left gave mine a squeeze, then resolutely withdrew again. The sweet life of Tara moved through the hall like a warm wave, we sat with our noses pressed to the window that opened on another age, perhaps not past at all, perhaps to come? Atlanta burned, sweet love met hard calculation, and Lena handed me her bag of sweets. Oh, that haunted house with all its fantastic passages, halls, wide landscapes, and the melancholy which I loved and found also in myself. Did your heart also tremble when you heard Nelly in *Quai des Brumes*: 'Every morning one thinks that something new is going to happen, and then everything continues as before.'

Yes! No! Here the loneliness was embodied therefore tolerable, the same dog that ran after Jean Gabin ran after the old man in Umberto D., that was lonely and harrowing, tears ran down Lena's round cheeks, one had to wipe away one's feelings before the always equally moving ending, to surface dry-eyed in a dead city on a Sunday evening when everything was beginning again: home, school, the days, the grind. Lena went on talking. Wasn't it sweet, the dog that ran after Gabin? How terrible it must have been in Atlanta, but it was lucky that Scarlett escaped. No, she hadn't read the book, it was too long. She didn't have time because of her homework. Next year we'll write one, Daniel! Imagine being as rich as Rock Hudson! But James Dean got his punishment for loving Leslie.

Cold gusts of wind blew towards us as we walked home. Lena looked past me a little, as though she were talking to herself. I felt like a worn glove. I walked with my collar up, I smiled crooked smiles, why could I not be a Bogart when Bogart could? We parted with a Bye! See you!, it felt like a relief. Something extraneous and critical began to penetrate my infatuation. The infatuation died with Umberto D. I ought to have seen it alone, seen loneliness alone. The pride, the poverty, the old man, the abandoned servant girl, all abandoned people, all the humiliations: how strangely familiar they were, close at hand, lonelinesses that brushed against one another for a few moments which the actors weren't looking. I saw them, they were parts of my growing-pain-aching body, and if, as I write, I stretch, I remember them, as though they had lodged themselves forever in my joints and limbs. What happened on the cinema screen was sharp both in the foreground and further back, in early dreams. It was all the eye's bright and airy pictures, disturbing human destinies, hate and love, the basic elements of existence, camera movements in the head of a schoolboy. Image became body, the body moved to the image's rhythm, for two hours time stopped. Whirling clocks were concealed in strange abandoned houses, on rainswept streets, in the gaze of someone persecuted or in danger, in the slow ascent of the camera-hoist, it takes in burning cities, brutal conflicts, the wind of history and the torment of love. What is happening to my room? Doors fly open, curtains billow out like pirate sails from black windows, an eye attentively observes everything that happens, it takes in the murderer, the drowning man, the lover, Hulot walks arm in arm with Gelsomina, Philip Marlowe looks up and observes you: you are under suspicion and at the same time see yourself, honour prevails over corruption, love is eternal and wide as the desert. There, in the cinema's darkness, a light that is comprehensible to all, and the forms living their momentary lives rise out of their actions and pass through you as through a hotel corridor, seeking their rooms.

I stand looking down at the rear courtyard from our bedroom window, perhaps a murderer is moving about down there, perhaps, if I make an effort, I could go on sitting here with a camera and observe, concealed from everything except the evil and the loneliness, the secret things that happen. But too many years have passed, some of the magic has gone, Humphrey Bogart is dead, Grace Kelly is dead. Only the unease and the longing remain, like a simple and artless song, by Nino Rota.

18 The Mount of Victory

Grandmother's staircase gleams with cleanliness and smells of summer. There are the the bluebell's gentle tinkling and the sun of the marguerite, and the darkest scent of lilac, as when shadows play. There, too, are the dandelion's poor-scent and the wild pansy's memories from bright rooms, with photographs of the dead dressed in straw hats and white clothes, children with bouquets of flowers picked embarrassedly and quickly. Flower-scent, like grandmother, requires time and stillness. On grandmother's door is the name Cedermark. She does not want to live with Viktoria, she wants to live alone, for as long as she can. Her voice is stern, like her hand, she needs only one room. She speaks of how she will soon be leaving, but she does not intimidate. She speaks the truth, she is a tree with deep roots. When she dies she will leave few things, but clear ones: some furniture, a few clothes, a photograph album where only Mamma and Viktoria live. She leaves one mild day in April, and her funeral is still and bright. Yes, even her seriousness was bright, as is often the case with one who has worked hard but has loved it notwithstanding. Of her peace Mamma and Viktoria receive a rich portion.

Just over a week after her death I stand on the threshold at home and look at Mamma, she is sitting on a chair with a fan-shaped trellised back, she is dressed in a chequered gown. The smell of timelessness is there, and I am seized by an emotion I do not understand, a mixture of sorrow and freedom: everything is so unaltered, and returns, in spite of everything. The light falls in from the window. The unease before the spring has stopped for a moment and sees: the twilight among the few trees in the courtyard, the smell of sap and melted snow, the wide sky. Mamma inclines her head over the pad, she is painting a water-colour, in front of her on the table she has two porcelain mugs, one containing water, the other her paintbrushes. There is the big Japanese brush with its domed point, with it one can touch the faintest horizon and plunge a whole seashore into darkness. It can draw both eternity and peace. There is the medium-sized brush for ripened, not yet awoken fields. There are smaller brushes, for hints at birds, flowers, mountain contours. If one's luck is good, they can capture the swift, blue shadows that are to be found both on the snow under trees in winter and under warm summer days, but perhaps most intensely now, when the spring is hesitating.

On the table in front of Mamma are a bowl of fruit, three oranges, a couple of green pears. But it is not them she is painting, she is painting Mont Sainte-Victoire. On the table beside her a book of Cézanne's watercolours lies open, her gaze passes to the book, she sees the mountain breathe and walks in the clear air on the paths near Aix. The lightness she seeks is all the weight of the accumulated years concentrated in a hinted line, a distance of tenderness. She hesitates, that is also a part of what has been seen and understood, this hesitancy which I received as a gift and have been struggling with ever since. The room seems to be listening to her silence. There is the old book case that smells of rosewood, and above her hangs a picture, a winter land-scape with black, flowing water. Mamma tests the colour against the shiny lid of the paint box, it has the orange of ripe autumn, it must come out towards winter, be thinned out in order to make the moun-tain hover. Mamma is not present here, either, her eye when she leans forward sees not the room, but the mountain, the meagre shadows, each insignificant part of the whole, of wide-open, hard-to-capture life. Mamma measures the silence all the way to the mountain's foot. That white surface must be divided into sky and earth, and weigh the same. The light from the window is just soft enough to correspond to the silence. The nape of Mamma's neck gleams white.

Over by the window stands Papa, in such strong light that he is almost invisible, a dark shadow only. He reads from Cézanne's letters: 'Nature is to us human beings more depth than surface, and so from it we must incorporate into our light vibrations, represented by red and yellow, and sufficient of blue to give the sense of air.' He reads slowly, translates. He falls silent and turns towards the courtyard outside. I stop beside Mamma, she looks up and smiles for a moment, her eyes are grey, but her gaze is averted. Then she goes back to her work. Along the floor with the simple, ugly, brown linoleum covering goes a narrow rag rug in white, with blue borders. I take an orange from the bowl and look at Mamma's watercolour for a while. I still have the book that is in front of her, it falls open naturally at 'Château Noir' and Mont Sainte-Victoire, it is the Phaidon edition, with Fritz Novotny's preface, in which he talks of Cézanne's late period with its distance from life, from human beings – as if 'all his landscapes were depicted in a complete absence of wind.'

I read it thirty-five years later, in the same stillness. The dead move about in the rooms of memory as though they were alive, more alive than the shadows that hurry out across the courtyard, that disappear along the streets. Only a hint of blue sky above the mountain – Mamma screws up her eyes, the light is so strong. That 'mood' Novotny turns towards and which he does not find in Cézanne, says Papa, is there none the less, as a life-mood, as the accumulated energy and emotion of a solitary existence. Is it his words I hear, or my own thinking, pale and quickly altering, and do I not hear at the same time the faint murmur from vernal springs, from the mountain's slopes or from the drainpipe along the wall, all an image that is conjured forth by time and is still there, outside. The limit between sound and echo floats, wind and water move there, green, yellow, purple, blue, but Mamma puts down her brush and knocks her forehead against her hand, closes her eyes. I feel the weight of the orange in my hand, the scent finds its way through the dry, hot landscape around the cool, unattainable mountain. Then the air becomes cooler, the image sharper. Cézanne's dejection greater, he walks away from the subject, dark in mood, his image is dissolved.

There is, in early spring, a cold current of air, an onsetting autumn. It brings with it signs of death. I don't notice it, only divine a sense of sorrow among those who have lived so many years together, and the sense of estrangement between them and me. Behind the bright image of them both, each in his or her own silence, appear changes, distortions, stains on ceilings and floors, colours that are beginning to run, curtains that are torn to shreds by gusts of wind, dark clouds that weigh the window down, as though a gale were approaching. There is a streak of blood from the sun that has set and a streak of blood from the sun that is rising. The day that just now was refreshingly cool now bites. Mamma's and Papa's voices can be heard from their room, excited, sharp, and, in between, a choking silence.

When I open the door, Papa is alone, he is stacking books in front of him, is almost hidden behind them, I see that he has aged, that he is a tired old man. He has caved in, the large pale hands barely touch the books, but his eyes are those of a child. There is a sorrow there that touches everything, from the beginning of time. The objects know it too, and therefore remain silent. But the mountain, the watercolour, the light is still there, so that one's eye is dazzled. Now Papa has also gone, only the spring light remains with its uneasy thoughts that move in and out of one another. For you, Maria, I quote with Cézanne: 'I have in a sense gone forward. Why so late and with such difficulty?' To see, to work, to train one's eye through nature, to find the culmination point in an orange, an apple, a ball, a head, the one that is nearest the eye, all this ought to exist in the language we speak, the words we send one another. Will we still have the same language, when you come back? The days hop 'like a yellow bird in April branches', to quote the excellent Dr Williams. Perhaps the best things in art and literature, when I cast my mind back, are a form of medicine? A family medicine chest for the lost or depressed, for whom the new medicines are not always the most effective ones.

Thirty-five years ago I took the university entrance exam. We sat, each one of us, in his own concentrated loneliness in the gym hall. There was an atmosphere of quiet desperation, and at the same time an element of comedy: that this should be some sort of indication of maturity and knowledge! I sit and choose: a religious figure, a figure from the stage, a landscape in memory. Christ as Hamlet in Paradise? The Banana, our wise old form teacher, looks straight at me, with a smile. What is he smiling at? The gravity of the situation? What is being demanded of me? Certainly not wisdom and imagination! If I want to I can open the nearest tall window and float out into the periphery, the wind is cool, trees sway reflectively, in there we sit like tin soldiers, there is a smell of mud and departure, soul-abrasions, between the clouds a blue patch is visible, a torn work-shirt. What white paper fields are these I am forced to move across, leaving my snailtracks on them? Now the sun breaks in, we sit in broad fields of dust and write, not for life, but for the school. We are hurled out into the unknown.

And now? How many unknown things there are left, as though some part of the wsidom had shrunk back then and been replaced by a sometimes fruitful, sometimes tormenting hesitancy. I sit at your writing desk, a day is at an end, it has been the first of May and I took a trip into the centre and saw the balloons, the masks, the students, the yelling, the colours, the spasm-like attempts at a carnival, a sense of spring. The icy wind tore at the thin trees, a gigantic barrel organ, transported here from some distant land, played old operetta tunes that froze solid in one's ear. Quickly all that disappeared, the student caps, the pubs, children ran with balloons, Lena and Jan grew up, first they shrieked with joy and giddiness, threw streamers, we carried them, then we led them, soon they will lead us into a new childhood, quieter, more colourless, more bitter. I am filling out your objective report from MIT with the most notable adventures, even you must have your allotted share. But they just remain sketches, stupidities. I think one needs to respect the lives of others in order to be able to respect one's own. I have put on a Mozart piano concerto at random, Jeunehomme I think, it fills my emptiness with a beauty we cannot live without. An exercise not only in listening but also in seeing, I fancy. Enough. Enough written, enough thought, enough fancied. I wish you a good night. Come, rest here by my side. Say nothing. Just be.

19 The Local Pub-Restaurant

I have not seen it before, the door in that dark gateway. Behind it can be heard a murmur as of people in distress at sea, a rising and falling wave. A glowing light filters out through the chinks in the door. If I take hold of the handle, perhaps a bolt of lightning will strike me to the ground. The door bulges outwards, like a sail in a storm, it breaks free of its rusty lock, it hits me in the face, out gush bawling and shouting, a hundred decibels of used-up voices and notes, beer foam and vapour, and a blustering crow lunges past me, scraping against the flaking roof of the gateway, and is gone, like a blow of terror in the eye. An enormous man with a small, ash-grey head, dressed in some kind of purple uniform, quickly hauls me inside and the door closes with a click, like a ladies' handbag. He gives me a shove forward, into the murmur and the mist. Out from the dark rear wall of the pub snakes a long bar counter, paper-white faces mix like soiled cards in the narrow cones of light from the ceiling; countless signs hang there, I can't see what is written on them for the mass of humanity that jostles round and pushes me onward. Dani! Dani! cries a wound of a mouth, it is the janitor's wife from the school, it is Majken, she is sweating and pressing herself against me, but quickly turns away in order to shout at three witches in fur: *Suksikaa vittuun!*[1] Over in a booth sits Uncle Olof with his profile dissolved by spirits and declaiming, swaying with his eyes closed, he is inaudible, his face plaster white and marked by death. A little man, almost a dwarf, is imitating a cockerel on the floor, fluttering with worn elbows, his black suit splits open, vegetable fibre gushes out. Klas with his round face shiny with sweat catches sight of me. Dani! Dani! This way! The black gap in his teeth widens, the whole of his

1 Get lost (Finnish) – literally: 'ski to the devil!'

mouth is filled with beer-foam and unarticulated words, two TV sets, one in each corner of the smoke-filled, flickering pub, are showing a boxing match, people stick together in clusters and roar at each well-aimed blow. A young boy with a wad of banknotes in his hand forces his way through to the bar counter using his hands as digging implements, around his neck a black crash helmet, a girl starts screaming, a hand is raised, a knife gleams, a figure crashes down and disappears, trodden into the floor. Olof Urwind lights his pipe in his corner and observes leaning forward, with greedy eyes, the stage against the far wall, where a blood-red curtain, more underskirt than curtain, is jerkily drawn aside to reveal a pale, middle-aged woman, sitting astride a chair; she opens her mouth and starts to sing an old folk-song, there is terror in her eyes, her smile frozen like ice and cut into her face, now the boxing fantasists are shouting and her singing is drowned in the general hubbub. I am sunk in my hole, on the bottom lie the invisible dead, this way, they cry, this way, and a woman with small pointed teeth clutches at my wrist. The sculptor with the shaggy beard is there, he tugs her towards him, he shouts with his small, gleaming pig's eyes red with exertion: Bacon was right! The supremacy of the imagination! The science of the imagination! The eternal recurrence! Grushenka! I shall drown you in coal, in coal! Everywhere I see teeth, mouths, fishes' mouths in an aquarium, everything is thunderingly quiet and sharks move there with eel-like movements, waiters with white paunches and black backs, on the crude wooden tables the circles of beer spread out, jaws chew, from the loudspeakers up on the dark ceiling the music booms, heavy and formless. The thin woman on my other side is a vegetarian, there's blood on the bananas, she whispers with a garlic mouth, blood! She is sucking a stick of celery, gnawing it with ecstatically closed eyes, she can walk through door-chinks, so thin she is, guess how old I am, she breathes, behind the makeup I can see the thousand years, the degradation, the blows, the hatred. Tomorrow she is getting married to a crane-driver, this evening she feels sorry for furred animals, tomorrow she will wear a leather mini-skirt, today she has elegantly frayed jeans, her age chops and changes like the gusts of wind out there, they beat against the leaden grey windows, she has a leather jacket, over her shoulder she carries a coquettish little shoulderbag, it contains her jewels, she loves working people, true socialism. She leans against the sophisticated connoisseur of wine, who is dressed in hand-sewn contempt, he sniffs at his glass with coloured eyelids, circles like a burglar around dream castles in France, sips, he is the expert, but the great Sculptor drinks schnapps, it vanishes into his beard as into a porous wall. The three witches in their furs whisper between themselves, their mascara runs. The whole room presses outwards in its terror of loneliness, the fear of silence whirls up in roaring laughter, glasses are thrown to the floor and smash in a rain of sparkling fragments, someone licks blood from his finger, there is Beda, coming out of nowhere, she has a brush and shovel, disappears again as if she had been swallowed up.

But now by the door over there sits Raskolnikov from the Ministry of Finance, he is sawing at half a veal cutlet while with half-closed eyes he watches a little girl who is dancing on the stage, fat drips from his mouth, children and old people are his favourites, his eyes are dead with hunger, suddenly he looks up and observes me thoughtfully, he is holding his knife upright in his left hand, supporting his head with his right, for a moment we look into each other, and he smiles. Then he turns his indifferent gaze away, lets it slide over the pub, over the tables, over the tumult, everything is in his eyes exact, positioned like a blood-red fragment of glass in an obscure mosaic through which firelight flames. Under one table a little boy looks out, vanishes again. There are mirrors on the walls, I only see that now, I thought it was all much bigger, that the people were moving, each and every one, with their doppelgängers, that behind the pub there was another pub, in the room another room, that the shouts, the groaning, the screams were coming from there, but it is here that it is happening, here the smells of blood and beer flow together, here the gentle songs resonate around the coarse ones, here we twist and turn in the mirrors' quicksilver, trickle down the walls. There, right at the far end of the scaly, serpentine bar counter sit Viktoria and Fredrik, my Papa, his eyes two black holes, she is leaning against him, I elbow my way over, I shout, where's Mamma? but Olof is there, gives me a kick on the lower shin, Idiot! he hisses, but Viktoria smiles: It's my little bridegroom, isn't it? Come here! But I am driven away by the mass of people, end up against the wall next to Bergsrådinna Petri. She gets up like a black mountainside, leans towards the Bergsråd opposite and screams: You! It was you who drove my son to his death! You!

The Bergsråd sits quiet, he considers her with a calm, malignant look, I settle myself as far in against the wall as I can in order not to see the double reflections, hear the double voices, live the double life that ferments around me. As from a bottomless well the yellow yelling rises towards the grease-blackened air vents in the ceiling, the air-conditioning rumbles evenly and steadily, we might all just as well be in an immense ship steaming into the darkness, and the camera's eye takes in the scratches along the bar counter, the claw-marks, the wounds on the bartender's neck, the light that flames up and dies down again, the eye that is visible in the hole in the curtain, the signs that hang from the ceiling and quiver in the drifting smoke, Barney's Pub 40 km, Next Novosibirsk, No Exit By Rear Door, Beware Of Falling Rocks, This Side Up, St James's Palace, Blood Bank, Please Keep Off the Grass, Rubbish Tip, Life-jackets Under Seat, Hands Up. Rüdesheimer Ingollstädter Spätlese, No Entry, Mortuary Across The Yard, Cul-De-Sac, they float like a dead flock of birds above the pressed-together mass of people.

In a flash everything suddenly goes quiet, as when one turns down the sound of the TV, mouths move but nothing can be heard, people drift out like smoke through doors and air-vents, the floor shakes, the rumbling that is now heard comes from outside, the copper-gleaming chandelier with its single burning light begins to sway, who is shouting, who is being carried away, who is bolting the heavy door, who is ordering silence? I stand alone in the empty rear courtyard, the only window with light in it is the skylight in the back room of the secondhand bookshop, there are pale stars and the city glides into a short, anxious slumber. A mist is rising from the stones. In my room stand the shelves, the books, the table, the sofa, the chair, the curtains are drawn, heavy vehicles are passing out there, torches gleam, a smell of doused fires seeps in through the walls, I sink into sleep like a drowning man, a quiet rain begins to fall.

20 Spring Days

Thus do days, weeks and years pass in my double-entry ledger. It is not only forty years that separate what I was from what I am, but the distance now, in the moment. Everything is strangely repeated, a new thing happens, something is unalterable, like a resignation in the soul. I no longer went to concerts with Mamma, Marina Miranda de la Cruz was an image that slowly faded in a haze, the illness sank its claws into her, her eyes became sharp, Papa's silence deeper. I conducted the Haffner in the circle of fellow students, but the first joy was over. And now it is spring, and the unease is here as before, can conceal itself no more. Those who pass one another in the street give one another a hasty glance and then lower their eyes to the flying gravel again. Anna and Fredrik, as they are called, as I want to call them with Viktoria, they have aged, I help Fredrik at the secondhand bookshop and go for long walks with Anna, she has grown restless. The joy, the sorrow, my failed exams, my troubles in love I keep to myself. Silence becomes a habit. Warmth is there, making no demands. The birthday children in the bookshop window each week have been a moderate success – Kierkegaard and Morgenstern, Martinson and Kraus, Schnitzler and Balzac, Lagerkvist and Emerson – always on the shelf there is some worn paperback or a yellowed version from the 1920s to put out, to take out of the window, to read, hesitate over, put back again. At night they converse, Freud with Conan Doyle, Undset with Plato, such quiet conversations that only cunning pursuit can snatch up a word here, a word there, heavy, impassioned will-o'-the-wisps in darkness, a strange pattern of light in silent nights. How can joy and loathing be so violently mixed? And the spring goes onward and reaches a point where the sun late in the evening casts its oblique radiance in over the work table, the Hermes Baby typewriter, the opened books. The spring moon goes its way in the sky, young leaves come out on the lonely trees in the courtyard.

It was a time that Fredrik loathed. He sat in the semi-darkness of the bookshop, conversed long with his regular customers, came home late in the evenings, a few simple words were spoken. I walked beside Anna down to the sea where the city was only audible as a faint hum, everything was open there towards the south, rocks, harbour, quays, clouds moved low above us, in the west we saw a blood-red streak, and Mamma looked at me, I was a child she was in the process of losing. Papa shuts himself in, she says to me, I hear her, you mustn't do that, you mustn't be like him in that respect, you must be open, Daniel. She takes my arm. The sharp sunlight makes me immobile, like Papa, I find it hard to read, I can't concentrate. Yes, she says, it's true, the sun is a thief, the moon is a thief, she stole her pale light from the moon, and the sea, the earth, the wind are thieves that rob us all, with the years we all grow poorer, have ever less to give, apart from our habits which are bad habits, but you haven't got to that stage yet, Daniel, have you?

There is something alien, bitter about her, her voice hard, I try to recreate her face in the twilight. We walked home along deserted streets where no will-o'-the-wisps or gatekeepers are about any more, she talked about her favourite author Hjalmar Söderberg, about his time, about the scavengers that still existed, marked by the war, damaged by drink they staggered out from sandpits and dark gateways, lay covered by newspapers next to the bottom of the lift shaft on our staircase, they stank, people stepped over them, they clanked away with their bags down to the darkness under the street viaducts near the harbour.

The stars are sharp, as then, I lie with my eyes open, the ceiling floats away, like a child pressed against the earth's thin crust I see the Plough and the evening star, doors and windows open on memory, the cool night wind is a life-giving breath. I think of Anna and Viktoria, the sisters, I think about my maternal grandmother, about the name Cedermark, about the cedars of Lebanon and that gigantic cedar Anna and Fredrik saw in England, they told me about it when I was very small, the shadow from the tree still falls over me, I think about wind and fields, about air and earth, about the sun's streak of blood in the west and the expanse of sea we saw together, I have also seen it with you, it is there eternally, a sign that the day is over, that the night is here. Urwind, Cedermark, Urmark, Cederwind, a warm wind full of earth and needles, an expanse of sea and a steady, moonlit, cool tradewind.

I will soon be twenty, somewhere I remain there, I drag everything with me and forget, but it is my life's luggage, it settles in my face, weighs down my hands, forms my movements, my voice hesitates, I force myself into the days. Thirty-three years have passed, I hear weeping from Papa's and Mamma' bedroom, soft voices, it is the last time we see Uncle Olof's wife Ellen, she beats on the kitchen door, does not want to sit in the parlour, does not want Papa to hear, Mamma sits with her, a little, dried-up woman who says she is on the way down, that no one can save her, she leaves a smell of spirits behind her, outside the sky is so mercilessly clear that all the shadows cut like the edges of knives. Ellen sits hunched forward with her thin hands in front of her face, she asks for money for accommodation, she does not want to see Olle any more, she hates him, he is a deceiver, a white-washed mask, a grimace, a betrayal, his lisping voice, his violent excesses, look! She shows her bruises, pinpricks, emaciated sinews, Mamma holds her arms around her and rocks her like a child, together we try to comfort her, but I don't know what to say. Now a door slams shut, Mamma comes into my room and sits down heavily on the edge of my bed, what help was money when there was no way out and the despair was so great? Yet perhaps Olle was not alone responsible, no one is, each and every one of us carries his own despair, that is all.

Anna looks down at the floor, the sun is shining out there, a book lies open and dead, I follow the lines but cannot understand them, Anna says with your voice: Are you listening to me at all? Are you running away again? Where are you really, Daniel? Here, Maria, here in my incomprehensible, weekday life, in my expectancy, in my longing for you. Is the spring more beautiful in New England than here? Does the house of dreams shimmer there, too, on moonlit evenings? Here the plaster is falling from our façade, patches of damp are breaking out, and the merciless sun sees all and reveals all.

21 The Dahlgrens

There was no simple route to Fanny Dahlgren's family. It meandered through the house as though it had not wanted to get there. It made its way to the summer as though it were my body; I hesitated. This heat that glowed as from a burning-glass! The May sap rose and the tree in the courtyard was full of bursting buds. More and more often strange men turned up, cast suspicious glances at house and walls, disappeared again, and at nights in a semi-slumber I could hear the wail of ambulances or police cars measuring the distance from safety to fear, a wave that washed through the finest of days, blue, open, infinite, like my emotions.

The Dahlgrens lived closer to heaven than we did, next door to Viktoria, they had a dark door with an invisible eye. It observed everything that moved on the staircase, in the hesitating darkness: distorted human faces, oval as eggs, spider-legs, all twisted by the certainty of being weighed and measured by an unknown, suspicious gaze. Those who were granted entry were led through a dimly-lit hall to a large room that smelled of cigar smoke. Over the windows hung skin-coloured curtains, up near the ceiling lace petticoats, and on heavy sideboards gleamed the family silver. You were received by Engineer Dahlgren, a genial, boisterous, cold-eyed man around whom Fanny and her Mamma moved like glowing planets around a planet that is dead. They were like sunbeams, casually borrowed from outside to lend a touch of life to those immense, immobile rooms. The cold they were unable to beat, it drifted like an invisible mist over the oriental rugs, under the oak tables, along the dark bookshelves, to stop in amazement in the doorway of the bright, warm dining-room with its white furniture; from the music room there came from the black grand piano a dissatisfied sound as of late, breaking ice. The windows stood washed and shining against the dizzying spring sky, and Fanny passed like a ray of sunshine along the dark corridors, barely conscious of the locked-in silence; she took swift dance steps, seized my hand. Her Mamma smiled but at the same time looked at her father who had sat down and lit his cigar. Everything breathed a slow Sunday, the conversation that circled around mad modern art, the lack of morals, sailing trips in the archipelago, and my studies, my future, the secondhand bookshop as a source of income. Every subject of conversation became a series of student essays; but behind father's spectacles there sometimes gleamed a wide-open, good-natured look, as though he wanted to say: don't trust me, I'm playing with you, I have my secrets. Roast veal, cream sauce, gherkins, ice cream, dishes that passed from hand to hand, and Fanny's narrow face, her lips, the mother's low, soft voice and the light from the window that illumined their hair so that the face's thoughts fell into shadow, everything was immobile and began, without anyone noticing it, to list: the people, the furniture, the room, it would all soon be hurled through the walls out into the courtyard and the crown of the tree that was visible through the window like a light-green mirage. Did they not perceive, I thought, terror-stricken, how everything was leading to a catastrophe, how the chandelier was already hanging lop-sided and the crystals tinkling, how knives and spoons, plates and flower-arrangements were sliding to the floor, dark as a receding ocean?

But the father got up as though nothing had happened, the mother carried the crockery through to the kitchen, Fanny danced on her way to the library, her father exhibited his gleaming drinks cabinet full of unopened bottles. From the cabinet with the built-in record-player floated Sinatra's *Songs for Swinging Lovers*, Fanny danced with her eyes closed, moving her thin hips, her father and I watched, there was something exciting and elusive about it, she held her pale face raised towards some unknown sky, her thin body was like a coil of smoke from her father's cigar, there was something suppressed, violent about her. It suddenly seemed to me as though in each of us another, more dissatisfied and truthful person were about to break through, the doppelgänger, not of one's own hot body, but of another body, unknown but like-minded, a shadow's shadow. And these strangers gave one another, in secret, an inner gaze, not of hatred or indifference, but of identification, in the way that power looks into the one who is powerless and the one who is powerless sees there his own darkness, and that both, in sleep, with clenched teeth, strive towards some kind of shared reality, a happiness, a harmony, the light of a spring day. Was there not a swarm of multicoloured sparks, beings, animal forms that whirled around the room and would have smashed us to pieces had we made one single violent and unintentional movement? Sweat broke out on my forehead.

When I opened my eyes, Fanny had stopped dancing and was reclining on the sofa, panting; her narrow thighs glistened as her father talked about his alcohol research. He had forty researchers under him. Self-evident things were, in his voice, elevated to the rank of Science. People of low education were more inclined to criminality than those with higher education. Poor people did not read so many books – not that he could find any great satisfaction in invented occurrences: facts were facts. Society was a mechanism that could be controlled. I sat like a child with listening eyes: so many pompous platitudes, so much certainty, so much good advice, and this awareness of his own weight and importance in the Academic and Scientific World. Outside, wild clouds were pursued by a wind that took no notice of facts. Chaos crept like rats in cellars and attics. Against the windowpane a large, fat winter fly began angrily to buzz, beat against the invisible outside wall, flew into the curtain and fell mumblingly silent. Engineer Dahlgren's cropped hair caught a glint of sunlight, he spoke of the importance of preserving rituals, coats and tails at doctoral disputations, women and children in black, and my untimely observation that all solemn occasions to a certain extent resembled funerals was met with silence. Fanny burst into laughter, flung her hand across her mouth.

But her father turned his head, listened: where is Mamma? Where is the ice cream? He puts down the table napkin, Fanny gets up, the house shakes, a tremor passes through the air, the father roars: Doris! Doris! Sunday stands corpse-still in the dining-room, in the parlour, in the kitchen we run through, the door to the kitchen stairs is ajar, the raw, cold odour of cement and secretly-hoarded foodstuffs rises like mist towards us as we hurry down, Fanny whispers that her mother usually disappears, she has 'her fits', her father jerks out Damn! Damn! What has she gone and done now? He flings open the door to the courtyard, it flies like the shrieking of white gulls, there is the dark gateway past the Stiléns' and the pub, over there by the wall sit three old tramps, between them a woman, the mother, she sits with her narrow wrists white as a child's, she looks up when her husband kneels before her, he whispers: Come! Come home!'

The old men gabble, a bottle is produced, a cold May wind is blowing and the soul shrinks to a stone the size of a hand. There is a child, he is standing by the door of my secondhand bookshop, he disappears, looks round, is gone, he has not yet been born, has not been there, time and space whirl like rubbish along the cracked asphalt, Fanny's blonde hair covers her mother's. She is so heavy, the father takes her under one arm, I under the other, she grows heavier and heavier, as though we were dragging a dead person. But she is not dead, through slit-eyes she gives me sharp look, closes them again. The staircase echoes with our exertions, it is getting darker and darker, Viktoria's door stands silent. We tug and pull, there are windows, banisters, stair-carpets, everything follows us, groaning, Fanny opens the door and we support the now sleepwalker-rigid body that blindly seeks its way into the big bedroom, fragrant with scent. She lies down on the bed and turns to the wall, the father sits down beside her, Fanny and I steal outside. Floors, endless black floors! Her hand is cold, the day's sick light falling in from the window, was not the father's hand cold, too, as he silently leaned over his spouse?

Fanny's room is bright, from her window I can see my own on the other side of an unfamiliar courtyard with one blossoming tree, it stands white in the twilight, faint gabbling reaches us where we stand. Then slowly we move, as though time had stopped us and did not want to disturb our silence. We lie down close to each other, there are our touchings, our exploratory activity, our pauses, embarrassments, all half-dressed and burning, from the radio comes faint Glenn Miller and I whisper: did you know that he never crashed, that he never went up on the fifteenth of December 1944, and she: Who? and her eyes are closed, she is no longer listening to any reply, she is rising in an arc, I see us, we are so far away, drifting over oceans, and I enter her, it is easy, a fulfilment merely. It is all accidental and planned in advance, heat and coolness at the same time.

But already a strange sleep weighs down our eyelids, we sink together, I am close behind Fanny, with my mouth at her shoulder, my breathing next to her breathing. I dreamt that I woke up in my study behind the secondhand bookshop, I was a mature, middle-aged man and you were there beside me, Maria. But when I woke up in my dream you were gone, only a small child sat there on the old chair, looking at me attentively, but then instantly vanished. I had the impression I saw this, I am twenty, I am there, she turns round, follows my cheek with her index finger, looks into my eye and says: You must go. Papa is standing outside the door, soon he will knock on it. It's always like that. Always! Always!

Her voice is like a warm spring breeze in my ear, as from a lost paradise. Always? Always? Have I been here before? How can I leave if her father is standing outside the door? Think of something, she whispers. I look towards the window, I close my eyes, open a door, I construct a fire-escape, I go out into the radiant May evening and close the door after me, slowly I find my way down to the courtyard, there is something I have forgotten but I can't remember what it is. When I am down at the bottom with one hand I wipe away the fire-escape, the door and the echo of my footsteps, the May sky is as bright and painful as only a dream can be. Racing clouds. Oh, life! There is no light in Fanny's room, perhaps she is asleep, she is getting older, she is moving far away, her mother and father are dead, everything is like the spring sky, open and hovering, a great dark wind. Beneath the tree some old men lay sleeping. In a narrow window down near the basement of the house opposite a green lamp was turned on. What was there in common between us all? Each day we were thrown between hope and despair, without seeing their meaning, without knowing whither we were bound.

22 The Human Angel

For those who have never dreamt of flying – or have forgotten the giddying attempts of childhood, the running, the jumping, the outspread arms, the walls rushing past, the final obstacles, windows and house-fronts in a dizzying rush, the bitter metallic taste in the mouth, the hum rising into a shriek, the soaring, the fall, Mamma's scolding, the turning of the playground aunties' eyes to heaven, the certainty that one day, one day – the first successful attempt will be merely a confirmation, a final acknowledgement of the bird that exists in us all, the eye it gives us, the sense of being carried on rising currents, the planing flight above landscapes that rush onwards into our inner selves, making streets and roads into swift extensions of our own eyes, and with the joy of soaring we can take in shores, roofs, tree-tops, gaping, upturned human faces, marine expanses, the glitter of sun, all in one single weightless voyage, secret, invisible, a conqueror of the winds.

From Fanny's flat it was only a few dozen steps up to the attic. There the great silence reigned, broken only by the gale that beat against walls and windows, and the light fell there like a forgotten river through the dust, illumining a cathedral of hidden, rejected life. The flats' wire netting lockers were there, some of them empty, most of them obscurely laden with baskets, skis, old chairs, rickety chests-of-drawers, zinc bathtubs, perambulators, kick-sledges, bundles of newspapers, plaster busts of presidents with chipped-off noses, paint tins, Egyptian mummies, tightly bound and rigidly staring, model aeroplanes, in their midst an old, forgotten DC3, portable field bidets from the war of 1808–09, old TV sets with still-flickering black-and-white pictures of long-dead beauty queens, exercycles, marble urns with ashen grey wedding bouquets, birdhouses, somewhere a silent, forgotten old-age pensioner with outstretched hand (very like the black boy on Papa's smoking table), a decomposed safety curtain, a consignment of old, rat-nibbled corsets, a telephone with a lifted receiver from which there still came a complaining, indistinct Hello! Are you there? like a pale echo of despair – everything was there, and in a corner the wings, the straps, the slender bamboo frames and the silver-gleaming cloth: I saw it as soon as the heavy, peeling attic door banged shut after me, it shone as though it possessed a light of its own, the dragonfly that would lift me high above my own confused emotions, to a cool, serene general view.

Above the attic door there was a spacious gallery, it stretched into the gloom, but from its creaking floorboards one could, through a stained, dusty window, see the city dissolve in plane upon plane of colour: an immense geometrical structure defined by the sky's blue tone, house after house, roof next to roof, and in the ravines of the streets people like insects. As I dragged my wings my eyes saw light, darkness, body, colour, form, place in space, distance, nearness, movement and rest, all gathered in a single thought: to fly, to soar. The dance, the movement in my body must be answered by the movement outside me. Why, really, should I be eternally bound to the earth? I have done my best to be a child. I have taken the university entrance exam, I have studied books, I have loved and love, I think, but I want to be a human angel. If I gather my thoughts, close my eyes, open the big attic window, conjure forth the carrying wind, thread my arms into the straps under the dragonfly's shimmering wings, will there not be a life there, more weightless than that of any other element, than those of water, fire, earth? I hear Viktoria's voice: Jump now, Daniel! It is quiet enough, and all brilliance, Daniel, comes from within!

Pine and basswood, cane and strongest silk fabric is my body, I am Leonardo's ornithopter. I hesitate. The city out there, the wind's whistling beneath the roof, it is all a mighty power made of silence. Music seeps through the gable window, pale as if it had been rubbed and washed, scraped and mangled into these light tissues of dust, these paths that fell through the wide world I was about to throw myself out into. Everything glides swiftly through me, spring air, fear, joy, I throw myself out, I fall through my life, I sink in the darkness, I bump against a crossbeam, I fall into an immense heap of dry hay, I am light as a child and happy as a summer memory.

Battered black and blue, dizzy, panting, incomprehensibly alive, unsuccessful, liberated, I get up and look around me. Lockers stand silent, chicken wire gleams in the May light, swallows fly shrieking through the air and are gone, a window gapes out at an ethereal tree-top. I see the immense attic, the smoke flues like a giant's arms, I am no longer caught in an invisible storm, I am the invisible storm! Daniel Hirundo Urwind! I am the insane lover to whom an airy nothingness gives a place and a name. I drag my shattered bird-form into a corner, there are still, even in that which is shattered, morning air and hopes, broken longing but still longing. To the swallows I must give my sermon: Fly on! See more! The people, they are gaping up at me, there are Mrs Rosendal and old Granny, there is Stig with his eyes wide open, there are Viktoria, Anna and Fredrik, they are all shouting: Daniel! My shoulders hurt, I wipe a little blood away from my fore-head. Was it I who dared to do this? The summer stands at the door, everything is sharp and clear, darkness and light equally apportioned, a calm rises in me, the whole of the silent house rests in this weightless light! It is like a swiftly transient sleep, smiling, without dreams.

Below me the heavy attic door opens and two people come in, I do not see them at first, only hear their breathing, the man's heavy panting, they stand near the light that falls in through the window behind me, it is Bergsråd Petri with the heavy spectacles which he now removes, he falls on his knees before the blonde girl, the beloved, sun-surrounded Fanny, the day stops and holds its breath while its heart continues to beat. He flings his arms around her knees, he presses his heavy dark head against her light-coloured jeans, he sobs Fanny, Fanny, but she pulls at his hair and forces his head back, she whispers: It's over! Over! And he: is Sten not enough? And she: Don't try to make it my fault, if he saw us then it was your carelessness, you swine, swine!

In the immobility, in the dust, in the smell of sweat and stuffiness the words flare like sparks that may set fire to the whole attic, they echo in the void, Fanny with her blonde hair, with her body's fragrance that he wants to force his way into, it is as though my face, my mouth were fumbling forward there in the dark, half-sobbing he shuffles after her, she recoils, I get up, I tear at the quilt in front of me, millions of feathers float white through the air, fall gently on top of the grotesque, ugly couple down there, invisible eddies take hold of this gleaming snowfall, Magnus Petri rushes out, a huge black insect, his carapace strewn with white flecks, Fanny remains, motionless, when I rush down the stairs, when I totteringly go over to her, when my conception of the world falls in ruins, when it is all over and cracks of despair open like wounds on my skin, I go over to her but she does not move back, she looks straight at me, she says: Go home! You that have a home. Go home! They are only words, they have no sound, they go through me, transfix me, the pain goes through me as the happiness did just now: it is inescapable. She looks at me, fathomlessly, I would like to rush forward but don't do it, she turns round and goes, the door closes. It is getting dark, the wind is rising.

23 In Rooms Dreamt and Real

The intractable door refuses to open. The light on the other side is too strong. On the whitewashed wall hang a steel lantern, a rusty barometer, an old icon. The odour of metal is as acrid as the brown water on the stone floor. From the stairs comes a cold wind of wood and damp. A cane chair lies knocked over on the floor. When the door opens the wind blows out the light in the room, it is immediately dark. An old cobblers' lamp with a green shade hangs low over a hastily concluded meal. The sound of flowing water comes remotely from a leaded window. The bowls of rice and meat have blue rims, the plates are dark, the water-jug gleams, untouched.

Further away in the wood-fragrant room one can see a finely latticed window that divides a forest landscape into clearly separate parts: trees, road, field, all enclosed by a house-wall. The wall grows and sets before me the familiar rubbish bins, the grey sky and time, the war, the rats, the night. Here the silence has been scraped together in a hurry, it rests by the legs of the table, hangs from the ceiling, smooths out the tablecloth but cannot manage to do anything about the breadcrumbs. Do I hear singing, like a floating in the air, a many-voiced voice? As a child I heard muffled churchbells, they rang in Sunday and its boredom, my dreams, white hours in May before school finished. From the newspapers narrow trails of blood found their way down onto the floor, everything came to an end each day and began the following morning. The room I am standing in opens downwards into the darkness where a fire glimmers. In one corner is the chair where the child sat. A meal is over, those who were sitting there have left, I am on a casual visit. Outside, a fresh May day awaits with shards of sky in every puddle, it murmurs in the water-pipes that meander through the room, there is the faint smell of birchwood, freshly-chopped and with white skin.

It leads me to you, to the dream about you, you are strolling about in Harvard and stop in front of an old wooden villa, we stayed there for a few days a long time ago, it was a hotel, we felt homeless in each other, we were so far away, a firewall stood in cold light, far away behind the window at the end of a dark corridor. I would like to follow you but you are not here, your determination is not here. The room sways slowly before my gaze, like the reflection of light in the water jug and the faint trembling of the glass on the table. I can't stay here, I have a lot to do now that the summer is about to begin: wash clothes, wash dishes, clear up after those who have left, keep the books, the inventory, make purchases, there is so much to see and experience, the days grow taller and taller, the tender green leaves are a miracle, were I dejected I would sharpen my gaze. Here too it smells of summer, someone has opened a window to air the room after their meal. So many contradictory emotions! Everything a confusion to unravel: the old who have vanished, I who sat at the table when I was a child, the rumbling of the mangle and the laundry room that I vaguely remember, it was the last summer of the war, the door stands open, the women pull and heave, the oakwood rollers gleam, the heavy stones shake, I crawl on, run bent forward, having rushed down a wide wooden staircase I find myself in a large, bright hall in the country, old men sit along the bench to the left, the women in their white aprons to the right, the curtains billow in the wind, the windows are open to the June day, everything is suffused by sunlight. The old folk have a world of their own, they hold silent children in front of them, rest their hands on their shoulders, there is an understanding there between them, I am outside, I walk with outstretched arms along an invisible border, they observe me, stiffly I direct my gaze towards the door in the gable, low whisperings follow me, I see myself at the journey's end, I rest with my hand under my cheek and see what is going to happen, the wooden table, the mangle room, how tall everything was, the stair-case, the old folk, the children.

You are outside, you have closed the door, you have escaped unhurt. Stone surrounds you, the rear courtyard stretches with masonry towards the sky, there washing hangs out to dry, huge sheets that dead bodies are wound in, children were dried on large linen towels, they ran between the fluttering shirts, the long johns, they whirled like dandelion seeds in a sunbeam, the women in their grey women's volunteer defence force uniforms carried baskets of bloodstained bandages down to the river, black water flowed in the gutters, the sea tugged at its moorings, new winds began to blow and all of it, attic rooms and halls, mangle and war years blew away down pale summer roads and along the streets of the seething city. I sat and read, buried myself in texts like a woodworm in wood, thirty years have passed, and were those years really what Söderberg calls the best time, the flowering time 'when the children have just grown up and the old are not yet really old'? Am I really old? Have I not always been old, an old eye, an old hesitancy on new, unfamiliar streets? Suburbs grow up, you can see them stretching north with television towers and rollercoasters if you stretch out of the skylight and hear the roof-plates rattling in the gale: the summer storm is here! It arrives, it passes over Kronberg Bay, sweeps across rocks and shores, tears the roofs from the stalls on the square, a huge whirlpool of Baltic herring glitters in roaming sunlight, is swept up towards the dome of St Sofia's, people creep around like ants in their dark carapaces, Satan himself stands on Sofiegatan raising a bottle of spirits to his mouth, June is full of the cries of gulls, the smell of mash, white clouds and cranes that reach to the sky. I run downstairs and outside. The gateway on the light opens with a boom. The city rattles past like a railway yard, and the heart skips like a thrown-away sandwich along June's waves and suddenly sinks, seven steps towards the unknown.

24 The World University

We always went to grandmother's when it was summer. She lived in another town and in another time. She stood with her feet on the ground, and the ground was full of invisible streams. For this reason she was called Bäck, 'brook'. She rested on her Cedermark and heard the murmuring of underground streams. She laughed, her almost toothless mouth opened in a gaping joy, then she closed it quickly and firmly. So it had been when I was a child, so it was now. She was indestructible. Mamma and Viktoria had wanted to take her in to stay with them, but she refused. She would manage until she died. Swift as a bird with small claws she ran from the parlour to the kitchen and back. Time could not run faster. She had her hair tightly drawn back, the parting gleamed white, her strangely pale eyes looked slightly past one, towards something that was timidly waiting. You may be a brook, but you smell of cedar, said Viktoria. I imagined the smell of cedar, the sunlight, the immense architecture of the tree's crown, the winds of the past stilled by its boughs, the air full of a spicy fragrance, of the shadows of Lebanon and the calm of English gardens, of Himalayan deodars and grandmother's glittering brook that sought its cedar mark; even after grandfather's death her life was full of him, the beloved one. The daughters had inherited his openness, in Viktoria amusedly ironic, in Mamma more silent, more gentle. In all three one could find that sudden silence that falls over people who have fought their way through sorrow and hardship and kept them to themselves.

As I sat in the warm June day and listened to their voices I hear them as though I heard them now, thirty years later. I sat and saw how young I was, and heard the silences, picked up a pen and wrote. It was a secret action that carried me a bit along the way. I divided the day into silences. There was the silence early in the mornings when everyone was asleep and you steal into your room, a pale, averted silence that must quickly be filled with sleep. The happy silence a little later, on a June morning, washed and cleaned, as a child is washed where he stands, in his bathtub, and is rinsed with summer water. Birds test their echoes, cool trees and brooks murmur solitary but never forlorn. The astonishing silence in the middle of the day, when the traffic suddenly seems to stop, the streets to empty, the houses to close: emptiness. The afternoon's silence that is full of repetitions, sounds, noise, voices and rejoinders fluttering by, and yet: always the same, indifferent silence. The evening silence in the twilight, the silence that bodes sleep. I listen to the three women who allow my silence to remain undisturbed, like the sunlight that falls in through grandmother's window, and stops by the rag rug on the floor.

In grandmother's room all is order, clarity, even at night when the moon does its best to make each object keep its distance and its estrangement. I have lain on grandmother's sofa overnight when Mamma and Papa were on one of their rare travels, grandmother had placed chairs as a protection, I lay and looked through the lattice work at the big moon, it too had been tidied away and hung up by grandmother, it was not dead at all, it had merely been damped down by grandmother so that I could lie in this borderland between waking and sleep, gliding on silvery water, surrounded by the fragrances of dark trees. Was it now, as I tried to capture the silences in my memory, that for the first time I was seized by the thought of writing, forming, noting down, seeking the right words that could give me at least a fraction of the image of myself I was looking for? My thoughts strayed, as when I listen to music, they did not gather into a centre, they were hurled out into a space of their own where chance texts acquired a hidden, magic meaning.

It is silent, even in the kitchen it is silent, here everything has been tidied up, the day cleansed and anxious about its stillness. Now they are talking in low voices, grandmother sits with her knitted shawl around her shoulders, a legacy from time immemorial, her warmth is objectivity itself. The small, hoarse voice seems to have feathers and wings. Her eyes search down into what takes place under the ground: we will have to learn to speak under the ground, she says. The strength she has possessed is beginning to desert her. The pale eyes look straight at me: what am I doing at University? What do I plan to do with my life? I try to tell her about my studies, about the bare lecture halls, about the cold light above the Alma Mater, about the soporific monologues of the professors, the dying texts, the gravel of accumulated facts, the compulsion in one's brain, the way in which the lyric and epic categories commit spiritual murder on living, bleeding words, the turning of imagination into hay, the turning of the theories into cement, turning is not the right word, it suggests metamorphoses, but here there it is not a question of metamorphoses – rather one of fossilization, gravestones over visions.

Here in grandmother's room, in the world university, the mind moves freely, a summer breeze passes through the trees outside, cries from the park out there acquire a sound of joy. The world is so silent, and so exact! The room with its order, the table with its bouquet of lilacs, the memory of their voices, grandmother's and Viktoria's and Anna's, reminds me of some lines I wrote down and pinned above my work table, they are Robert Walser's: 'The passionate desire to depict life in words arises in the last instance merely from a certain exactitude and a refined pedantry of the soul.' Daniel is reading, leave him alone, he can have his coffee later, says grandmother in the kitchen, the low voices follow me along the years, they are enduring moments in eternity, vanished and present, like dragonflies from the time of young summers. Time? It was almost effaced, as a dream effaces reality. The world was an open book to be read, and the text emerged more clearly beneath closed eyelids, now in light, now in shadow, as space emerges before the one who lies in a meadow, looking at the sky. The real was composed of tangible and intangible, the dream concealed in the fresh kernel of everyday life, the undemanding carried me, carries me. I sit in my world university, a green lamp burns near my text, it feels as though you were moving about in the next room, but I know that you are far away and will not come home for the summer, you have to carry your project to its conclusion, I am gripped by such unease. But that is far away in time, this is here and now, I knew nothing about it then, I am at my twenty-four-year-old beginning and trying to learn to read myself, a never-finished task.

Grandmother came into my room, she sat down by the window and beckoned me to her. We stood and looked at the fresh light-green trees, it had begun to get dark, the room's fragrances surrounded us. Your mother's father, she says in her lightly singing voice, your mother's father used to sit on that white bench down there, a few days before he died he described to us how he saw himself sitting there, being led to his catafalque, saw us standing around him in mourning, many people have seen the same thing, President Lincoln, an aunt of mine, from lofty heights we see ourselves, and he said that he was gripped by such a sense of sorrow and freedom at the same time, he could do nothing, and who can? Do you see him there? Everything has stopped, the people are not moving forward, the sun has stopped in its path through the sky. That old man there on the bench, I don't know him, he could have my features.

Grandmother puts her hand on my arm, it is thin and dry, a claw, almost. Over in a corner of the rear courtyard, behind the tree-tops, some old men have made a fire, the smoke coils through the branches, trees come hesitantly into leaf and from cellars, holes, garret boxrooms, staircases, rubbish bins, road viaducts the wretched ones creep forth, the sun begins to warm. It is June and silent in grandmother's room, she has gone without my noticing it.

25 Midsummer

I can count four trees within the house walls. The inner courtyard has a twilight of its own, and the wind there rises from invisible cracks in the asphalt, from cellar windows, blows like white washing out of the dark gateways. There are lamps between the trees, benches and crude tables, people move about there, bright moths in the midsummer evening. Children play, run after their cries and shift like happy shadows over the thin lawn, in and out among the beams of floodlights. The grown-ups stand in a queue by the long tables with beer and steaming pans of sausages, the old folk sit smiling with tired eyes, they have seen it all before, but it is all once again new and full of mystery, light summer evening and city noise at a distance, garlands of motley-coloured lamps and gleaming brass of horn and tuba: red and sweaty, a small brass band pumps out its marches above the murmur, while confused pigeons fly to and fro, cling to the window-ledges or disappear into the darkness under the roof. Mr Rosendal fights a hopeless battle with his bass tuba. It is imprisons him, it coils itself around his swelling body, it gets the upper hand, he vanishes into its hard, coiling arms; someone has poured soapy water into the gaping funnel, slowly a gigantic bubble rises from its black mouth, gleaming with gas and summer sky, children shriek, grown-ups point at the shiny sphere, majestically the bass tuba raises itself towards the sky, hesitates, sinks, everyone blows, the wind lends a hand, wind! I cry, *urvind*! but my voice is drowned in the murmur from a thousand throats, the entire courtyard swells like a damp grass mattress, and the balloon with the desperate Mr Rosendal and the groaning bass tuba sways in the evening wind, yes, it rises towards the nearest tree, a soughing passes over the world, mankind holds its breath, all is despair and expectation, the moon itself is effaced by the bubble, it is a whole world of rainbow-shimmering colours, it wants to be free of the treetop and the chimneypots, but a long narrow branch cuts a notch in the dream, the city shakes, the earth quivers, with a dreadful crack the balloon bursts and the bass tuba falls, gleaming, snakeskin-cold, and clings to the crown of the maple, Mr Rosendal has short red socks, white legs and a voice that is choked with rage and horror. A ladder is raised, there is tumbling and rattling to the accompaniment of loud cries and booming salvoes of laughter, the music begins and the stars are pinpricks in the deepening sky.

Beer and sausage, heaven and hell! I want to throw myself out of my window, my loneliness is a snakeskin, a sausage-skin, I plunge across distances that are only a breath of wind between the house fronts, I rush down the staircases. But down there at the bottom, inside the door, stand the gang, they turn round and look at me, jeans, pony-tails, dark glasses in the middle of the night, blind and deaf, with knives. There is no way out. They follow, chewing gum. The murmur in the courtyard makes the silence here unbearable. My body consists of disparate joints, all of them disordered, unfeeling. Stiletto on skin, incision on throat, I have felt it, I feel it, the catastrophe comes like the lightning-swift fear in the midst of joy, I stretch out an arm, they laugh. Do I shout, or see everything in emptiness and silence, the door opens and the Pietinens come roistering and laughing in, lads, they shout, off you go out and celebrate, it's midsummer eve, what are you standing here for, and I slip outside, a black rivulet. I bump into Herman Stilén, his hair has turned grey, his moustache is drooping, his parting is in disarray, but his eyes still have their piercing brilliance, they protrude slightly, he stinks of beer. Eh? What? Daniel? Out chasing girls like Stig? Pale about the gills, is he in difficulty? Stig was asking after you. Birds of a feather, ha ha! Not everyone can have a good head for study, but hard work will take you far. And you have to have something here, too! He points to his crooked arm, feels his invisible biceps, pushes me playfully, as though he were about to hit me, he wipes his mouth, I haven't seen him like this before, all the people change suddenly, show a hidden side, something confused and crazy charges the still air between the house fronts with sparks, I walk past myself and over to the people around the dance floor, there is dancing between the four trees, hands fumble along backs and bottoms, cheeks are placed against cheeks, eyes are closed, it's an old-time number, I've got you under my skin, a clarinet fingers its cool rosary, later it will be twist and shout, the old must give way to the young, I stand in between, look around me, that so many strangers live in the house, including myself!

It is warm and light, the midsummer night, I feel like a stone that has been hurled towards the starry sky. Aren't you going to dance, says Mamma. Midsummer only comes once a year, says Papa. Don't sit with us old folk. Remarque, I say. Akhmatova, Orwell, Rousseau, Pirandello, I reply, I have changed the books in the window, I can begin. I ask Mamma to dance, how light she is, birdlike, I don't remember dancing with her after that, it must have been the last time, everything is full of evening shadows, she dances so lightly, it's a seamen's waltz, she gets quite giddy, I lead her back, her face is pale, there is a premonition of cold in the air, the night forms a great vault above the courtyard. I do not know on which heavenly body I must hang up my immense longing, my desires, will I ever be able to live my life to the full, can the light be preserved now that the year will soon be inclining towards darkness and the image of the rear courtyard then can be united with the courtyard now. The people ever more silent, the trees ever further away, the lamps being put out, the music falling silent and each person going home.

I was looking for you but had not yet found you, Maria. I remember lying in the semi-darkness, listening to the rain beginning to fall like a faint, consoling song, did not need to get up to see the raw planks of the bandstand gleaming in the feeble light from some lanterns that were still alive, smell the fragrance of young leaves just come out, hear the last voices say farewell to the lightest night of the summer, feel the entire courtyard expand into a space for devotion. And was there not also another faint music, pale, and scraped, criss-crossed by the singing of some nocturnal bird I could not recognize? I can hear grandmother's voice, it is saying: God created the birds and set the mountains in their places. He also decided to create man, but then abandoned us, and we must seek him, as the children seek the one who has hidden. Her voice is rough and warm, her skin almost yellow, with moles, she died in the spring, she has closed her eyes, her bed winds slowly around her shoulder and floats away, above the courtyard, above the roofs of the houses, until it is smaller than a star. Her Junghans strikes three tranquil chimes, the pendulum swings, measuring the motionless time, all are asleep in their own invisible world, seeing in strange dreams what their days lack and their lives do not dare.. Far away, on the border between sleep and waking, I hear the thunder's distant boom and echo, a room, clean and lonely, and see a child turn round, look at me, and in an instant vanish.

26 In the Old Hospital

I did not know that unsuspected wellsprings murmur under the house. Perhaps a great dark river moves down there, making piles and foundations slowly sink. Has no one noticed anything? The raw damp smell of sea is smoothed out by the summer, the warm weather is here. From the expanses the great steamers glide into the port, the city darkens with parks and silent streets, and the sick turn round laboriously, wet with sweat, and see the distant heaven. It is not yet for them. More or less concealed, isolated, lie the rooms for the forgotten, the lost, the sick children are also there, even when the summer is in full bloom; perhaps it is a mourning bloom, perhaps even now the first shadows of autumn are falling over the dazzling grass; they do not see it, a white light from the motionless curtains and the tall window surrounds them. People who have no errand here avoid the antiseptic corridors, the echoing doors, the television room with a few forgotten, motley dressing-gowned patients. In the wards the beds stand close together: this is an extremely old, enlarged, altered, modernized building, but the rows of old folk are the same, the thin arms, the closed eyes, the vases of flowers, the silent day is the same. At nights they glide away into their dreams, ice floes on dark waters, each with his tormented body, his crucified form, barely visible under the white sheets. Once they were all our neighbours. They were there, they have just gone away for a bit, we say, they will return.

There, behind a screen, lies Mamma's cousin Ludvig, snorting, wild, he has lived alone all his life, about women he stammers and dreams, his eyes move past all objects and stop before unseen spots on ceiling and walls, his blond wisps of hair stick out, he has tried to teach me to paint. He has dragged himself along with a small inheritance, painted flattering portraits of directors and chief surgeons, professors and celebrities, he has made a name for himself that is now forgotten but not yet buried, he writhes in his forgetfulness, and we are only a reminder of the world he is in the process of losing. Everything is alien here. I see that Mamma has grey hair, streaks of silver, only now, as she bends over Ludvig do I see it, everything here is focused on aging, fading, death. And the summer that stands so beautiful outside the window, refusing to come in! On hot summer days Ludvig sat in his shirt-sleeves swearing at the canvas, at the palette, at the hand that obeyed him all too well. Once upon a time he had been obsessed by paint, he had eaten paint, dreamed about paint, but the paint did not care about him, it withdrew back into indiscriminate, grey life, or miscegenated in an unwarrantable fashion so that it all became poisoned, snuff-brown, nauseating purple, garish green, bilious yellow, hatred rose like sour marshwater in his body, he locked himself in, his body wasted away to tough wood, his arms that had always waved wildly around him took the brush and produced portrait-like, rigidly staring faces, his joints cracked when he pulled his fingers, they were like bars in front of his face; only when he saw children was his face lit by an inner light.

But it was the unknowns he captured, commissions piled up, he would have nothing to do with his exhibitions, he said he lived in a dead town. He dreamed of becoming an actor or a musician, anything but a painter, towards night he huddled up like a shell with two holes for his burning eyes, but he had grown fat from lying in bed, his thoughts had also grown fat, from the shell someone else oozed out, feverishly active, he was constantly hurled between two people, one mobile, the other immobile, and now the mobile one lay fettered immobile, with saliva running out of his mouth, in a shrill voice he asked after his room, his files: he was a collector, a photographer, his thin hands took us in, cut us off, we were glued into his album, our faces, our faces flamed past, all of them incomplete, poor quality, torn. Then he gave up photography and took up knitting: strange creations, coarse-knitted pink cupolas with earflaps, to be used by Tibetan monks, spiral-shaped winter woollen hats with tassels to frighten wild creatures with, nasty little black berets to pull over low foreheads, gigantic magpies' nests on top of gigantic hair-dos, pill-boxes and scoop hats for older ladies who have given up all hope of a better life, horribly aggressive American-inspired peaked caps, hunting caps with Tyrolean motifs, small cherry-coloured flying saucers pinned firmly to straggling buns, black terrorist masks with red lips, joined-up pan-gloves with chin-bands, feathery balls of cloth in all the colours of the rainbow, coarse nets with metal decorations, veils of mourning for a new world, all woven out of furious joy and mistrust.

He stood with his door ajar, and when he caught sight of me he soundlessly closed the door or hissed out a Psssst! and pulled me into the hot room where the easel was, the bed pushed against the door to the over-cluttered kitchen, the bookcase with the photograph albums and the two rattan chests with the work of his hands, swelling like thunderclouds. Through the dirty window one could see a firewall, a grey-painted sky and a black roof. Those who came to sit as models were drawn like helpless flies into a spider's web of suppressed emotions, it rendered his violence-subdued portraits strangely alive: eyes stared like small welding-flames in motionless faces, barricades against encroaching life.

What he succeeded at was of no value. He lay and looked at us, his hand slid over an invisible membrane of glass, in a hoarse voice he spoke of the necessity of a total world order in which everything had found its place: paintbrushes of varying sizes in jars of varying dimen-sions, parallel lines in rooms that tried to rise up in rebellion: the ward he lay in was ideal, beds in straight lines, everything in order; when I visited him for the first time at the hospital he called to me: Look! I've produced this! Straight lines! Forward march! Ringing and rejoicing! Mamma strokes him on the forehead, he falls silent, the thin hands pluck at the sheet, always those hands that move in such alarm even now that the body has abandoned its refuge and is on the way, out, I could see it and feel it. Screens partitioned off the most seriously ill. Trays of lukewarm food, hardly touched. The white, friendly nurses, often overworked, and the heat that wanted to penetrate inside and was blocked at windows and doors by an interior, intensified chill. The sick were cranked up in their gleaming metal beds, they saw the summer outside and turned their faces to the wall, the world slipped away, the light stood waiting, even the scent of the flowers on the bedside tables stopped around the patients and was taken away when night came. Someone lamented far away, all night I heard the unknown woman's voice, everything that had to do with the world of the healthy here was here mute, without response, the whole of the brightly-coloured city with murmuring trees and fountains, unreal and abandoned.

Here, among the sick and rejected, life acquired its true proportions. The nurses became the last links with life, their warmth lingered
in the room, there were barely perceptible changes from dawn to
twilight, all those alien faces became one and the same, a living token
of something which existed outside and which Ludvig, minute by
minute, was wearily starting to leave behind. The summer blazed,
sometimes hurling a warm breath of sap and leaves through an opened
and again swiftly closed window, those who were healthy looked so
alien, he observed it all with the strength of a dying man; his body gave
off a sickly sweet odour, he whispered: we don't really need anything!
Mamma nodded. She kept her hand on his. He turned his head restlessly, then fell silent. A great white silence reigned in the room.

I saw the glistening doors to the hospital staircase, the gleaming
corridors and the yuccas in their corners, the silent lounges, each
sound was swiftly muted, outside the summer's heat struck us in the
face, houses lay like batteries of stone along dusty streets, the shadows
were short and bleached by the sun, the city roared, placing distance
upon distance, above it sailed indifferent clouds. In bed, Ludvig drew
his thin legs up towards his belly, they could not be straightened out
again. All this was a rehearsal, it would return when Mamma died.
Behind us we left room after room, the whole building seemed to
contain people who lay waiting for a visit, who with their absent hands
stroked their alien faces, so far had they had gone, and must go onward.

27 The Funfair

You write that you are spurning the summer and burying yourself in your work, perhaps that way you can shorten your time in the States and come home sooner. Perhaps you are deceiving yourself, something in your letter tells me that, some tone there makes me wonder, feel a vague doubt, an unease. I can't afford to travel over to see you, all is quiet in the bookshop, but I keep it open, in summer the books are always unusually reticent, seem almost superfluous. In the autumn they begin to live and find their natural reading darkness. I wrap myself in the city as in a weightless twilight garment, I walk along the shores and see the sea expand, a great empty surface, and white cruisers head out, gigantic, filled to bursting-point with people. I often fall asleep on the sofa in the study, the book I have been reading has fallen down on the floor, the skylight is open, the door to the courtyard also, Orpheus meets Morpheus, a faint music comes into being there, that follows me through the days. Towards evening the unease wants to break out in earnest, I look at the telephone, it is not concerned with me, no one rings, I ring no one, the people I could ring are in the country, who are they? Did I leave the dishes unwashed yesterday only because I had nothing to do? Have I changed the display in the window, will some summer stroller stop and look at my Milosz and my Hesse, not to speak of my Kafka, there is such a loneliness around him and his long, narrow figures that he absent-mindedly scratched in the margin of his mercilessly clearsighted life. People walk by, here and in Prague the horrible obtrudes, it has no face. Sometimes a moth gets in by mistake and circles blindly under the green lampshade, and I remember Olga Knipper's story about Chekhov's death, it is that time now, hottest summer, and he turned away after having drunk a glass of champagne, shadows lengthened, a horrible moth whirred in the room, the heat was stifling, in the silence the cork flew out of the half-finished bottle with a pop, it was over.

Yesterday, tired of the July quiet, I passed the dark gateway to the street and saw a large brick-coloured iron door that I had not seen before, it stood ajar, and behind it I could hear what sounded like the roar of a thousand voices. I stepped into a clattering world of popcorn and wilting lilac, into a mellow July evening when the worst of the heat is over and the sky is pigeon-blue above black tree-tops. A large funfair spread out before me, with garlands of multi-coloured lamps, they were like the screams from the giddy roller-coaster, I pushed my way forward through the dense mass of people. Children sat on the lawns with their peppermint rock and candy floss, from the shooting gallery came rapid firing, people were carried past, the violent clattering from the roundabouts and the miniature trains made the funfair slowly revolve, the market stalls and tents flicker and change places, the silhouettes of roofs all round twine like a ribbon around my forehead. A wilted maypole flew past, this was not a casual frenzy, this was permanent happiness, dearly paid for. I did not know where I was going, where I was, I thought I saw the dead Olof Petri flit by, there was a woman who looked like you, I followed her, when she turned round her face had disappeared, all that was left were black shadows, a grotesquely smiling mouth.

At the ghost train there was a long queue, I joined it, children screamed for ice cream. When, as if under duress, I got into the two-seater carriage beside a groaning man who looked like a wrestler, it was as though I were trying to drag with me all the weight of the crowd's babbling and the compressed, confused yearning for adventure that drifted along spookily illumined passages. In the cave we were hurled into all the sounds were stretched out, an echo chamber was filled to the brim with fearful roars from invisible animals, luminous monsters rushed over us and vanished again, suddenly the carriage careered into a thundering waterfall, at the next moment to be engulfed by fire and rush towards a rock-face; the man beside me chewed popcorn, then threw the bag into Niagara. I wanted to cry out but sat soundless, was led through an empty darkness, through a jungle of wet lianas, I felt the acrid sweat from the man beside me, his rasping breath. From death we were hurled out into life, into the human flood that surged around me, shadows that dragged small children along, whistles shrieked, giant pandas waddled out, there were grinning masks and false noses, and children ran shrieking around the open-air dance floors. Plastic lawns gleamed, there was a sparkling round the dodgem cars as they bumped into one another, there was always a darkly resolute boy driving against the stream, he was a knife in the belly of happiness, high on a tightrope walked a white figure with his long pole, the great evening held its breath, he was across, he stretched up his arm, the public applauded hesitantly. Right at the top of the giant wheel, where the night wind beat against my face and the city spread out its ribbons of light, everything stopped. I swayed gently to and fro in my basket, I was alone with my giddiness, all unease and longing left me, I did not choose but was chosen, did not accept but was taken into my own calm, as though there were always a possibility of returning. I did not ask, merely saw and lived, released my convulsive grip on the iron gate before me. The darkness around me was mellow and full of light. Far below life murmured mechanically. I was close to the stars, and had no name, it was an inspiration, an insight into healing.

When I made my way towards the exit I passed the hall of mirrors and went mechanically inside, it was natural: that I should see myself like that, in various forms. The hall lay outside the amusement park proper, as though it had been built only for me. There were no visitors, only an old man who has half asleep in the ticket window, he looked at me with eyes that were scarcely open. He turned his tormented face away, mumbled something about closing time, but I knew that he had only just opened. What did he want to prevent me from doing? Where the air had been filled with colour and smell, with sausage-stand vapours and sulphurous clouds from the shooting galleries, with trampled summer and dance-floor stamping, here it was quiet. I made my way into the gleaming, slowly rotating, peculiarly ghostlike world where faces were lengthened and shrunk, where one's body assumed grotesque forms, where one's smile froze to a grimace and the mirrors demanded distortions, in pleasure and horror, all equally mechanically. Those pale, pasty features, elongated to the point of unrecognizability, the body swollen, the neck a giraffe's, the eye a runny egg-yolk, the ears like swollen handles, myself approaching, myself backing away, bending my knees, mirrors pressing me to them, filling me with loneliness and darkness in which I could make my forehead flow out into a formless peak, my eyes and nose press together into a pig's snout, teeth and lips grow mooingly enlarged, chin be hurled out like a hairy spear from a dwarf's squeezed-up body. I dragged it with me, I twisted and tore, I could not get free, tottering I made my way out. Right by the exit there was a mirror, covered with mist, gazing at me indistinctly was a dwarf, a shrunken head, a spherical torso. Then I hurried out into the dark July night, slipped like a shadow along the streets, gangs of hot-rod teenagers moved yelling aside, like a soot-flake I was swept onwards, a bat, a stunted creature, was no taller than a child, half-ran through gateways and across courtyards, up staircases that reared up before me, managed with the last of my strength to open the door of the flat, heard rain beginning to fall outside, hurried past the mirror in the hall, went back, could not see myself properly, hesitated, went into the bathroom, the light struck me in the face, I raised my eyes, I was there, had grown older, my hair wet with sweat, my face furrowed, alien and confused. I rinsed my head in cold water, I had survived, exhausted I crept into bed, sank into a bottomless, dreamless torpor. The dawn was there, I awoke some hours later, stretched cautiously, lay motionless. Day returned.

28 City in July

How are your elementary particles faring in the July heat? You have been in Maine, you write, you have been to see the old fishing cemeteries, you have sat on the Alcotts' verandah, you have walked with Thoreau, you have rested under the big, cool oaks, with whom, with whom? Leptons and Mesons, Baryons and Nucleons, Hyperons and other invisible Persons have been whirling around you, you have watched them with your calm attention, can you not see how they also fill the air here with their absence, how the boundary between dream and waking, all this openness, receptiveness, boundlessness awaits your arrival? The city in July is full of tourists, everyone else has moved to the country, as indeed we used to move, too, now I rejoice in silent streets.

You took me in hand, that first summer we were together, you were hesitant but securely rooted in yourself, even then you were clear about your goal, your work. The year is '68, how many things happened then, the world roared in with its passion, its violence, its revolt, we are hurled between the headlines, they become ever more unreal, the murders do not stop, the surface of evil is immeasurable and invisible, people break it with screams that echo ever more remotely, like things betrayed trees, air and silence remain.

You are here and now, in my empty summer room, impatient, determined and irritated you wake me: Wake up, Daniel, I have to go to work, aren't you going to open up the shop, are you going to let your father take care of it all? Stay still for a bit, I say, but you don't stay still, you move about the room, I catch at you, hold my arms around your hipbones, they are quite cool, almost hard, you free yourself gently. The sun falls on the house-fronts opposite, deepens, it will be afternoon, intolerable Sunday without you, empty hours like an illness ahead of me. Where this feeling of loss comes from I do not know, sorrow and love talk constantly to each other without us hearing it, they surround the most everyday objects so that I shall see them more acutely. Your lips are dry when we say goodbye. There are always these empty distances between the bed and the table, between the bookcase and the window, between the shell on the window-ledge and the glass on the table, between hand and hand. Each object needs special attention, they turn away when they know that we do not see them, when we walk past them or thoughtlessly use them, as though they were a matter of course. One day they will take their revenge, tower up around us, drown us, suffocate us, we have collected them, amassed them around us with sharp nails, we have started to dream about them, they force everything else out, they pass under our skin, we transport them out to stinking fields but they stand outside the city gates, the refuse, all that has been abandoned, in the July heat it all flames up like fire towards the sky, and the smoke drifts between the concrete of the suburbs.

I am a child, you know it, I am extremely old, I long for you, you know it. Something unsuccessful stands waiting, it cuts me off from myself, from what I think is myself. I sit, a stone, unthrown, on my bed and see the emptiness and uncertainty behind maturity's surface. I see that the paint on the windowframe is peeling, that the door has been clumsily painted over, it has stains. I walk over to the secondhand bookshop, there the shelves stand like an accumulation of dead words, have you noticed that piles of paperbacks have a stained paper-smell of their own? Yellowed paper, waiting, decay. That which gleams out there, the puddles on the asphalt, the rain-beaten windows, the deepening sky, the vapour that is rising between the empty houses, it is like a too-early autumnal unease, it feels as though I were suddenly standing face to face with the darkness. One week in the middle of the summer everything changes, the light abandons us, the child sits in the country motionless in the afternoon, the sun sets with a lonely brilliance, the green leaves have stopped changing. To be imprisoned in the viewless winds, and blown with restless violence round about the pendant world!

So: I am arranging a programme for my future. More work. Greater precision. Greater openness. Routine. Facts: we take turns at cooking the meals, Papa and I. The kitchen looks on to a beating-balcony that no one uses any more. There is no courtyard party this summer. The courtyard is a dark background, and the light falls hard in some other direction, falls suddenly in when I open the door to the kitchen stairs, the sun shines like a river, forces its way into all the rooms, carrying off Mamma and Papa, astonished they sit in their beds and think they are dreaming, so unaccustomed it is, the light. Even Mamma brightens up, she walks, supported by us, over to the bookshop, sits in Papa's chair in the room at the rear and listens to the few summer customers looking for thrillers in the paperback basket. Look! says Papa, what a wonderful week, all these great men who were born: Leino and Proust, Thoreau and Bruno Schulz, next week Babel, Singer, Keller – isn't it fantastic? He spreads out his arms, he has lost weight, his shirt is soaked in sweat, Mamma leans back with her hand in front of her eyes, it grows quiet in the world, where is our summer? I shrink, table and chair become intolerably small, the words become blocks, blocks of letters for building towers with and demolishing again. Are you there, Daniel, she asks, she he has lain down on Papa's chaise longue, it is too many years ago.

It is late, and from the TV flows an indifferent stream of sufferings, murder and death to eternal background music. Sibelius suits everything. The world situation and the country's decline and fall are analysed by a horde of researchers and experts, chewed up and spat out, and behind them we sense, we see all the oppressed, the unemployed, the old, the debt-encumbered, all this darkness falls over the children and the young, and their eyes grow hard and look past us. There sits Per with his wooden mallet, striking the table, Sture is taking his revenge on Minna, they sit in corners and under tables, they are all small, when they are big they will have motor cycles and leather jackets, they will hurl themselves thundering across streets and squares, but they are still small, look: Petra is drawing a government minister, he looks like a doll with outspread arms, he has fingers like Granny's claws. The summer was everywhere, in the body it shone, ran with chapped legs out to the jetty, there the old pike lay with its jaws open and swallowed me, but in the cellar underneath the house there is a smell of darkness – potatoes, they have survived the war, the sun's in its heaven. But the wind is getting up, the wind is increasing, everything will soon be swept away: light rooms, the children who ran around playing, the hut in the tree, the evening meals on the veranda, the things that were repeated and were yet new, Jan's reflections on the rock as the sun was setting, Lena's unease, their sorrows, their joys that we shared, we walked along paths that are gone now, there was so much to lose, did we know it? And what have I learned from this? To fill some sheets of paper with signs, conjure you forth, have you here with me, we sit round the green lamp for one eternal moment.

29 On the Way Yonder

She sits in the shadow of the tree and knows that she does not have long to live. We have brought her down to the courtyard, and she looks around her. Her precision has increased, she takes note of the sky's depth and the shadows the sunlight throws over grass and asphalt. House-fronts that lie in shadow have a special blue tone. Which authors died in July, she asks Papa, but he doesn't know, he only knows the ones who were born, Petrarch was born then, on 20 July 1304, you remember we read him when we were in Italy, *L'erbetta verde e i fior' di color' mille, sparsi sono quel'elce antiqua et negra pregan pur che'l bel pe'li prema o tocchi* – and she smiles, my foot scarcely manages to bend a single blade of grass, but the tree gives coolness just as well as an old holly – they sit together and I have to turn away, moved and despairing. Of course, there is always Chandler, says Papa, he ought to be a good watchdog for the beloved Laura. You've been a better watchdog for me, says Mamma, and soon you can hand over the role to Daniel, he will take charge of you. Her grey eyes seek mine, the unease that has always characterized her has evaporated, just as the July heat has for a few days left the city and been succeeded by thunderstorms, rain and, now, fresh coolness. I will climb the mountain of victory, she says, I will see it in reality, it is so much clearer than all the copies here, there I will meet Cézanne and have a serious conversation with him, he is not fond of jokes, I neither, and what is more, he also loves distance and oblivion, he was uncertain, everything stood open and unfinished, sometimes we don't know whether we're living or just remembering, there's a strength in knowing that, isn't there, a strength in knowing that, isn't there, Fredrik?

She falls silent, Papa nods. It grows silent. Swallows hurtle past with their cries, cool lines of notes like rays across the sky, the city is withdrawing. Hesitant contacts, of the hand with her hand, of the eye with another, wide-open eye, the gentle giddiness that comes from the swift flight of a whole life, the contact of the trees with the sky, of the brush with the surface, life rendered visible, an inspiration that is approaching, something that is never concluded, yet weighs the same as what is to come, for us all, it is a bowl to be carried tenderly, flower-petals quiver on its surface, great coolness approaches from the forest of cedars, the twilight is a cool hand on the forehead. I have made progress, says Mamma, the last mountains are not so silly, keep them, destroy the earlier ones. What was it he always said: why so late, and with such difficulty? That was before he died. And he also said: it is always sad to renounce life while we exist on the earth. I find that hard to understand. Where else would we exist? In the aether? In the vestibule to another existence? One gets tired of thinking about it.

She leans back in her chair, exhausted. She closes her eyes, she breathes so quickly, it is as though her breath wanted to follow her yonder. We lead her back, she lie on her bed, turns her face and looks at us, smiles: Go, I'll rest for a bit. Later she wants to meet Viktoria, they sit talking softly, short sentences interrupted by silence. She looks at me but I don't hear her, I sit by her bed, she is leaving us, Marina Miranda de la Cruz, from where I got that name, it rushed out like a bird, its song was only a part of a greater song, life is so simple, merely a sorrow and a candle, minor and major woven into each other, her prelude was the fifteenth one, a happy summer of shadows, and death that is there, knocking discreetly at the door, or is it life that still wants to delay death for a while; she loathes the expression 'raindrop prelude', there is no rain, only a great wind bringing with it shadows and leaves, the room stands open and is at last completely clean and empty, completely white and cool, and quiet.

Sadness, where will that emotion find an enduring abode if not now, when life's greatness and brevity stand before an ever deeper darkness. That emotion exists also, but stronger, more bitter, the irreparable feeling of loss. Worn-out objects, mute stairways and court-yards, the city pale as an old negative, Papa and I silent, facing each other across the kitchen table, hands moving mechanically, Sunday in July. The soft voices from the bedroom. Ceiling, walls and floor enclosing us in their darkness. Kitchen sink, gas stove, butter and bread on the table.

30 The Lift Journey

The heat has reached inside Viktoria's staircase. Every time the door to the courtyard is opened, an asphalt-heavy breath billows into the gloom of shining stone and distorted elegance around the gleaming, juddering lift, an ornament to every lift family, a revered older member of that unnumbered horde of human cages which, decade after decade, has raised mankind to ever higher levels. The summer has turned and is now falling, in spite of birdsong and mighty greenness, towards its close: a week in July, and everything has changed. I who thought I would be able to go back without disturbing time, find that I must go forward, dragging with me all the rooms I have visited, like an old bargeman with his barge that is filled to the gunwale with scrap and possessions, mercilessly exposed in the flooding sunlight. I cannot take one step forward and at the same time one backwards: then I go stiff. What do I know of the stars' constellations and what do I know of the human ones? In order to be able to come back I must find my way forward. When Mamma died something happened that cannot be made up for: one of the sources of security in our lives is gone. I try to remember her face, her eyes, her voice when she said: I am so proud of you. I remember the evening of the Haffner, and the triumph, strength and beauty of the first movement. That evening I felt like the hidden light of the world. It is gone. The light penetrates up there, and I am the one who must fetch it, I stand in an empty well, see through a water-mirror the light up there, how it constantly moves, I must rise upwards with the whole of my body. Slowly I become what I see. Finally up there, what do I see? Days, days, and myself a little older. 'O God! I could be bounded in a nut-shell and count myself a king of infinite space, were it not that I have bad dreams.'

I sit with Papa in the room at the back, share his work, he is often at home now and I stay the night with the green lamp shining through the summer nights. We often go to visit Viktoria, sit at her sky-blue table that is now the weak focus of our lives, but a focus at least. The dogdays are over and rain has fallen. Towards nightfall the wind gets up and goes out, wanders along the seashores the way Mamma used to. We are closed off in her big room, with the marine horizon like a floor-limit, rocks and forest like dark walls, the vault of heaven like a ceiling.

We go across the silent courtyard and press the button for the lift to come down, something happens up there, a faint clattering, cables run up and down in the gloom, and into the lift behind the three of us comes Engineer Dahlgren, he gives us a quick, cold look, then his daughter Fanny, we don't look at one another, what are they doing on our staircase? Are they on their way to see Berg the builder? But what about Fanny? She looks sunken, pale and turned away. Finally Mrs Rosendal with her two plastic bags comes puffing in, the latticed door closes, we stand there breathing, Mrs Rosendal somehow gives the impression of having been seated throughout the whole of her life, she ploughs her way through us and now also sits down on the small, narrow mahogany bench beneath the mirror, the lift keeps shuddering. She sat moaning in her mother's womb, she was born sitting, she sat her way through her childhood and girlhood and finally sat down groaning on Mr Rosendal, bags and all; Mr Rosendal is dead. Engineer Dahlgren has a white shirt, Fanny a white dress, they are like a silent bridal couple, Papa says something softly to Viktoria, she smiles with absent eyes, there is nothing more embarrassing than to rub up against people one does not know in a lift; all stand with their thoughts intertwinedly mute and would rush out into the realm of privacy if only it could be arranged.

But the door is closed, all hope is lost, the lift begins slowly to judder upwards, the first floor, the second floor, a gleam from the courtyard down there, a fragrance from Fanny, how much do we weigh altogether, I remember Stig Stilén who boasted of having managed to seduce a girl in a lift, perhaps it was this one, first went up, then down, fastened the zipper of his flies when the lift came down, the girl rearranged her hair, they got out. Fanny's face has grown thinner but acquired a rounder shape, I suddenly look at her, straight into her eyes, we are wide-open, there is a faint gleam there that passes through me like a blow to the pit of my stomach, suddenly the lift stops between the third and fourth floors, Engineer Dahlgren explodes. Out gush curses, softly, then ever louder, he beats on the wall of the lift, the door will not open, he presses the alarm button, nothing happens, Fanny begins to laugh but soon falls silent. Then Mrs Rosendal gets up – has she no first name, Euphrosyne, Kunigunda, Lillemor? We are pressed to the side, she takes a leap into the air, it is incredible, her flowery summer dresses, her heavy breasts, all hurl themselves into the air and down again, and the lift revives, sets itself in motion, increases its speed, exposes its rattling tusks of steel, the mirror is traversed by reddening spots, it passes the third and fourth floors, there is no fifth floor cries Engineer Dahlgren, he is unusually worked up, his neck unshaven and blotchy, Mrs Rosendal hisses: that's men for you! and Viktoria agrees.

Up, up we go at speed, old lifts are as strong as old Fords, up, up through the attic floor, past frames of joists where my old aeroplane still flutters like a withered dragonfly in its corner, up through the roof, up towards the radiant sky, the clouds have dispersed, we are grains of dust in an iron cage, below us the city spreads out, the Empire city, then the sea, a mighty breathing in, the parks, a gleaming church spire, above the horizon a light purple veil, the straight streets, the television masts, the blinking lights, the gentle wind, our group welded together by giddiness and horror, clinging to one another, our heads bent down, hands seeking support against the walls, clutching for support, eyes staring rigidly, bodies with breath like iron hoops, higher, higher we climb towards our effacement.

In situations like these the individual is put to the test and displays his specific character and dissolves in other individuals to the point of effacement, or breaks loose like a wild desire to free himself from everything that weighs him down. Papa presses, icily controlled, both the alarm button and the button for the basement. Viktoria is violently inquisitive, presses her face against the side-windows in order to take in an experience which she with good reason supposes she will not encounter again in her life. Engineer Dahlgren has sunk down to the floor, stiff in his terror, Mrs Rosendal stands speechless, plastic bag in hand; like birds we rise lit up by the setting sun, an insignificant reflection merely on the deepening sky. Fanny shouts with a shrill voice, it shouts down the wind: It's not true! Not true! Not true! I hear and see, everything is fragments being hurled up into the air and drifting away, I see our black cage drifting in the strata of air, see us there, clinging together, and the lift seeming like a diamond to cut a narrow streak across the glass of the sky, so that the window on eternity can suddenly break and a greater, more bitter darkness behind it flood in over land and sea. A gentle breeze makes the lift-chamber sway, I try to find out how much strength and how many cables are holding us up, but I can't see anything, all that happens is that a faint myriad of stars bursts out, the branching of a tree-top, it is a greeting from Anna, there is a smell of cedar wood and a great bright room opens.

Now Mrs Rosendal demands to get out, she has had enough, I don't intend to put up with any more of these stupid jokes, she says, whom she is addressing is unclear, her eyes are veiled, she tries to push her way to the lift door but we prevent her, a glowing understanding permeates us at the hour of trial, the post-war spirit has not yet been forgotten, we breathe in the same air, the same city spreads below us, everything gives us new, wild perspectives and the sense of balancing at the hour of danger on the walls of the abyss of an opened street, and of keeping houses and eyes together.

What I noticed was the light and the weightlessness, the euphoria, the freedom, the whole of the childish city below us with its toy houses, a few paltry old districts, the immense suburbs' endless rows of blocks, the necklace of lamps along the motorways, the water moiréd, islands like hurled stones, the haze in the north, all this concerted giddiness created an exalted atmosphere, welded our group together, we were seized by a wild joy, it, too, light and floating. Someone struck up a song, I'm swinging on the highest branch, or There sits a little bird, perhaps the latter, my memory is not good enough, I can still hear the intense emotion of the last verse. 'He flies until his wings break, he sinks into billowing sea, and the evening smiles in roses, and the star on his grave's golden lea.' Mrs Rosendal has a warm, supportive alto, Fredrik a clear, sonorous tenor, Fanny's voice is a bit shrieky, but a soprano is needed, Engineer Dahlgren gets out a few shouts in the higher register.

While we are thus being borne along or rather aloft on wings of song the regular plane to the south overtakes our lift and falters in surprise. Pale faces are pressed against windows, a hasty ascent and the plane is past, in the cockpit the pilots sit speechless, I can imagine their disbelief and the radio officer's messages to the ground. But now Papa succeeds in his efforts, the lift begins to descend, returns like a metal balloon down into its dark shaft, and the roof closes over us, the silent attic glides past, Fanny gives me an oblique glance, then the lift stops at the top floor where Viktoria's nameplate glows with phosphorescent light in the darkness. We all stagger out, Engineer Dahlgren disappears down the staircase with Fanny, I see her narrow back and her surprisingly powerful hips, feel their shiny coolness in my hands, Oh oh, says Mrs Rosendal, I have no words, and she too takes her leave, tears glisten on her cheeks, wordless she disappears, but no longer weightless, no longer free.

Viktoria invites us in, we sit round her blue table and talk hesitatingly about what we have experienced, about other events in our lives that could be compared to this one, if only Anna might have experienced this, she says, and Papa: perhaps she has been through something similar, something of that beauty and greatness, that fear, death assumes so many metamorphoses, and as for the city, we have acquired a different view of it now. At great heights human beings lose some of their grandezza, Viktoria asserts, they look like lice on a bare scalp, and I try in my turn to call attention to the amazing interplay between the four elements, between air and earth, sea and the fire of the sunset. We wondered if we should carry our observations further and take up the matter with the lift company – after all, they must bear a certain responsibility for what has happened, and the lift had only recently been inspected. We decided to let the matter rest, thinking not so much of our lift exports as of the belief that now, here, at Viktoria's fragrant coffee-table, permeated us, that the inexplicable should remain unexplained, so that life should not be completely impoverished, for what more then would we have left? At the same time I was gripped by a peculiar, strong sense of sorrow and compassion, compassion for Fanny and her Papa, compassion for Mrs Rosenberg and her pathetic plastic bags, compassion for Viktoria and Papa, compassion for myself for having just lost Anna, my friend, my Mamma, and it seemed to me as though everything I had seen and experienced was merely accidental and doomed slowly to be effaced, as the night effaces objects so that we no longer see them, and we ourselves sink into sleep and oblivion and are no more.

And as happens with children or old people, my eyes were filled with something hot and wet, I leaned my head against the table-top and sank into an all-effacing weariness and blessed oblivion, only waking up much later. Viktoria had put a quilt under my head, she gave me a gentle shake: the telephone had rung, it was you, Maria, you stood in the telephone kiosk around the corner and wanted to come back into my life, did I have any objection? No, I had no objection, we flew towards each other and into each other, like voyagers of discovery who have finally found what they sought, a spring, a star, a new continent to study, or only the scent of a flower. The wonderful thing they had scarcely dared to believe in, what they had dared to believe in. I said: I was up there a while ago, and made a gesture towards the sky. And you answered: Now I have drawn you down to earth, and here we shall stay at least for a time. May I sleep with you tonight? And every night in future?

I write to you, here and now, about my silent days that are endlessly empty, and about the mysteries that fill them.

31 The Weight Man

The man sits at a table, which has a white cloth, it lights up the dark room with its old-fashioned wallpaper. He is short of build, his eyes are barely visible in their dark sockets, he gives an impression of weight. When he speaks his voice is hoarse, now and then he yaps in a friendly manner, that is his laugh. From the window an empty street landscape can be seen, houses, a grey sky, a meagre rain. You remember that the summer that year was short and cold. He telephoned you, he was a cousin of your deceased father, he had emigrated to the States in 1928, at the worst imaginable time. His name is Roald Berg. Beside him stands Mrs Rosendal with a hand on his shoulder, there is a deep mutual understanding there. They live in poverty, and so he has finally plucked up courage, and phoned you. I look at you, you seem more curious than frightened, you are pregnant, we have moved to the three-roomed apartment and Papa has given up both the secondhand bookshop and his dwelling, he dwells deeper, further into the darkness, in a narrow room on staircase D. The perspective from the Rosendals' windows is a surprising one. Roald Berg has worked as a masseur in Florida, as an orange-picker in California, he experienced the stock exchange crash and the drought and famine in the Mid-West. He has dragged his way along, he is one of the forgotten, he has been neither pimp nor smuggler, he has not become rich, for years before he moved back to Finland he made his living in a circus, as a weight man. Weight man? Yes, he is immovable, he can make himself as heavy as a stone, he is rooted firmly in the inexplicable, he has that quality.

We interrogate him about his life. He replies in friendly fashion, he expects nothing of life and human beings, but here, since he arrived three months ago, he has experienced love. He has lost some of his weight. The emptiness he felt has now been filled, and he is ready to pass away, happy. He has hesitated to come into contact with human beings, most people have ready-made pictures of foreigners, and he is a foreigner, an immigrant, settler he calls himself, he wants to go down into the earth of his homeland, and stay there. Hedvig moves, like many fat people, silently and swiftly, between kitchen and living room, she brings the dishes in and clears them out, and the silences that exist are light and natural ones: that is due to them both, to the simplicity and dignity that they show both to us and to themselves. You ask if he has any memories of your Papa. He remembers summers they shared, fishing trips, a warm friendship, decency, a life with no overriding ambitions, but with dreams, of course. Even then he could not be moved, got out of the way, no matter how your Papa tore and pulled at him. He smiles. He has always had a horror of flying, what if his weight were to drag the aircraft down to earth? Hedvig strokes her hair and gives me a glance, her eyes are the bluest I have ever seen, they reflect the sky, have they always liked like this? Why have I not seen it before, only her clumsy shape?

Roald is seventy-five years old and spends parts of the day at the city library, in the reading room. There he reads the newspapers, then borrows a book he finds suitable. What does he find suitable? He gives it a feel, he feels its weight, even if it is slim in volume. It is books about travel in foreign countries, Kalm, Linnaeus, Nordenskiöld, Hedin. What he pays attention to in their work is the descriptions of nature. However poor he might have been in the States he always tried to save in order to be able to buy the *National Geographic Magazine*. He studies the landscapes carefully. If he concentrates, they begin to surround him, so that he can live in them. He prefers descriptions of the Arctic and the Antarctic. Because there are so few people there they become graspable and open, welcoming, as though he belonged there. All the changes, the wind, the moonlight, the silently falling blocks of ice, the seals, the walrus, the flight of the snow-geese, the few but brilliant flowers, the great wide resonance of purity altogether form a room one can feel at home in, an enormous room, it must be admitted, but a room at any rate, timeless in its way, because the seasons repeat themselves in the same slow, unperturbed rhythm, so that they too become a part of the very atmosphere, as it were. The closest he has come to this peace was in Alaska. There he once saw a solitary polar bear on the move, where had it come from, why was it so sovereignly alone? It was a part of the landscape, much more so than he. He would have liked to understand it, and in that way understand himself better. The light, the black water, the snowfields, the icebergs he saw from the ship, the sunlight almost unreal and peaceful, all this he remembers with the same clarity. Among the greatest experiences he has had he counts the Aurora Borealis. Those fantastic waves, that flaming wall of light that slowly changes, as if touched by a wind from the earth, the solar wind above the earth's magnetic field, the rays that are hurled upwards and effaced, that he has seen and preserved. Then he felt weightless and outside himself. Perhaps that is how one feels when one is dead, he adds, almost apologetically: he is no philosopher, and not religious either, but he believes in this immense experience. It is a feeling he has also experienced on a smaller scale, in the memory of a fragrance from when he was a child, or when Hedvig is near. Also, sounds that have vanished mean a lot to him. He tries, there in the book, to make himself listen, on the icefield or in the fragrant forest. It is all a mystery. The innermost meaning is perhaps that one leaves it in peace. For landscapes have their own languages, they are open rooms; we go, Hedvig and I, down to the sea as often as we can. All kinds of things fall away then.

They sit beside each other, expanding the room and making it light. What light they have they have also given to us. Forty-three years, he says, what are they, what have they taught? More than what one day in absolute stillness can teach? What he and Hedvig lack is children. He has lived alone. And now it is too late.

I have come here, he says, met Hedvig, she has taken my weight. But you just try to lift me! Come on! I can see that you are tough.

I take hold of his waist, I groan, fragments of light gleam past my eyes, I must lift a man to the heavens, my body trembles, Roald smells of sweat and poverty, silence and solitude, I heave and lift, my arms quiver, the world rushes out in all directions, the room is left behind, is it the house itself I am trying to lift from its foundations, the stone base, the cables, the rafters, the masonry, is it myself I am trying to tear free, I cannot move him, he has grown firmly into the ground, I must give up, I stagger back, wipe the sweat from my brow. You stood with the twins in your belly, Maria, you too are heavy, immovable, I only a feather in the wind. Roald says: I still seem to have my weight. Perhaps I could earn a fiver in some country circus?

I hear his voice, his dry laughter. Hedvig and Roald, they soon moved away, they came and said a brief farewell, we helped them to pack their things, August came and years after that, and we did not know where they had gone, the cards we wrote came back: addressee unknown.

32 Sergeant Pepper

The half moon passes quietly through the clouds, refreshing the autumn evening. The twins are asleep in the sling chair, Jan with his fist on his mouth, Lena with her arms stretched out. We make our way forward into a world of sleep and bedtimes, feeding, nappies, views of the floor, far from the twins' constellation in the Zodiac. Life crawls forward, leaving traces of toys, spilt milk, pulled-down books, great surprise, light of clear eyes, undressings, dressings, warmth in soft skin, semi-sleep, semi-shadow, sunlight and movement in the grass, four hands, four feet, they are both so different, the one dark, the other fair, forever in motion when they are awake, crawling in different directions. Never have we seen the room, the world from such a worm's eye view, chairs gigantic, tables with great darkness underneath, each lost knife or fork a threat to the order of the world, gruel and mash, unease in one's sleep, dreams and nightmares, unknown and amazing, everything new and exhausting, wonderful.

They sleep, they sleep, the sky deepens sleeping, the stars only pale pinpricks on an airy ground. The metal roofs gleam mutedly after a brief rain, the trees' greenness has stopped and is waiting for autumn, yes, there is a faint breeze of the decayed and the overripe, there is a smell of earth and that which turned in July, nothing is any more what it once was, Lena and Jan fill our arms and days, feathers with weight, continents lighter than breathing. If one sniffs, one can hear the sea. The music flows faint as moonlight out to us on the balcony, Lucy in the sky with diamonds and we know the words, John and Paul, and Sgt Pepper, the world with all the people, we have the LP, it is getting worn out, it crackles in the atmosphere, in the evening, 'Picture yourself in a boat on the river, with tangerine trees and marmalade skies. Somebody calls you, you answer quite slowly', the lonely hearts play, you call to me from the bedroom, I answer quite slowly, when we put the twins to bed they don't wake up, the music is a coil of smoke or a light cloud, a white nappy eclipsing the moon, the Milky Way close to and miles away.

Sometimes, when we have to go out to town for a bit together, Cedermark & Urwind go into action, Viktoria or Papa, or both, they crawl about on stiff legs, put on bibs, wipe mouths and bottoms, sit and observe the games of the moles, the leaping of the weasels, the happy grunting of the pigs, the screaming of the gulls, we rush back, the children take turns at waking us, they lean their sleep-drunken heads like fruits smelling of milk and sleep against our shoulders. If I hold them on each arm I am filled with the earth's gravity and agitating peace. 'Look for the girl with the sun in her eyes' and the boy with his own darkness, she with the sky-blue, he with the deep blue, we follow them both 'down to a bridge by a fountain where rocking-horse people eat marshmallow pies, everyone smiles as you drift past the flowers that grow so incredibly high', and only later do we realize that Lucy in the Sky with Diamonds may be a reference to LSD, now the flowers are growing, the wild vine in its pots, the dahlias with their velvet colours around us, the city mumbles sleepily at our side, 'newspaper taxis appear on the shore, waiting to take you away, climb in the back with your head in the clouds, and you're gone'; but you are not Lucy, you are Maria and near me, Lucy is there in her dream among the stars, our time is measured and tested like the gruel on the edge of one's wrist, not too hot, not too cold. Every day filled with simple, clear actions, baby-sitting concerns, work, distribution of time and waking, troubled nights, visits to the doctor, tears, cheerful toys, and the silence when the children have gone to sleep. Your closeness, wise and energetic.

There was a postcard from Jan in Kenya today, those wild perspectives, that inexplicable freedom he is looking for outside himself and has not yet found, he is only a bit over twenty, Lena travels down here now and then and stays for a night, we go out to some simple eating place, then sit in the kitchen afterwards talking about the world's egocentricities and her hopes, studies, it is as though I grew a little younger each time, or do I just imagine it? What I hate in the passage of time is all the sentimentalities it gives rise to, they become more and more difficult to avoid the older one gets. Do you remember how our summer terrace began to hover when we sat drinking our white wine and let ourselves get intoxicated, also by the warmth from the family circle? You have been gone too long, something is going on, I can read it between your words, objects turn towards me and give me constant reminders. When I was about to take the rubbish bag out, its bottom fell through. When I got up from the devastation I struck my head on the door of the airing-cupboard. I got a blinding headache and discovered that the aspirins were finished. I was halfway to the chemist's when I realized that I had forgotten my wallet. It was that kind of day, there is nothing to be done about it. The gods turn their backs. Later on, a fuse blew, and I started to rummage in the tool box. Rolling about in there is all life's ignorance, old typewriter ribbons, nails and screws, measuring tapes, peculiar implements that gape at me, inert and rusty, wooden knobs from unknown doors, dried-up tubes of glue and suddenly erupting ones, old medals that must have been Papa's, a remarkably ugly miniature glass, candle stubs, string, a long-lost paperknife, torch batteries from the early years of the torch, old electric flexes, fishing floats, no fuses.

We all have our crazy tool boxes, our gruesome nails, our hammers and screwdrivers, our old broken spectacles, our passages to non-existent doors, our old pill-bottles, limping chairs, our collapsing four-poster beds, twisted chandeliers, unusable heirlooms, dead lamps, dead windows.

I turn off the record player and *Sergeant Pepper*, it is over, it only vaguely reminds me of our life. I remember Papa standing here, at the window, after the funeral, saying: It's gone, all of it. That is incomprehensible. What can one reply to such a remark? The autumn stands at the door, it will always be welcome, it never promises too much and does not need to take anything back. The year has turned, and with it something in my life. The old goes backwards, with its back against the wind, in order to be able to breathe.

33 On the Stage

The August evening was already sufficiently dark and warm for the doors and windows in our great, labyrinthine house to be imperceptibly opened. A smell of sandalwood and too early autumn rose up the staircases, filling attics and passages with motionless and gentle expectancy. People who met in the courtyard or on the stairs went past each other smiling, as though they shared a common secret. Windows that remained dark towards night slowly reflected advancing clouds. The oval mirror in the hall reproduced our faces as if they were those of strangers. Had you and I changed at all? Your face was already showing the very first sharp lines, drawn by time around your mouth and your eyes, and in me some of the confused childishness had yielded to a more mature, darker uncertainty which the day's work concealed. In the living-room the babysitter sat, reading the books for her exams; the twins were asleep, their breathing barely audible. How could we leave them, how could we steal some hours of their time in order to visit the underground theatre on staircase F where the Metamorphosis theatre group were performing their Improvisation for two voices? Did we want to measure our voices against theirs, listen to a new sound, was it because we had met them before and been fascinated by their seriousness? Or in order to try to get Papa to come with us to see something outside his room? He had dressed for the occasion, in a white shirt, his neck stuck thinly up out of the too-wide collar, his dark suit made one think of a funeral: around him hung old age's smell of pipe-smoke and gentle decay. We held him under his arms as we made our way down into the creaking lift and along palely lit passages under ground to the door with the piece of paper on it that said in untidy block capitals: Metamorphosis; behind it one could hear a faint murmur, and when we made our way into the black-painted cellar room we saw that the stage was already open and that the two improvisers stood motionless, looking out through a stylized window at a black rear courtyard. How many floors down, how many years down, how many darknesses down must we find our way, in order to perceive with the actors that behind the windows there was only darkness?

There was a smell of cement, and the simple wooden benches were indistinctly filled with people we recognized: Viktoria, the Pietinens, the Stiléns, the Dahlgrens, all with pale faces turned towards the light on the stage. A few simple spotlights had been mounted on the ceiling, illuminating a rough table with glasses, plates and a bottle of wine; the two people by the window came back and sat down opposite each other. People moved impatiently on the benches, then it grew still. The man and the woman did not look at each other, they ate, talked now and then about the simplest things, about food-buying, work, the weather, about the quiet that was so good for one, like balsam, like medicine, here, in the country, in the peacefulness, far away from people. They leaned back and their shadows lengthened; outside a faint rustling could be heard, as from trees, gradually as from a dense forest. The room's simple white walls now slowly began to darken and blotch. Around the two people dead thickets, black branches slowly grow, and the flickering candle on the table is blown out by a stronger wind. The two people turn their faces towards the audience, why have they turned so white, why have they sneaked on masks with anxiously staring black eyes over their living features? They look at us as though we were the ones who were sitting on a stage. I am gripped by uncertainty. No ropes, no dust, no props, no cyclorama protects us from the play's momentary life. Sometimes it resembles our own. Slowly the woman and the man become older, one can see it, they gently fall together, one can still hear what they are saying to each other, but more and more often they turn towards the window that is illumined at regular intervals by a blinding white light. Soon it will be autumn, says the woman, she has to raise her voice, and the man does too, he can hardly hear her for the gathering wind, he had not expected it yet. That must be the sea rising, says the woman, it sounds like the boom of a waterfall.

Now they have started to shout at one another, but we can't hear their shouts, we can only see their lips moving, the make-up beginning to run down their cheeks, the noise must be very loud now, but we can't hear it either, it is invisible, omni-present, the two people have got up, they are calling to each other, they are seeking protection from each other. The window is now illumined by a growing light, façades, props, ceilings and walls vanish into it as into a blinding furnace, the woman and the man shrink, cling to each other, there is only a black shell, the light penetrates and fills the whole room, the stage, the cellar room, the house, the audience crouch, half get up out of their seats, suddenly, with one blow, everything is dark. Light, shouts Mr Stilén, I recognize his falsetto voice, light! And slowly the lights go up, the woman and the man come in and take their bows, did they not burn to death, why are they here, what kind of a falsification is this? There is a patter of unenthusiastic applause, the Pietinens' boy blows up a paper bag and bursts it with his fist: the show is over.

Papa gets up with effort, we make our way outside. Here, says Papa, this is where the air-raid shelter was, the beams, this is where one sat, and I did too sometimes, when I was on leave. He mumbles, falls silent. The white light , the light of fear, still shines in his eyes, he takes my arm and yours, we walk along an unending corridor, people hurry past, out in the courtyard we take deep breaths, stars have burst out like finest gravel on the earth of the sky. We follow him home, he closes the door, at home he pays the babysitter, sits in the kitchen for a while, has a beer, eats a sandwich. Sometimes we listen but can't hear anything except the usual sounds, a car starting, footsteps on the staircase, Jan calling out, but when we go in to the children's room they are sleeping calmly, we can scarcely hear their breathing.

34 The Way to the Library

While the inhabitants are asleep, the heavy demolition lorries arrive,
the excavators and the battering rams, gliding airily through the dawn,
and begin their work. Façades, roofs and interior walls are removed
with dreamlike swiftness. When we wake up, we can see a long way.
Everywhere people sit up in bed and find themselves hovering in
space without limits. We see our house stretching like airy planes
towards the pigeon-blue sky. The entire neighbourhood forms a
world of observations. The young lovers try, wide-awake, to cover
themselves, the children are prevented by their mothers from going
near the sky, the old sit and accept what they have always known: that
the day of total openness has come. And yet each person must go his
own way, over high bridges or through dark mineshafts, in order to
attain the reality he creates. What surrounds us is a slumber. The
white stone hovers a hand's breadth away from us, and sinks when we
sink.

And then the everyday is there, and outer walls, inner walls and
roofs stand in their places, apparently immovable. They tremble
without our noticing it, in the wind; or is it perhaps an unexpected
earthquake that makes our security acquire these thin, branching
cracks, bursts subterranean pipes and lowers roof pennants in sudden
calm? The children wake us, the children direct our existence towards
the present and demand our attention. They scamper around us like
ferrets, stomp proudly away, their liveliness compels us to run after
them, and the days must also run, between playgrounds, day nurseries,
babysitters and wakeful nights: sturdy it all is, ingrained ways of doing
things, changes of clothes and sleep without dreams. The schools have
started, and gaily-coloured creatures shuffle along the streets with
laughter and shouts, but Jan and Lena are so small, they go into hiding

and rush out again, they invade our beds and every crevice of our lives, and the years disappear, as swiftly as a change of clothes. And we thought we lived in the past and in the present, so we didn't count on the future rising up at our feet, as though we were standing in a marsh. Did I think I would find my white stone in the midst of such great unease? Did I think my hand held the world when it weighed a book? Maria says she has heard of an inner room, a secret room in the library, where the ultimate wisdom exists, is that not something for a second-hand bookshop owner to strive for? I wonder if she is joking? What inner room is she talking about? Ought she not as a physicist to address herself to swiftly expanding space, to particles hurled out into an unfathomable universe, to our dwindling insight into the laws of chaos? Look at the twins' room: chaos. And yet we hold the days together, every day tidy up; it is like balancing on a rainbow.

You will smile when you read this. So quickly does time pass, that now, at this moment of writing, it seems shorn of significance, deprived of its façade and its roof. The room, my room, closes around me. Here is the table with the green lamp, the grandfather chair, the bed, the cooking stove, the bathroom mirror that reproduces a heavy, stupidly staring face, covetously imprisoned in sameness. Work and time leave their marks, and the dream sweeps them away again. Anarchy reigns at night, during the daytime habit quietly shines, grey and hardwearing.

But if I open the door in the house that the years built, the dark hotel corridor stretches before me with its trays of leftovers, half-finished bottles, shoes without owners, TV explosions behind closed doors. There is always some man with his face shadowed by the brim of his hat who comes towards you with his hand in his coat pocket, he gives you a suspicious look, stops in front of your door and knocks, you go on, turn a corner, begin to run, rush down an emergency staircase, see a door, suddenly find yourself in the large hall of a library. People sit quietly at their desks, the bookshelves stretch for miles, on their ends hang peculiar signs, Roman numerals, triangles, squares, circles. There is no way out except one door far away, a strong light, from which a strong light penetrates. I look around me, but everything is silent. The shelves sag with books, old folios, whirling dust, cracking spines, a faint lament that grows in strength, a chorus of voices from centuries of words and thoughts, ever more heated voices from the books unwritten, the yearned-for, the lost, they jostle with the others and weigh down the topmost shelves ever more threateningly, the whole library totters, I jerk open the white-glowing door, close it, stand panting with my back to a cold wall, there is a cold room and a sombre man behind a table, he looks up, is not surprised. I cannot see his eyes, I stammer out my name, that I am being pursued, that the library on the other side of the door is on the point of disintegrating, that I have had enough. Enough!

He says, drily: Did you think that you could go out of the library unaltered? Did you think it was a question of texts, printers' ink on paper? Do you think that you can read without coming into contact with bleeding life? This building trembles with the movements and whisperings of lovers. Beauty and horror climb up all the bookcases. Did you think the library was a place of refuge? A simple medicine chest for consolation? Here thousands are in hiding, in flight. Do you think that you will find the book, the one that bears your name. Urwind? Daniel? One moment.

He leafs through his card index, the back of his head is quite shiny, like a that of a deathshead. When he turns round I see that his features have been carved with a knife, the dark eye-sockets, the high cheek-bones, the bared teeth, the jawbones' clutching-tongs. He says, in his soft, clear voice: You are not here. Here are only those who are able to express themselves, who have a language, who are at once dead and alive. I can only find you in the telephone directory. That is your book. Look in it. Dial the number. Perhaps someone will answer.

No, it isn't fair! I shout, we're alive, we're not dead, we answer, we speak, there is always someone listening, we are the biggest library in the world!

He smilingly hands me a telephone receiver, he has dialled my number, I hear the ringing echo in the empty room, in the darkness I sit up with the beating of my heart on the outside of my body, reach for the telephone on the bedside table, I must have imagined that it was ringing, there is no one there, I put the wet receiver down again. The room is silent, the way through the darkness long.

35 The Full Moon

The full moon slowly rises above the roofs of the houses, gets caught for a moment on the tower pennant of the corner house, tears itself dreamily free and pours its light over the communal yard. Metal roofs and people are turned silver; a dark city is magnetically attracted to the immense, pale disc: pale with tiredness, perhaps, you say, yourself surrounded by this chill that emanates from the heavenly body above a floating city. The earthly yearns for the cosmic, and the trees stand inundated by their flowers. Because everything is still, the moon's slow journey seems all the greater and heavier. We see its mountains, we see its hieroglyphs and detect its smell of metal and stardust. 'Many a bright moonrise in the North calls softly to me like a muted reflection. She becomes my bride, my alter ego. An exhortation to find myself,' I say. That is Klee, and if you see his full moon, you see four trees, our wonderful hovering house, divided, but not splintered, into a dark, warm geometry, into an architecture reflected in the eye of a child. If you look there, our window, our curtain, the garden with its fruits, the mountain and paths of memory, all beneath the magnetic silence of the full moon. Klee sits bowed over his memory, the moon is the centre, but there are three smaller, red moons, like echoes, dispersed above the angular houses, the building blocks, the cross gleaming narrow and white in the darkness. Higher, higher the moon rises, and the sky is free from clouds. The same moon that opposed Goethe's birth, he had to wait until it had made its exit. You do not see such a red and beautiful moon every night. *Velut inter ignes luna minores* – and the lesser stars shine there, like children or sparks by its side.

In order to see it in all its splendour we go down into the courtyard. People are walking about in silence, Granny frees herself, doubled up and spluttering, from the darkness and shuffles like a black insect with a tucked-up metal skirt out into the silver flood, like the snail she leaves a silver track behind her, turned to silver the tree-tops stiffen, but here and there a window burns with sudden and inexplicable heat, as though it wanted to offer answering fire to the frost that is slowly rising from soil and asphalt, to the wind that the courtyard itself conjures forth, it grows slowly, dislodging the immense moon-wheel from its crooked path. Yes, 'now a wind comes and touches the tops of the groves,/ see, how the earth's satellite, the moon, has crept out./ Night, the fanciful one, approaches and full of countless stars,/without a thought for us, distant, strange,/she already shines up there, a stranger in the realm of man,/ high above the mountain's crest, sorrowful, with mighty brilliance.' He stops for a moment, Hölderlin, then goes into the shadow of the gate vault, a stranger, he too. And leaves us to the full moon with all its names, the disc, the cymbal, the round loaf, the saucepan, the piece of cheese, the ball of wool, the silver coin, the bowl, the astrakhan, the old man, the dog. Maria looks at me. Do you know what my grandfather, who as you know used to be an old seaman, used to say: that the moon eats clouds and shakes wind?

Oh, you know so much more than I do, but don't always bring it out, you are moonlight and moon-voice, moon-darkness, moon-fire. We make our way inside, Papa calls to us, he breathes heavily, he says: During the war it was dangerous, the moonlight, Daniel had not been born yet, you lay in a cardboard box later on, like one of my books — ; he laughs and has a fit of coughing. Maria leans him against the white quilt, we listen to the children but they don't wake up, I am like an uncut, clumsy, heavy stone, I borrow my light from Maria. Now you must sleep, says Maria, but he moves his hands uneasily, he says: it was hot then, the heat coloured the moon blood-red, the books seemed to melt, we kept quiet about so many things then, no, all that is dead is not wonderful, Södergran is wrong, everything is not inexpressible, it must be said, it must be expressed, he did that himself, after all, a dead leaf and a dead person and the moon's disc, it is so heavy, as though the courtyard were full of black water, you've seen it, haven't you, the black water rising and the moon setting in it, reeking of blood, I had bought the secondhand bookshop from Janz, he fled after that, Sweden, America, he was a Jew, completely alone, perhaps one becomes so there, in the back room, be careful, Daniel, I can't hold my thoughts together any more, help me, Maria —; and you cover him with the blanket which he has thrown off him, he closes his eyes in exhaustion, we go silently out of his room, undress silently, our skin is quite cool, we sink into each other and into sleep as though we were seeking protection for the world that forms a vault above courtyards and squares, above cities and seas.

A tremor passes through us, we have seen the shadow of death among the others in Papa's room, a tremor also passes through our bed, with eyes closed we go gliding out through the window, the house has sunk down into the earth, the sea to the south is full of a gleaming moonstripe, the children seek their way close to us but the wind drives us out on the open, cold expanses, sheets flutter like sails, curtains billow from open windows and hide the moon, it races among the clouds and to the north one can see the burning light of silent lightnings under a dark cloudbank, houses are sucked out magnetically into the moonstripe with empty, dead window-openings, to the south one can see a high wave with an icy, gleaming edge approaching, it is coming to smother us, it will soon be over, that is predetermined, the moon racing through the tattered clouds, the raft, the storm, the wave, slowly the bed turns round and I stand with my face to the darkness, alone, and fall down like a child, wake up on the floor confused, Maria's side is empty, I crawl up half-blind and see through the open door to the living-room that she is sitting there, that she is listening to the faint music that is flowing out into the stationariness, into the unease, her face is wet, I fall to my knees before her, put my arms round her hips, *Weichet nur, betrübte Schatten*, and we listen to Bach's cantata, most profoundly to *Schlummert ein, ihr matten Augen, fallet sanft und selig zu!* World, I will not stay here any longer, I no longer possess any part of you that my soul would desire, here I build only pain, but there, there I will see sweet joy, quiet peace —. And Maria says: I can't get your father out of my thoughts, and with him all my dead folk, it's the moonlight's fault, I don't know why I am crying, don't ask any questions, put your arms around me for a bit, soon it will be morning and the children will wake up and we have hardly slept at all —; grief-burdened shadows, go!

I switch off my green lamp and read your letter once again. You are homesick. Aren't we all?

36 Gabriel's Heavenly Geography

From the children's room a hidden door opens on to a darkness-smelling staircase that reminds me most of the tortuous journey I made as a child with Viktoria past Hannes's half-open door and the mysterious cries and whispers that percolated out of it and at night gave the whole house a glow, as though a great fire beyond our control were raging and could only be perceived by glimpses as a gleam of light flaring past behind our silent, closed windows. But each morning order was restored, and when Viktoria sometimes invited us to Hannes's studio it was large, cool and tidy, an airy room in which the paintings, gently vibrating, stood on their easels and naked models with cold-blotches wrapped themselves in heavy blankets, their gaze stiffly directed towards some time unknown to us where everything stood still and only on the canvas acquired a cruel, violent life. Cold and fire were parts of a world that expanded every minute to be restored by Hannes with a hard hand to its proportions, its semi-abstract life within tenters and blotchy lengths of passe-partout. His dark beard now had grey patches; thus does life paint us and cross us out and scrape us with its knife in order to make us live, grow old and surrender. But Hannes refused to be content, he raged between the studio's whitewashed walls, sometimes flew up against the glass of the studio window, yet without daring to smash it. Sometimes he lay on his bed for days on end and stared at the ceiling. Then only Viktoria could rouse him from a vague vegetation in which indistinct forms hovered as in a private, dark universe. There a limitless swarm of ever-changing, grotesque faces moved past and blended with one another, until Hannes at last rushed up and with charcoal on paper set down this face, a Christ-figure, suffering, crowned with thorns, its gaze always turned to the ground. He overworked that face so much that it finally vanished in its own blackness, with gaping mouth and rubbed-out gaze.

While Hannes stood as if paralysed before his drawing and then in rage tore it up and began a new one, I walked through the September light towards the door with that living strip of light that opened behind the room with the paint tins, the brushes, the canvases and the tenters. I had not seen that door before, behind it there was a great and magnetic silence, there Gabriel sat writing words and kneading out a world of intractable visions; he had been in despair about his life and now walked into the landscapes he conjured forth like a drowning man rising to the surface and gaspingly taking in air: everything is light, tormentingly illumined violently yearned-for reality. If I was in despair about my life I had here a muttering, silent fellow-sufferer, free as a dazzling white bird, huddled over his well-balanced lines, in his chubby hands he lightly held the sea's air and the stones of anguish. Surrounded by piles of papers, books, brown envelopes, he charged the air with tobacco smoke and static electricity. His picture screen flickered with ever-deepening perspectives, swift journeys along shore-lines, over forests, along rivers, out towards sea and sky. At a tangent that only he knew he made his vision crystallize into a few simple, open, freedom-condensed lines, purified and precisely balanced. Behind his table he observed me with the passion of a mineralogist cutting from the bedrock a suprising, unheralded sample of the imprints of millennia. You observe my sea-view, he says, jammed in the window it is wider than you can dream of, in gales it sprays its salt on my paper, I go rushing around but then sit down, stillness becomes a vital necessity, silence likewise. Do you understand something? Do you hear the booming under the house's foundations?

He directs his wrestler's hands downwards, as though he were commanding the powers of the underworld to rise up into the light, he laughs hoarsely, his stubbly hair gleams with early frost. I give him some lines of childish text which I have produced with agony, he wrinkles his face, ash falls on the table in front of him, he reads and moves his lips, all that he writes is inwardly spoken script, his eyes are deeply hidden, they are like his window, out of the darkness they open on the heavens, but what do I see through mine but a back yard? Ah, a portrait of the devil, he says, a picture of the Prince of Darkness! He puts my text down, looks at me. Suddenly he leans forward, studies some point immediately beside me, blurts out: Evil, to make a figure of the devil from evil, that is the wonderful treachery of every cursed petty bourgeois philistine, his barely conscious ability to conceal himself and in all decency continue the evil, ah! Those arch-executioners and mass-murderers, Stalin and Hitler, the whole retinue, and those millions who followed them, they were not blind, they could see, that was the terrible thing! They were one of us. You, you are still young. Do not raise evil on to a pedestal! It becomes too distant. They were not and are not unique, the executioners, they go freely among us and continue their infamies, there is a piece of them in us all, we despise those who do not have the same opinions as we do, we attack the defenceless with knives or taxes, man is for ever in pursuit of fresh victims, waiting for the right moment in a dark alleyway, and then he strikes. Ah!

Gabriel snorts, hauls out a bottle and two glasses, we drink in silence. Listen, says Gabriel, what can you hear? No, I don't mean the water tap or the neighbours' dog. Not the wind or the people. You can hear everything you have been robbed of. The courtyard singer, the clatter of horses' hooves, the beating of carpets, the squeaking of cartwheels, combine harvesters, the silence, you have to travel miles to hear the silence, you get up and listen, the September sky is deep, to be sure, but can you hear the stars? My computer can hear them, it is a faint, crackling sound, as of celestial gravel. It is like a language, fragments, you understand, but dense fragments, only the most important part becomes visible. How was it your Papa used to put it: Work more. More precision. More openness. Order. Oh yes. Something to reflect on in silence until despair grabs you by the scruff of your neck. Aren't you going to say anything? Do you notice that my table is beginning to rot away, that shoots are sprouting from the knothole in the wall, that there is a smell of food, burnt paper, what else is there to do but cross out, cut out, there will be bloodstains but you can wash them until what you write is like spring-water, as changing, clear and unfathomable. The meaning of life? It is life, it is my orange plant, it is a bundle of paper, it is my stomach pains and my dreams, it is this room here. You see, I am growing into the floor, soon I will have worn out all my opinions, the older I get the more naked I become, until everyone can see through me. A cartographer, that is what I would have liked to have been. I have some old maps which your father sold me, cheaply. An angel sketching in new lands. Here everything dissolves into moments, toil and drudgery, sandwiches and beer, and why, oh, why must the fork lie on the left and the knife on the right, and why is the hostess self-important and I submissive, even though it is I who am the guest of honour? I try to see without being offended, it just takes a bit of energy. Poverty, what is poverty? And all the hypocrites who sentimentalize poverty, it is lack of money, of will to live, it is a half-life. And all those who go on about the shamelessness of taking money from the state, Hannes, too, there they are with outstretched hands when it suits them, the grumblers. I refuse to write treatises. I refuse to sign programmes. Absurdities. And people who constantly separate discontent from bitterness. They have eyes in their heads, have they not, they can see what a September day looks like, can't they? Damn it! I stand on a mountain, I preach sermons to the birds, one day I will be one of them, go hence and explain their song! Listen to my prophecies, more you will never get. One is forced to live in contradictions, if they were erased life would collapse. There is no answer to the most pressing questions. The philosophers gave up long ago, they devote themselves to hairsplitting. Mysteries! Mysteries of life! They are the ones I would chart! My heavenly geography! The one the Eskimos carry with them, invisible. Have you read Uvavnuk, he never won the Nobel Prize, how does it go again, I used to know it like breathing, almost, yes: 'The great sea moves me, the great sea takes me away, it bows me like the grass on a stone in the river. The height of the heavens moves me, the strong wind blows through me, takes me with it so that I tremble with joy.'

Gabriel falls silent, then murmurs: 'joy'. He leans back and closes his eyes. I don't know whether he is in his room. The strong spirit fills my mouth and throat. 'Joy.' I get up to go. He gives a start, follows me to the door. Against the intense light that fills his room he is completely dark, I can't see his features, he raises his hand in a greeting, door, walls flutter away like mighty sails.

37 Victoria's Blue Cathedral

I woke up last night to the sound of infants crying. Yes, there were two of them, in their distantly muted wailing. Now it was scarcely audible, now its sound increased with the power of despair. It echoed through the house, over the city, it penetrated the universe, that fear and sorrow, and empty windows, deserted squares and dark corridors listened: the autumn darkness grew thicker. I did not know whether I was hearing that despair in a dream or in reality, here, now, in our bedroom. I sat, as at the beginning of this long, painful journey, and felt again the silence of a room and walls that closed around me. You are not here, and neither are Jan and Lena, you are scattered to the harsh winds of heaven: perhaps you have to follow them? Just now I held the children in my arms, buried my head in their pure, soft smell, felt their warmth like a part of my warmth, they are five years old, they walk around, move in and out through us, look at us with searching eyes, and suddenly an onwards-rushing time has snatched them from us like daylight robbers our valises.

I get up from the bed in order to close the window, where the Venetian blinds are knocking against the window frame, a wind is blowing outside and a new day is on the way. As I move past your old dressing-table with its adjustable mirror I see that the mirror has turned towards the sky, that it encompasses a space above the roofs, that up there secret graphical signs and galaxies are on the move —: perhaps the wailing I heard came from there, I pass through the image like a burglar or a ghost, but when I study the mirror more closely it is covered by night and mist and effaces everything. Only the darkness and the light from the window remain. No image, no figure. Only silent rooms and the light falling in from the rear courtyard remain when we are gone.

I was seized by such an unease about what was now happening or going to happen to us, as though the silence and roving thoughts I experienced were a foreboding of some approaching, unknown catastrophe, that I had to go through into the kitchen, light the lamp above the coffee table and make myself a cup of tea. I sat with my hands round the cup, looked at the empty window where a black weather-vane somewhere squealed in the wind and people fell, one by one, down a black precipice; when I had gone to back to bed again I myself fell, with floating body, down into a deep sleep, as though I had absorbed all the wailing's weeping and weight and with them descended through layer upon layer of apartments, corridors and rooms, outside the house-fronts in my own cold, open and imperceptibly swaying lift. Right down at the bottom, in the inner doorway where the Stiléns' door banged in the restless wind in its passing and where the smell of freshly slaughtered animals seeped out from behind the metal door of the early murmuring, gigantic pub kitchen, I saw Granny Stilén bent double by old age being sucked away towards the street like a black raven's wing with broken feathers; from the World Kitchen came laughter and the clatter of steel and metal, a violent, derisive hammering.

In the empty flat the ringing of a telephone flares up, there is Viktoria's hoarse, tottering voice: Do you want to come up, Daniel, I'm sure you are lonely just now, come and see what I have made!

True to habit, she has left the door ajar. She studies me as usual, her complexion is full of liver-spots, her eyes covered by a light film, but in her room she has built the blue cathedral of her dreams, from cardboard boxes, shoe-boxes, wooden boxes, matchboxes, a transverse section through the world of the lonely. And inside these countless rooms: floating spheres, pyramids, stones, shells, fossils, here and there a glowing immortelle. Her room is very light, the cathedral stands in the corner by the window, a geometry in the air. Perhaps you are thinking of Schwitters' Merz, she says, he had opportunities to continue his life in other rooms, he built out through the window, down on to the street, so great was his longing, mine is less but just as mysterious and dignified, don't you think? When one grows old one must become one's own heaven and church. You see, I have taken down the bookcase in order to make room for the miracle. Isn't it quiet? As quiet as a room by Vermeer? When the light falls from the window it creates shadows, you see, there are stairs leading down and up, there is the hovering sphere, there is the cone, there is your mother's beloved mountain, small, of course, there is a woman sitting with her back to us, do you see, there are lots of rooms in a row as in Hammershøi, do you remember that Russian film when Lavretsky comes home, the doors that open in the old country house, the old servant who goes first, the pigeons that fly up, the timelessness, how does he put it now: 'He began to listen to the silence again without waiting for anything – and at the same time he was waiting for something' – yes, that is what it is like, the poor man was waiting for love, but what are we, your Papa and I, waiting for? And in the meantime he reads and I build my rooms, passages, chapels, the light, the stairs, the shadows, the music, the silence, the purity – the dark purity, and the white one: is that not a fine background for an old woman's dreams? I wish Anna had seen them. Perhaps she does? Fredrik sits here sometimes and looks at the whole, he doesn't say much but seems to walk around in there, Olof was here for a bit, drunk as usual, the whole rubbishy thing made him furious, he couldn't stand it, it can be seen like that too, as a labyrinth one can't get out of. I suppose it's a pastime. It passes the time. Here time has vanished. Look, there, the concertina stands like a pagoda in the light from the glockenspiel, hard to get a candle in there without burning the whole place down, there is the viola da gamba with its noble voice, next to it is the room with the forgotten things, the astronomer's ancient measuring devices. And there you have the torture chamber with wheels and thumbscrews, racks and white-washed ropes, I could paint them blue, and there the waterwheel has stopped, you see, it is low tide, and the too-doll there looks at its cramped room, see what blue eyes she has! If we go up the stairs here we can hear all these strange old instruments, the rebeck and the viol, the reke and the giga, and the brittle frets of a theorbo. Listen!

We listen. From Viktoria's cathedral emanates a faint but clear music. It speaks of a great calm, beyond childhood, beyond death. It smells of wood and glue, but also of something unknown, more obscure, more bitter. It contains so much completed longing. And what does your cathedral look like, Daniel?

I only have the beginnings of a pure, white chapel. There a woman sits on a chair with her back to me, she is awake, or, if she is asleep, her sleep is light and bright. She is alone and present, the waiting and open one, the receptive one, you pass through her as if you passed through yourself, she is the enigmatic and wondrous one. That distance in space we call blue is mirrored in her eyes. She is the invisible, and does not answer questions, the limitless that we shrink away from.

That is why I have built my cathedral, says Viktoria. Come, let us go inside. Be careful you don't trip on the steps. Here is a door that is always open. Here is a house, it hovers in space. If you listen, you will hear someone listening back. If you forget your name, you will acquire everyone's name. It is your own innermost name.

38 Granny is Dead

Granny is dead. She lies huddled up with her bun of hair motionlessly hovering above the sheet, her eyes are open. She must be nearly a hundred. A high wind knocks open the windows of her room, the curtains flow whitely out into the darkness, and the cold snaps her shut like a winter fly, sending her straight out into eternity. The Richter scale registers a mild earthquake, and from Viktoria's blue cathedral an acanthus leaf detaches itself and falls slowly like a token of autumn and corruption; a faint sound of bells can be heard. Hannes pricks up his ears in his studio and sees the night penetrate into the white room he is painting. Clouds great as enamel dishes with blue edges roll past the pale new moon and Granny's bed with its masur birchwood ends swings slowly round. Those whose lights are on notice them flicker, and the scent of gall rose finally dies out there, beside the dead woman. Herman Stilén kneels, suddenly ducks down under the bed, tries to take hold of the old plywood suitcase with the worn strap that glows like a pat of butter, concealing Granny's secrets; she has brooded over them, she has spread her silken wings over them, she has furiously defended them against every assault, her claws have scratched deep scars in the creaking floor. But Herman gets stuck, he shouts as though he had been lured into a trap, and his small feet drum. Half in my dream I hear it, and think that the rain is at last here. Beda, faintly glowing, hurries to his aid. She pulls at Herman's legs, she seizes hold of his hips, with a concerted groan they crash backwards into the central heating radiator beneath the window, which answers with a hissing.

The plywood suitcase lies immobile on the floor, from it emanates a silent hatred of the inevitable. Herman tries to extricate himself from Beda, one button of his waistcoat hangs like a torn-out eye above his dangling turnip watch, he pulls the withered strap off with a tug, tears the lid away. The pale moonlight meets the bundled rows of parcel grips, carefully preserved lengths of string, five wads of rouble notes from tsarist times, and, wrapped in tissue paper, a whole napthalene-smelling collection of children's clothes. Beda buries her face in it, her shoulders tremble, Herman consolingly puts his fat hand on her back, but she leans backwards, the tears flow, she laughs, sweat and tears mingle, she can scarcely utter a word, Herman kneels, a whole family grieves, a whole nation is seized by the gravity of the hour, the sky is silent and can only gently close the windows of the mourning room, the clouds can only roll past and windows with dead panes watch a grieving town.

I wake up and hear your gentle breathing, go silently in to the room where the children are, Jan lies wrapped in his sheet like a luminous butterfly pupa, Lena is sleeping so silently that the whole room is listening, downstairs, far below us Gabriel puts out his lamp and studies the coil of smoke from his stubbed-out cigarette billowing in the radiance of the moon and slowly dissolving, like a too-accidental text. He sees the rear courtyard arching like a shield between the house walls, this creature of stone stretching the legs of its annexes in all directions, corridors, staircases and rooms melting together into a single, heavy body that is merely waiting for the chill of autumn, for more high winds. It is all the same to Granny. She is sleeping longer than usual, with her are dying the memories of a forgotten time, of Viktoria and Fredrik as very small children, she herself has shrunk, like a child she is flying into eternity to meet her Erik, there you can still smell the roses and hear the waves from her childhood, the smooth rocks, all the pictures, all the old ships, the boats, the nets, and in among the nets the old women with their aprons, the parish paupers, the horses tossing their heads as they draw the wooden ploughs across the meagre soil, knives and forks on the cabin's timber walls, the wooden bridges over to the town, the tollgates, the barrels, the trailing skirts, the room groaning swelling with beds, a glimpse of the Tsar, the red bandages, the white, the sparks from the horses' hooves, granny's granny going on falling, falling, falling down into complete oblivion, and now she, now we, now the great clamouring world awakening to a new day.

Exhausted, Herman reclines in his grandfather chair, Beda shuffles wearily out to the kitchen, she must telephone Stig, she must tell, whom? the police? she must go to a funeral parlour with Herman, now she must brew coffee, strong coffee. More than ever she feels alone, she feels that her heavy body is growing down into the earth, she would like to let go, go hurtling down, a too-heavy lift in a too-dark shaft, she must sit down on a chair and do nothing, the world is full of unimportant objects, each with its own weight and warmth, yes, its heat, even; and the sun that merely goes on rising and setting, it is easy for it to shine above good and bad. It occurs to her that she must tell me about Granny's death, Fredrik is probably too tired, Anna is gone, Daniel is there, after all, perhaps she ought to go down to the secondhand bookshop, the three steps, from the courtyard side of course, outside the day is brightening up, the swallows left long ago, but the pigeons are still there, and the gulls, perhaps Stig is not out on a gig, there are streets and houses everywhere, and they bump into her, just like Herman, watch-chains and cuffs against eyes and hooks, braces, always braces, and the small child in its pompous little body, the bloodshot eyes, and she who always started to think about food and hunger when he lay with her, plenty of salt, plenty of spices, stir it, the result half-cooked, she thought she would not think like this, Stig had cursingly hammered the sheets of plywood between the brass bedposts because Granny could not endure the latticework, as though she too had been caged in, sat in her bed like a moulting bird, fluttering her sharp shoulder-blades, now merely a shell.

Beda imagined herself standing watching the funeral procession, the dense crowds of people lining the street, the state funeral, the arch-bishop talking about the significance of cleaning, if she had cleaned the same floor and wiped the nose of the same children the floor would not have existed any more, would have become as thin as a leaf, and she would have gone crashing down to the floor below, done the same work there, and of the children's noses nothing would have bee left, the government's wreath was laid by the prime minister, the Finnish tango 'Kotkan Ruusu' filled the Cathedral with its wild desire, ah, Granny would have loved that, and two spavined work-horses from the interior of the country draw her freshly-scented coffin past, knot-holes through which she could look out at the grieving multitude, the TV set in its usual place, she had always been on good terms with the son, like a dwarf at last, with immense strength, gone ahead like a vacuum cleaner, leaves had whirled in from the trees, a trelliswork of thundering vacuum cleaners by the graveside, so heaven would be clean and tidy on her arrival, probably had the plywood suitcase containing the most essential items with her, in the funeral procession after Granny she and Herman of course, waving to the people, black veil flying behind her, and accordion music so that even Herman's feet in those black lacquered shoes writhed and wriggled, as at the dancing school, swinging in the air. The whole house follows, the ragamuffins, the civil servants, the field kitchen with the funeral meal, vapours and fragrances of burned leaves in the cemetery. She sees it all as if from below, the feet, the eyes of those who are walking past. Ninety-three years old. I am too tired. I won't manage it.

She sits in the old chair at the table with the green lamp, pulls at the sleeve of her cardigan and mechanically wipes the dust from the lampshade. I promise to tell Papa, we'll be at the funeral of course, if there is any way I can help? She shakes her head. This is only the beginning, she says, her eyes are anxious, she looks about her timidly. Would I have a verse to put at the bottom of the announcement? Not the usual thing. Doesn't need to have anything to do with Granny, but with the other side, people don't think about it, but we're almost living there already, aren't we? I promise. When she has gone, I rinse my face in the shower room. I have small grooves of self-pity around my mouth, there is something untidy about my face, my eyes unfocused, something runny and vague. Where does sadness come from? Papa has handed it over to me. He sits in his room, looking up: Has someone died? Am I a mirror for what happens? It will be a grey day, says Papa. That is the colour every shade of which we learn when grow older. Grey. And the smell of gall rose. All that will be left of me is a faint smell of paper. By and large I have failed in my life. That is also an education. But the smell, the smell – he breaks off and we sit in silence.

Yes, where does sadness come from? From early lonely mornings, from summer twilight, from something that existed early, in the shadows, behind people's talk, built into the rooms, into the oblivion, into the objects, into the violent scale of the colours themselves: something enduring, not black and white, but grey: calm grey implacable days, with that healing stillness that is also a part of sadness, like the clown's somersaults and solitude. From the harbour one of the great ferries sounds its siren: granny is dead.

A poem, says Papa. Oh, that poem, the death-poem, it stirs everywhere, in the brightest connections. Listen here, and I try to translate directly, from Roethke's 'Words for the Wind', is this suitable: 'To have the whole air! The light, the full sun/ Coming down on the flower-heads,/ The tendrils turning slowly,/ A slow snail-lifting, liquescent;/ To be by the rose/ Rising slowly out of its bed,/ Still as a child in its first loneliness.' Can't you see Granny before you, slowly rising out of her bed, the gall rose, the pensioner of the entire nation —; and listen here, the last lines: 'to look into the light that lingers, the glitter that stops on the sea's surface./ when the sun has set behind a wooded island;/ to follow the drops that fall from a lifted oar,/ while the rester draws his breath and the small boat silently glides towards the shore;/ to know that light falls and fills, often without our knowing it,/ as an opaque wax fills to the brim,/ fills and trembles near the edge but does not run over./ still holds and feeds the filled flower's stem' —.

He is hoarse, he has to clear his throat. Oh, Papa, I say, go over and sit down opposite him, the room, the world listen, it is the inescapable richness, it meets us every moment of our lives. The silence when it is stillness, such a great consolation. Have you still got Albert the bear, says Papa. I gave it to Lena, I say. She loves it. So my dream of the great open sea has not been lost, says Papa. He looks towards the window. Autumn equinox, he says. Fine clear days to pass away in. Beautiful, what I remember. A few more years, Daniel, then the wind can also sweep this leaf away.

The funeral, you remember it don't you, the twins were there, sat wonderfully still, Lena with Captain Albert in her arms. A Bach solo cello sonata. Papa, so lonely. Reminded me of Mamma. All very quickly gone, and irreparable, even the least of servants. On the way out, Viktoria on one arm, Papa on the other. The fragile, stubborn life. The gentle autumn.

39 The Farthest Place

One dark morning near the autumn equinox, when I could neither sleep nor manage to stay awake, Mamma came down the slope of Mont Victoire, carrying her watercolour case, and even though it was gloomy and dark I knew that it was her. She stopped and looked at me wonderingly. Daniel, is it you? she asked, and I could scarcely answer because of my sorrow. I see that you haven't forgotten me, she said, when you do, the last traces of me will have disappeared. That is the way life goes, and there is nothing we can do about it. I was so afraid you would come to harm during the war and even more afraid when it became the fashion to despise those who fell so that we should go free, ex-servicemen, war invalids, women's auxiliaries, while the traitors were elevated into heroes; you did not join in, perhaps you were too old for that, or too wise. You were quiet, but I sometimes heard you shouting from your cabin, and I came to comfort you, the way I always comforted Fredrik: you have acquired his loneliness and his sudden squalls of fear, and with my gift of unease you went cautiously out into life. Did you never think of anything but of taking over where Papa gave up? It's so dark there in the secondhand bookshop, the window on the courtyard is so small, when Papa and I sat there I would have liked to have opened all the doors, but the war came, doors were closed, what I dreamt of became so small, and then I began to paint, first in my imagination, then, with my brushes, on the paper: it was my way of daring to touch the dreamt. I sat with my eyes shut in a clean bright room and felt you moving inside me, and went walking with you in Provence, in Cézanne's landscapes, and sometimes Papa came with us, but often he was far away, too far away. I wanted you to acquire some of the sharp visual sense he had, the distance, life's fields of colour in balance, and yet all of it radiant, radiant with air and wind.

The thing that grandmother had, too, do you remember? There it looms, the mountain of victory, unattainable and therefore wonderful, and beautiful. So much became so ugly, after the war, blind and strident; then I moved to what remained, and when we took our evening walks, you and I, the shoreline, the sea, the wide perspectives, then I also wanted to give you what I saw: how the dream is here and now, elucidated and created before our eyes. I tried to praise life, that ought to be our task, don't you think, Daniel? Did I give you anything? Did you see how the mountain hovered, how he made it beautiful and gave it meaning? Not from certainty but from hesitation came those last watercolours, which I tried to mimic in my way. When one asked him which subjects he preferred to devote himself to, he slowly moved his fingers towards one another and clasped them. At the point where reality forsakes us there is another, deeper, more intimate, outside time. The one that is also in Chopin. You're not cold, are you, Daniel? All that fragility, and then the image, the sign, the striving, the vibrating light, pungent and dark, from the earth, near Le Tholonet. We used to walk there once, Papa and I, among the olive-trees, and under the plane-trees in Aix. Passion and strength – we possessed only a fragment of it. Of doubt, more than enough. And of failures. Your Papa thought he had failed in everything. And you, Daniel, where have you reached, what have you experienced? Does Maria protect you now when you make your flights, so that you don't fall bloody on the hard ground? Where does it come from, this fundamental sorrow that Fredrik suffers from? Have you acquired it, too? I know that you, like I, possess those golden days, those happy hours when all you see, encounter, talk to, mention, listen to, all the things you touch, landscapes that open to you, acquire a radiant meaning of their own, a light that comes from within, as now, when the autumn is at its most beautiful. Against the fundamental sorrow I place the fundamental joy, in spite of everything, the amazement that there is so much that is beautiful, so much to learn, so much that we pass blindly by —. Oh, Daniel, that is how I would like to live! What you are seeing right now, I would like to see. The most beautiful thing I experienced when I was alive was what the moment gave, and the place, the landscape, the silence. I became quite a fair connoisseur of silences, Daniel. Perhaps it made me lonely. The mountain of victory became merely a hinted line, scarcely visible. But from there I could hear the warm wind. The colours did not deceive, they merely faded. All the scrimping and saving, all the unimportant things fell away. Fredrik tried to follow but could not, there too he thought he had failed. You, little Daniel, how are you? Do you remember what I said to you about a sharp visual sense, the inner one, the important one? You are writing? Yes, I know that you are writing, that you are trying to keep the books of your thirty-nine years, your memories, the passage of the years, I know. Right now, at this moment, you are trying to conjure me up from the dead. But now, when I am here, what have you to say to me? Perhaps I am not a dream at all, perhaps I am the living reality and have attained my final place, while you are still seeking, groping your way through open rooms, have no permanent place, only a labyrinth, echo chamber, the great wind that blows away names and actions, so that only a symphony, a book, a watercolour, a thing of beauty recalls a love that was. I remember how I knitted a jersey and a cap for you, I had managed to get wool from somewhere, you were so small, I could carry you, now you must carry me, oh, you have another road to travel, distances to overcome, silences to break before you reach yourself. I see that you are beginning to get impatient: one shouldn't associate with the dead for too long. Everyone has his furthest place. I am waiting for you there.

With these words she touched my cheek, looked at me for a long time searchingly, with a warm gaze, and was gone instantly.

40 The Barrack

From the silent we are suddenly hurled out into sound and light, from the habitual to the unknown. A wooden door opens, and towards me gushes a warm, wet odour of sweat and stove-smoke. Along both sides of this barrack room run benches, painted grey, made of wood, and metal lockers with padlocks. On the table with its paper cloth, plastic cups and a thermos flask. This is the eternal, temporary life. It moves with heavy, hard bodies, with the unease and anger of those who have not yet been eliminated, it glows in latticed windows until late in the evening, the suburb sinks into sour thoughts and wild hopes, the children lie there in rows. The shabby pack of cards thins out and is worn to death, while the tobacco smoke thickens. Towards nightfall there are violent quarrels, someone is thrown out, police cars wail and are gone again, the dreams are filled with groaning, walls collapse, but not the innermost ones, doors are knocked in but not the invisible one, this is the shared existence, the overlapping life, the iron beds, the muteness and the catastrophe: sooner or later someone will get a passport, someone will be robbed of his parsimoniously accumulated worth, the great brooms will sweep, the steel-hard winds will blow, you will be beaten, eliminated. The mad people in the locked wards double up, do not move any more, on the trees' branches birthmarks appear, sometimes glow blood-red and twisted in the chill October days that are now breaking in. The room I live in among all the others pushes against me, my body is too big for the room, as a child I filled the smallest cabin, now the dreams are too fervid, dripping with sweat, and when the brännvin comes out across the tables the men begin to dance, like bears, spread their arms, shout meets shout, we sit on the benches, strike our hands on the table, stamp on the barrack floor, the stove-lid flies up and bares its red, panting maw, limbs twist and lash out, we live in the house of the immigrants, the isolated, the strangers. How many people have been born here: none. We move invisibly and therefore shout at the sky, our home is somewhere else. Incidental space fills them, they themselves becomes incidental spaces, everything is used up, is temporarily patched up, windows, doors, cracks through which the night wind howls, peeling walls with their pornographic images of women, everything tormented and lonely. The despair gives birth to violence, where there were living green leaves there is now cement, excavators dig for our intestines, chimneys spew out our lungs, watercourses slowly dissolve our bodies, in the patches of oil on the road a solitary, black cloud is reflected.

I sometimes dream of walking with bare feet in innocent grass, but new rooms cut the clear air between the chopped-down trees, there is a slurping in water pipes and taps, and mist unfolds its blind cornea on the windows. To go on living demands immense efforts, silence, wardings off. Those who succumbed moved on a slippery surface, slid outside, fell from rock to rock, were borne away, some got staggering to their feet, were found huddled up in their bunks. Those who lived squeezed into the same room knew nothing about one another, they played cards, drank, fought, were silent, hated, sat, strangers with strangers, and time was just the present moment, the day rammed into the moment, a muddy stake. Every hour the body's space was robbed of some of its power of resistance. There had to be a room-order, wardrobe, bed number, barrack number, pecking order, cleaning ladies, slopped floors, sauna-glowing skin, fists with bottles, swinish stories, raucous laughter, war stories, thumbed photographs, national songs, rituals, so that life could be lived. And those homeless people could not find so much as a fistful of earth there at home, only an indistinct, swiftly past-gleaming image of a river, a clear lake, a child at play, the dim eyes of a slaughtered horse that follows them into the dream.

In this land the population sits with a cold lamp, staring at the ceiling, they dream of a crystal chandelier, surrounded by cold light they live. Tables, chairs, beds, cupboards, all can be dismantled and moved in a moment, thrown out by the landlord or evicted by the state, no sooner are they awake than they find themselves in another place, drunk with sleep they see through the open door the mist on the fields round the town, a red sun, someone shouts: Shut the door damn you! Unemployment, poverty stare them in the face, public assistance goes with its gaze fixed on forms to be filled up, in an adjoining room sit three men, refugees, in another something secret is going on, the three are listening, muffled blows and cries are heard, they lug everything with them; the dying children, the abused women, the burning drought, the burning houses, among us the young people have energy and initiative, pointed boots to kick with. Lena and Jan come home silently from school, they look past us, don't want to talk about it, we try to protect them, on TV we listen to modulated voices that promise us a brighter future, patience, they say, will to co-operate, thrift, but before the lonely man in the hotel room all those who have bled here, been silent here, drunk here, loved here come jostling out, they sit with their suitcases under the bed, how can one fill a suitcase with an entire life? The hand-basin with its brown bottom, the corridors with their worn carpets, the light pale as old skin stretched over bony legs: all this must be the wrong room, for I know my house after all, here there is no distress, no fear of tomorrow. But the sound of blows from the next room? The child that weeps and is then silent? That peculiar repulsive crowd of small winged insects that penetrates through windows and doors and whirs around even when darkness has fallen, as though we had cobwebs in front of our faces? I have my routines, my habits, I keep myself to one side. All it needs is one blow from a stranger, a kick from a teenager, a coarse hand pressing your head back, the sweaty odour of a leather jacket, and reality changes colour, from grey to black, the fear hisses out of the mattress, the bucket lies overturned on the floor, a stretcher is rolled hastily along the gleaming hospital corridor, a grave lies prepared, man is man's wolf. Do you think your language protects you? Do you think you can exchange your life?

It is late. I think of you and the children who are so far away, of the silence that is never silent, of the voices that are heard through every wall, of the life that awaits us when we grow old, of those whom we love even after they have passed away.

41 The Great Leap

The scandal of my life was the great performance of *Giselle* or whatever it was at the Opera where I was prima ballerina, says Viktoria, she takes deep drags on her cigarette and blinks at me with one eye, it almost falls out, the wrinkles round her mouth are like a small fan, she is even paler than usual but her eyes are always equally inquisitive, equally alive. Like Mamma's, but even sharper. She has torn down her cathedral, walked through the blue passages, taken with her steps, pillars, windows, open spaces, begun from the attic and finally effaced the last door, abandoned her room and moved into the old people's home, there her stories grow like the cigarette smoke, the directress is furious, the old ladies listen devoutly, something forbidden, violent and saturated with colour percolates into them via Viktoria's hoarse voice, they gather in the lounge but often the TV remains mute, Viktoria takes them on strange journeys, all is smiling wisdom and exaggerations, the beauty and horrors of far-off countries, and those mystical transformations right next to their own rooms, the crystal vase that tinkles in the midst of silence, photographs that begin to glow; from forgotten hiding places flaming blouses suddenly peep forth, people whom they do not remember suddenly rush in and fill the corridors with their happy voices, children run around and tire them out, towards nightfall all the old ladies sink down into a murmuring slumber, the dead visit them and are accompanied by Viktoria's peculiar creatures, a masquerade with black eyes, white faces, red lips opened to smile or to bite.

But always there is an inner joy, a hope, a stubborn thought: I live! I dream, I exist! Previously the 'Home', as their place on earth is called, was so grey, so grey. The communal breakfast with all those chewing jaws, Pastor Berglund's flowery visits with Bible talk and the beyond, the knitting junta with their long, pointed needles, oh, if they could only vanish into the big palm pot and bear an abundant fruit of blouses, cardigans, scarves and baby clothes when next summer comes, what a delight that would be! Viktoria's fantasies dash around like the best of cleaning ladies, out fly old medicines, mouldered routines, in comes a fresh breeze, almost a breath of spring, for outside the window time balances the scales evenly between spring and autumn. Even the very silence refuses to present itself at definite times, voices whisper behind half-closed doors, and the visits to the theatre, to concerts, to art exhibitions become ever more frequent, the watercolour course steers towards ever wider and ferocious seas. Without you, my ladies, our culture would collapse like a house of cards, says Pastor Berglund, and everyone laughs.

But days arrive when Viktoria rests in her room, everything in the Home breathes stillness and freshly ironed laundry, when Maria and I visit her her face is birdlike, her body scarcely visible beneath the blanket, she listens, but doesn't hear, she has been gone too long. She just lies in a strange peace, does not dream, is absent, doesn't care about today's newspaper, about the radio programmes, about the evening on TV, about anything, she is so light, so floating, doesn't know where she is bound for. There is a big silent house she can move over to, there is always someone there, invisible, who will give her consolation; then she is one of the absent, the ones whose minds are light. She sees the living and the dead, they greet her with smiles, they talk to one another, do they all know one another? They must do, everyone knows everyone else here, but they make no encroachments, they all go their own way. How does Shakespeare put it: it is all so fresh and cold, my old age is like a hard winter, cold but fresh. But sometimes one does get cold.

She smoothes her hair, her blouse, goes out to the others, they are sitting in their chairs, Viktoria, sit here. What have you been up to recently? Tell us something. What was it like when you were young, when you danced? Who did not dance in their youth, says Miss Malmsten in a bitter voice. They didn't dance the way I did, says Viktoria. And be glad of that. You have escaped the scandal of your life. I went through it, at the Paris Opera. The immense stage, the gold ornaments in the gloom, the flicks of the ballet master's whip, and finally the climax of my life, the solo, was it *Giselle*? *The Dying Swan*? *Swan Lake*? Swans everywhere. Anyway. After the arabesques, the pas de deux, oh, he was so strong, he lifted me so lightly, you see it before you, this serious game, a game of weightlessness, and finally le grand jeté, the great leap, everything gathered, concentrated, infinite tension, my leap, years of training and more training, and then the leap! I rose, I hovered there, in the ether – and remained there! Remained, hovering, there! And that dreadful silence in the auditorium before it exploded, before the audience got up, before I heard the screaming and the shouting, before the director rushes in, the curtain falls, a ladder is dragged out, a sweaty stagehand pulls me down, the enchantment broken, the fall, my foot broken, a career in pieces! You can imagine the headlines the following day, Scandal at the Opera, The Hovering Ballerina, Misplaced Magic. Oh, the fury of the opera management, the journalists who besieged my door, the flight, the contempt, shouldn't you have had a broom as well? And those few of my friends who remained, the mystery that could not be solved, the shame and – the sense of happiness. Yes. The happiness of having got up there, fought my way free, defied the law of gravity for a moment.

Viktoria is suddenly silent, abruptly gets up, goes to her room. The mirror is there, she studies herself, makes a grimace: time makes ugly. Only in our inner selves can we expect stillness. Unnecessary to expose oneself. Wipe it away, wipe my face away! As one wipes away steam. Life is strange. The days get shorter and longer at the same time. And all the people! Now one must take them to oneself, now push them away. And everything that is replaceable. Riddles.

42 The Messenger of Autumn

The ambassador of autumn is here. Klee painted *Der Bote des Herbsts* in that rich year of 1922, you remember the reproduction I have pinned to the wall in front of the writing desk. The colours from a clear, calm day come into the room and wait to position themselves round the gently glowing tree. Nuances of blue, violet, six vertical fields striving for light, step by step, the autumn landscape I recognize within myself. You have strolled there with me. There is a state of mind there, as at parting, but without sorrow. There is no longer any striving for greenness; what we have lost in words like 'fate' and 'completion', 'stillness' and 'consolation' are found recreated here. The hand grasps the brush, the clear water receives the whirlpool of colour and light and concentrates itself into a living, deep surface. The insight comes slowly, accepts without demands, the eye walks in parks, in Brunnsparken or along the streets of Harvard, the great trees burn so silently, as though they had nothing else to tell us but that beauty is a gift, full of secrets, as existence is for a child. 'In order to capture a living harmony in a painting it must be built from independent parts, combined into a harmony only by the final brushstroke.' Slowly Klee approaches the wisdom of the child. It is to go into nature, see the wide fields and the tree that stands alone, a chosen one, an emissary. Weimar resounds autumnally to the echoes from Goethe.

The light falls over the old buildings, it also reaches my room, I walk with Klee, with Herr Formmeister, he talks of the subconscious, leaves are falling, the day is high. I do not form the autumn, he says, I make forms rise, a tree, a room for the clear days where they can rest, a quiet for myself. Only gradually do I know what I have built. I do not begin from nature, I begin from my painting; nature follows. There are planes to move, timeless entities bound to their own colours, thus do I create my autumn. The language I seek is invisible and is sucked up by the tree, how much water is needed for a tree to grow, how slowly it prepares itself for the autumn, the winter, for apparent death. Long after the image is finished, I give it a name. It has already existed somewhere, right from the first brushstroke. Everything is open, nothing complete when the painting is there. I produce a creative process, a birth. On the edge of winter it is especially intense. The painting is not born with a brushstroke, it is built like a house. A house made of stone and wind. It is more important to become than to be. You must start from the beginning, always from the beginning. Creation lives like a genesis beneath the visible surface of the work. All intelligent people can see it when they look back. To look back – into the future – is something only the creator can do. Nature, the biggest of rooms, leads us to freedom. The genesis, the creation, the origin is found there. I let myself be flowed through, amazed, like a child. It sometimes seems to me that only children, madmen, primitives can see into open nature. But it is a matter of translating what is seen into form, of thinking in stillness. Colour is mystery. First the canvas must be prepared. I consider the canvas, I listen, it speaks to me through my eyes. It is important to be calm. Consider the leaf, how life flows through its veins. How the autumn touches it. There is a net of light. Is the original source still there? I gather what rises out of the earth, I am the trunk, I go onward to the radiant crown. I am not the beauty of the crown, the beauty has merely flowed through me. I do not reproduce the visible, I make visible. The emissary of autumn comes to your simple room, he is clear, calm, he speaks to you, and the autumn's fever subsides. I make a green moon light up your house, Daniel. I am a part of the earth, a part of the universe, I am a star among stars. In Hannover I met Schwitters. He goes in and out of his imaginary Merz. There is room for us all. I met your aunt, Viktoria Cedermark, there. A young, fair-haired girl, with a calm grey gaze, autumn eyes. Do you want to send her a greeting? She was a young danseuse, she almost hovered. As we all do, in the universe, on our earthly planet. I remember that she talked about Cézanne's Mont Sainte-Victoire, about the last watercolours. I wrote a poem then, it goes:

> *There are two mountains*
> *where everything is bright and clear,*
> *one is the mountain of the animals,*

the other, of the gods.
But between these two lies
man's vale of shadows.

If anyone looks up
he has a presentiment
of a perpetually unfulfilled longing,
he who knows that he does not know,
for those who do not know that they do not know
and for those who know that they know.

And now farewell! Remember: the painting is looking at you. Once more: see, listen, feel!

So, Maria: go to Yale, visit the University's art museum, stop in front of *The Messenger of Autumn*, see that architecture of light and darkness, and the tree that stands there, outside the window, here in my room that waits for you.

43 The Skating Rink

It will soon be winter, and at the top of a tree in the courtyard a burning leaf is whirling, whirling in a wind that only the tree pays heed to: a small pennant that is stubbornly trying to cling fast, absurd and comical. The first light snow has fallen. People leave black footprints. The radiator in the secondhand bookshop goes on strike, smoke comes out of the customers' mouths, they flee with their freezing books in order to thaw them out at home, watch the language slowly begin to glow. The little boy has not appeared in the grandfather chair, I seldom sleep there. Last night I heard the sound of a tensed string, woke up and missed you so intensely that I immediately fell back and saw you standing in the doorway of the livingroom. You said: Shouldn't you also put the great scientists in your window, too? Darwin, Einstein, Medawar? Oughtn't you to know something about the laws of physics?

I reply: Einstein thought that a diffracted light could be beautiful, Poincaré solved the riddles of mathematics in his dreams, ought not more scientists to know something of the laws of aesthetics and art? Around the Nobel prizewinners' TV interview table it is most often the writer who is missing, he is not considered to have any part in the world of intuition and imagination, what does he do, really? Create clouds? And yet recently a seasoned old chemist went up and declared with tears in his eyes that in the end it all depends on – love! It is the driving force in our work! Love is the origin of everything!

You look at me and say: It isn't just old chemists who say it. Old secondhand bookshop owners can suffer from it even worse! What did you say? What did you mean? When I want to reply to you, you are gone. The room grows dark, the cold penetrates through the walls, the heart wobbles like the last leaf on a black tree, wobbles and wobbles between joy and sorrow. Suddenly a day from the past stands before me, my memory chooses without plan, or with some concealed divining-rod: it was when the children were small and I despaired of the secondhand bookshop, I asked you if you might have a job at the institute for me as a caretaker. You're too old, Daniel, you replied, couldn't you start to write or paint instead? Actually, you're quite good with your hands, you could be a carpenter. A shipbuilder, I suggest, bark ships, I could start making toys, they might bear a close relation to my general disposition. Don't you think?

You produce a hard-to-read grimace, look at me as though I were poking fun at you! It's me, myself I'm poking fun at, damn it! It was the same day I promised Jan to go to the skating rink with him. It lay pale beneath swaying lamps. Jan was thirteen, moved on the ice with lightning swiftness and habitual ease, my legs always used to sprawl in all directions, my ankle joints would double up, now in, now out. Snow crystals gleamed in the air, I used to hang on the partition facing the figure-skaters, the girls who practised their figures-of-eight there. There hovered the beautiful Sonia, I had once seen a film of Sonia Henie, Sonia cut her deep, narrow traces in my heart, as she passed me she gave me a quick, burning look, I was lost, wings carried me over the bar, from the loudspeakers came a waltz by Waldteufel, the wood demon had me in its grasp, I glided over to her, put my arm around her waist, we went whirling off, I was her burning shadow, she my breath, close to each other we floated off, in a flash the skating rink disappeared behind us, we gathered all our energy for our famous devil's spiral, the people, the rink, the house fronts, the dark church there on its height whirled round in white terror and triumph, and with a cry Sonia was hurled out of all coherence, down into the gigantic snowdrift at the side of the rink, her legs stuck up so comically, kicking about, as if she were trying to dig her way unaided to the centre of the earth. And I fell, through the darkness, I would never see her again, she would never leave me, I was outcast, my soul shrank and stiffened like sheets in the frost, I woke up on the floor, Mamma came in and wondered what was going on.

I stood and watched as Jan displayed his technique, everyone in the team running around with their helmets and sticks, shouting, passing, Jan raising his arm and waving, I going home. It was quiet there, Lena was out at the pictures, I took a turn down to the secondhand bookshop, unlocked the back door, lit the lamp and took out my Keats in order to try once more to translate his poem O thou whose face hath felt the Winter's wind:

> *O thou whose face hath felt the Winter's wind,*
> *Whose eye has seen the snow-clouds hung in mist,*
> *And the black elm tops 'mong the freezing stars!*
> *To thee the spring will be a harvest time.*
> *O thou whose only book has been the light*
> *Of supreme darkness, which thou feddest on*
> *Night after night, when Phoebus was away!*
> *To thee the spring shall be a triple morn.*

That was ten years ago. By chance I find the poem in a old folder in my writing desk drawer, take out Keats, the dictionary, sit down and bind the years together:

> *O fret not after knowledge. I have none,*
> *And yet my song comes native with the warmth.*
> *O fret not after knowledge! I have none.*
> *And yet the evening listens. He who saddens*
> *At thought of idleness cannot be idle,*
> *And he's awake who thinks himself asleep.*

Keats sent the poem to Reynolds in February 1818 and wrote that he had been led into these thoughts by the beautiful morning and a sense of idleness – 'I have not read any books – the morning said I was right – I had no idea but of the morning, and the thrush said I was right –'. I listen, but hear no thrush, it is October and dark, but light for him 'whose only book has been the light / Of supreme darkness' – strange, lonely, comforting words. You write that you are coming home soon, it seems to me as though I had been waiting too long, forgotten too much, what I thought I was looking for perhaps I did not have. No, I don't fret after knowledge, I fret after your nearness. But an uncertain chill of heart is hidden there, somewhere within me, a foreboding, a great unease.

44 The Filming

The house stretches out a new arm, a recording studio, rumours circulate about its violent, autonomous life, people coming and going, doors banging shut, shouts and silences behind closed doors, the smell of electricity, cables, spotlights, the savour of something violently, resoundingly new, gum-chewing managers, script girls in mini-skirts, control rooms, monitors, producers, directors, the avalanche of dead images rolling out on viewing screens jammed into every nook and cranny and swelling in every room, the droning voices, the clipped, roaring laughter, posteriors and tossing hair, wild shooting and stupid question-and-answer games, earnest professors in close combat with lank-haired interviewers, all of them in make-up, swiftly guided past endless corridors, past the cellar theatre and the conference room, past rows of empty boxes with names and without names, gleaming fluorescent tubes and furious ticking over, paper mugs and technology, sudden twitchings in the brain, coarsened, diluted, smoothed out, only the most important things left: the horror, the blood, the giggling and rubbish; we are tired of it, we are all tired of it, we sit with the screen's flickering light projected on the rear wall of our brains, the children stare at naked thighs and dying villains, the grown-ups at playschool aunts with balloons, we are slowly ground down into the mire of stupidity, we sink down into a premasticated pornography of disaster, our hands grope for the plate of food that is going cold, one might as well eat straight from the can, bragging quizzes and aerobics, only sometimes a living, lonely face on the screen, quickly wiped out, on with the piano-tinkling and pillared coulisses, the artificial staircases and beauty queens in pink draperies, the autumn continues but not all the heroes have fallen yet, not all the suffering children have been discussed yet, the days go by and as I am about to open the door of the

Antiquarian Booksellers' Society's old conference room I am hauled inside by two men I do not know, it is a big dark room with spotlights that are directed at me, half blind I am led to a chair, a fat man with a thin face and a checked cap leans towards me and says: He'll have to do. The best we can hope for. Let's get started. Can you read?

Is he crazy? Am I surrounded by autodidacts? In the semi-darkness, among cables and cameras, shadows are glimpsed, someone is shouting, someone is going round with a pad, what is there to ask about? A warm mouth whispers at my ear that it is the last day of filming for a TV science fiction movie about the end of the world, in the lighter style, but gripping, good that you showed up, you can read the closing words off the monitor, do it quite naturally, as you've always done? Before I have time to react, a board claps, a red light goes on, I see some words in the darkness, I read: 'The music rose out of the rubbish as though it had been hidden there all along. It rose like a low, then slowly growing note. It was like a small choir of voices, a white-and-grey wind, but perfectly still along the fragments of life. Human larynxes could not produce such cold music, the sign of an eternal betrayal. Why was this music wailing, then —' Damn it, where's the music? shouted the man with the camera, a crane was slowly hoisted, something droned from loudspeakers, I closed my eyes, the heat brought sweat to my forehead, a woman appeared and began to work on my face, it slowly stiffened to a mask, I had known it all the time, this game of directors, scriptwriters, cameras, cutters, mixers, producers, assistants, make-up girls, designers, wardrobe assistants, script girls, those thousand cooks around Everyman's Stew, everything centred on the desperate hope of capturing the hunger, the desire, the hidden death right now, of covering it up, laughing away brief life, igniting stars so as for a moment to attempt to illumine the flat land where no beauty grows. Where was the great Disposer? What were these cables, ropes, blinkered spotlights, tasteless backdrops with topsy-turvy artificial staircases, marble bathtubs made of plastic, Corinthian pillars on Doric feet, gigantic bouquets of exotic parrot flowers, false sauna benches, spangled pianos, giant teddy bears dressed in skirts, old taverns made of cardboard, swaying between withered birch twigs, tuxedo-clad young men with pony-tails, female singers in miracles of tasteless screaming, what did all this mean, why was it all turning shadowy, whirling up dust in the beams from the glowing lamps, echoing beyond all life, sinking down into the grave of oblivion that was dug in the middle of the stage: the central point of the play, Yorick's fixed point; but we're not doing *Hamlet*, the director shouted: where's the author got to? and a middle-aged man with a scraggy neck and lank hair came out and said: I've got the text mixed up, you damn well know it, it's an inside job, and the director clambered up like a monkey behind the cameraman on the crane and shouted: let's go! Shut up! Silence! Stop! Music up!

And the breathless silence when something created grows forth, when something dreamt and designed bursts into flower, when a vision goes into its can, when the darkness of a studio condenses to a small red eye, the complete concentration, one of the shadows suddenly emits a fart, the breaks, the roarings, someone missing, take, break, take, the music slowly being turned up, sobbing violins, syrup for the masses, into the microphone I read, as though I had never done anything else all my life: 'Why was this music wailing then? For it was the triumph of death! Why was it rising from the ruins, this singing that was not singing but a guttural sound? For many had heard it before, seen it as rising eddies of dust from the tumult, the screaming, in all the signs of violent, discontented, hated life: this music that was moving towards an ever denser darkness, an ever heavier, more vulnerable world, a music for abysses. Why was this music wailing? Why was it rising like mist from the earth —'

Damn it! shouted the director. Cut! Where's the mist? Are there only idiots here? The mist, damn it? Let's roll! Retake! And you, read those damn words with a bit more feeling, will you? After all, it's the twilight of the gods we're describing, we want to give them a proper dose, and by that I mean a blast at the planet, a dose in their backsides, remember: more feeling! Pull out the stops, damn it! There was a hissing from the floor, a cold, white mist spewed slowly out, came rolling towards me, I read: 'Why was it rising like mist from the earth, the breath from the mouths of the dead. It rose and remained, not an echo but the very voice of the crushed, this song of death, a storm-wind over the ruins —'.

The music was thundering now, I could no longer hear my own voice, dark forms loomed ghostlike out of the white mist and vanished again, it's in the can! someone shouted, in the monitor I saw myself raise a pale face, those dead eyes, the crane took me in, I glided further and further away, stop! I shouted, stop me! and right up to me came a close-up, the eyes, the face a crater landscape, those dreadful wrinkles, the mouth opened to cry out, but not a sound, then suddenly, from the loudspeakers, a booming laughter, the mighty screaming and rejoicing of the rabble: along the studio walls, on fragile iron balustrades, clinging figures, strangely familiar, Bernt in clown attire, Viktoria in a gaudy beach costume *anno dazumal*, Hannes wearing sunglasses in the dark, Beda Stilén grotesque in a striped bathing suit, Granny shuffling with her head forward down the studio's spiral staircase, Sten Petri hanging from a blood-red trapeze, Fanny walking past naked, accompanied by the wolf whistles of the studio hands, and there, on a cast iron bench, Roald and Hedvig, motionless, silent, with wigs in their arms. I start up, run over cables and wires, between scenery and hangings, along fluorescent-lit passages, come out into a big, silent auditorium where only a few lonely TV screens flicker, dropping their snow. How cold it is out there, darkness is falling, people's windows are glowing, the earth is divided into fields of light and dark.

45 Old Age

Papa sits at his old writing-desk. It is as though I had never seen him in an easy chair, an armchair, always at a task, behind a protective screen. The slightly heavy and clumsy body I inherited from him has grown thin. He sits with his hands motionless before him. He looks at me with a gaze that is in some way bent. Do all old people's eyes begin to resemble one another? Do they see something we do not see, or are they simply somewhere else, in their memories? Papa sits in his own solitude, he has got rid of 'everything superfluous' in the room, there are his old writing-desk, the bed, the bookshelves, the Jugendstil lamp; there is the grey November light from the window. He says: I can't maintain that my old age is like a hard winter, cold but fresh, as I think the Duke says in *As You Like It*: my old age is a burden, and I want to be rid of it. Winds without views, ur-wind without wind. No! The only things we old folk cling to are secrets and strange dreams. I dreamt last night that all the roof-gutters stretched up towards the stars and sucked them down like a rattling torrent of silver coins into their jaws, like gigantic vacuum cleaners. The whole rear courtyard was filled like a bathtub with silver, and that was what people had been waiting for. They came rushing out, I among them, and began to scoop them up, they shouted and made a noise, and everything was at the same time horribly quiet, and I felt dead tired. Why shouldn't I? I am eighty-five, and the secret schadenfreude in living on and on feels bitter in my mouth. I don't see many people, apart from you and Maria and those blessed children. I can't remember what you were like as a child. Quiet, with violent squalls. I feel like hiding from everyone's view, and crowing as proudly as a cockerel when the occasion comes along. The occasion never comes along. I see the world going under, but I don't. I float around like a piece of wreckage. I get along quite well with myself, whoever I am. What was it Maupassant said of himself in his old age: Monsieur de Maupassant va s'animaliser. One's eyes start to give up, but still go on looking for the great secret, the meaning of existence. I sit at the window and observe clouds and twilight, how long, how protracted it can be, and people don't stop to see it. Sometimes there are several layers of clouds: completely light ones, like veils, behind them fiery red knife-sharp cirrus clouds lit by an invisible sun, and lowest down, nearest to me, big heavy dark violet clouds, pumped-up and threatening. One's thoughts wander, the brain's office shrinks, it contains only worn-out furniture, and the light there is dim, and soon it will be night. I wonder if Kafka would have like that image, the worn-out room, the fear? He could write about it, in plain language, I have never been able to. I have failed in most things. Certainly, I have managed my own affairs, I think that Anna and I, we had the same features, but where I tried to shut myself in, she tried to go out, restlessly, all those uneasy spring evenings. While I sat and read. And still do, perhaps with a little more discrimination. Now I have studied the great modern masters, Broch, Kafka, Musil, a little Trakl in between. I feel as though I were one of them. They are like children, so old. It is the wind that is the last element in *The Death of Virgil*. Perhaps you think I have been what Broch calls 'reality-blind'? Yes, perhaps. But there are realities and realities, the most common one is perhaps the most vague, the least real. When I am gone a reality is gone, the one I transformed into myself from the texts of the great. I imagine that I have always been the creative reader, that is but a meagre consolation, but a consolation none the less. When I am gone Broch's 'promise and insight' is gone, and no one can see it. You know yourself, Daniel, that through what you read you see yourself and the world a little more clearly. Not yourself? Then you must make one more journey through the world in order to get there. You doubt? You despair? I cannot comfort you. Intolerable life is like a story babbled twice into the ear of a drowsy man. If according to Broch Virgil doubts in his poem and its power of self-renewal, how great then is our despair, we who have not created, have not invented any expression. If only you could get started. I know that you have the passion, the strength within you. I think of your Klee, your Schwitters, the 'white Jews' as the Nazis called them. Huguenau has forgotten the murder he has committed, all he remembers is his successful business deals. So that world ended, the world of the humanists, the dreamers, but some went on. We must be the walking cemeteries of our friends, as Sperber said. It is a question of listening, to each jarring note. Kafka did that. When he talked he thought that he sounded like a complaining cat. I myself sound like a howling dog, sometimes I wake up from my own complaining. Self-discipline! Self-discipline! I think of Anna's beloved Chopin, and of Kafka. For him, writing was a form of prayer. He saw himself as a body stretched like a bridge between two rocks, beneath him he had the abyss, he was a sagging bridge, someone stamps on his back, crushes him, he falls. He felt kicked away, like a dog. Don't laugh, he said, don't laugh at the tenor singing his long final aria about the fact that he is dying! The whole of my life has been a death aria. And mine has just gone on, since Anna died. Do you remember Mamma? I mean, do you really remember her? To penetrate right down, to the darkness, layer after layer, floor after floor, all the way down, to what Broch called the dark regions of ego-development and ego-efface-ment. He was in pursuit of the divine. What is that? There is only one yardstick, said Virgil, and it is the work's goal, not the work of art, not the artist. The goal. If one doesn't know that one prolongs the twilight, and becomes like the shop-owner outside his small shops on the street, in Broch's books, one forgets to close up. How is it he puts it: the man who at a distance longs for his wife or merely for his childhood, he has begun his sleepwalking. We have started early, I suspect, with that walking? When were you born, again? The same day as Keats. And I the same day as Musil. What if every human being has his unknown companion in world literature? Eh? When I see the snow that has fallen, effacing people's footprints in the courtyard, I sometimes have a great desire to go into the snow in the dark, go out in my pyjamas, and like Ulrich long to feel the cold air in my hair. That would probably be a solution to many problems. To stand barefoot for a while and know: this is the beginning of the end. The silent white courtyard, the dark sky, to feel both delight and sorrow, or neither. To feel the 'daylight mysticism' that Musil dreamed of. To stand in front of a mirror at night and see that the darkness there is different from the darkness in the rest of the room. All these strange moments! Now I long for the last one. The patience of old people. The goal. What goal? Was Anna happy with me? Were you? And Maria – Maria is like a good steady breeze on a hot summer's day. When I see her I get a bit envious of you, and senilely prurient. Blind with loneliness. Those frail wooden bridges. God is near, and hard to comprehend.

Today the spirit's ardent flame gives birth to an immense pain: the unborn generation. Grodek in my heart. How was it Kafka put it: 'I am nothing but literature and will and can be nothing else.' And he created a world, the one that is, terrible, around us. No, don't go yet. Sit here for a while. Now we have November. The long dark weeks. The evil silence, and the good one. I am weary of them both. But we like sitting here together, don't we? Imprisoned in the viewless winds.

Papa laughs, leans forward and pours more wine into the glasses. My monologue is finally over, he says. Did you know that Herman Stilén died? Right on the spot, the lucky beggar. Why beggar? And what sort of beggar? Daniel? Are you here? Good. Now let's drink a toast.

46 November

The sky's great door shuts. The fields lie empty outside the city, where the houses creep closer together in order to lend one another some of their warmth. The children run to and from the school, their faces closed. A child came into the shop here the other day asking for sci-fi. Found some thumbed serial magazines, I gave them to him, he had such a thin, pale face, with large eyes. The street outside was almost black. There isn't much to dream about. That precisely today – a Monday – the books had concentrated themselves in such an averted silence, such a compact resistance, stood there each with its back to me, each with its secret, but with a common smell of dust and mace, is no coincidence: Mondays are like that. November behaves like that. But the smell of paper is a good smell, it is as though a ray of summer light were to fall into a warm summer room: the dance of the dust specks in Hammershöi! Through them run the children, they stand or fall, the strong and frightened kick, the submissive keep away, the lonely are lonely. You see them at the kindergarten, they sit under neon lights, cutting, painting, hammering, dancing in a ring, falling, getting up, waddling about in their red and blue dungarees in the courtyard with the slide, the ropes, the playhouse, the slush and the mattress sky, they are like potatoes in a potato box, pour out plump and peeled across the floor, go rolling around, the hair of the girls is like little waterfalls for climbing, I remember it, and Mona cutting off a piece of Lotta's hair, all the screaming, and how all the lively activity slowly froze beneath the classroom's white lamp-globes, and the desks that slammed shut around the groaning, aching, combat-ready, clumsy body that still felt too big there, in the trap of table and bench; they run through me, their teens are angular and coarse, forgetful and heart-rending, we want to enclose them in a great, eternal warmth, but they stroll away out of our lives. Doors were always opening, or closing, new silences we were not used to came to stay. They are here, in every room, on every staircase, those running footsteps, the breaking voices, they cannot be swept together like small children, the TV can capture them, we sit on big blocks and there is a fat uncle with a beard who is telling us something and building something made of paper and paste, if only we could pour the jar of paste all over him, then we were allowed to play rowdy games, then three punks sing a song, we are like pins in a pincushion, we are candle flames, and someone tries to blow us out, and at last it grows winter dark, and we go to a bus that takes us home.

Were the dead there, listening? They were everywhere, lurking, on TV they fired wildly, and small children ran around with grenades and swollen bellies, they had flies in their eyes, what do we learn from that, we aren't learning for school but for life. On TV everyone is already dead, they are just pretending, that is why they laugh and smile all the time, there I see myself on video, I am completely alien, I am full of expectation and a complete changeling. Leila won the big children's quiz, we were supposed to hug her and kiss her, but we wanted to scratch her and kick her. We formed a circle round her, there, in the studio, the camera didn't see, but we ate her, all that was left was her doll's dress, her doll's face, and of her prize – a large teddy bear – there was no trace. A playschool aunt with a big mouth screamed, soap bubbles came out of her mouth, if you pressed her stomach she only squeaked.

We ran between cables and cameras, we rampaged around in the big fortified stronghold, there were endless empty corridors, little mouse-holes where here and there a mouse stuck its quivering nose out, this way! shouted Stig and we ran after his burning hair, in a corner men and women sat drinking coffee, they looked up in surprise, we gobbled them up with biscuits and Coca Cola and all the rest, we rushed through conference rooms and rest rooms and studios, went storming along iron railings and up and down spiral staircases, a torrent of lava in a gigantic abandoned rubbish factory, everything was shining new, fantastic control panels flashed and giant loudspeakers snuffled, there is Aunt Inna shouting Danni Danni what are you doing, can everyone see what we are doing or can they not see us at all? I am back on dizzy bridges, in rooms with stunted furniture, in the eyes of Lena and Jan I see something bygone, something defiant and desperate that was once there, tenderness was there, too, now violence is here, the children describe it, without comments, how someone kicked, how the teachers talk to them, it can be quite enjoyable to see how the grown-ups behave, and some in the class are quite tough, no one can get the better of them, you see: they are the ones who like kicking, something happens, at least something really happens when you throw your weight around. The worst thing is silence, we drown it, we go into the forest with a roaring transistor radio, there is life and sparks, everything has changed since Stig and I passed over abysses and Granny was alive, it was before the time of the great revolts. What you had to do was throw yourself over. It still is. By other means: switch off the flickering picture screen outside and inside you, sit in stillness, listen and just be in the healing stillness.

Things are quieter outside. The great cold is approaching. Even the barking of the dogs in the ravine of the streets sounds distant, feeble. The one who travels sees his distance within himself. I long to get home. Papa called the secondhand bookshop his home, then Mamma became silent and turned away. He did not notice anything. Now they are both gone. An unreal moonlight penetrates through the window, it was bright and gentle before. The dead look appealingly at us: Do you remember us? All those years with us? In their silent sorrow there is no accusation. Their image is far away. In childhood they were quite near, I ran around in the house of magic, storing moments without knowing it. There was a great security in their voices, in the low-voiced conversation in the evening, in the smell of the lamplight, everything was worn and near. The things I could stop I observed. Children collect the near and worn. Viktoria stopped me and said: Behind your eyes an old man looks out. Shall we get married before the old man dies? She laughed. When I think back I see what great sorrow all distance gives. There is nothing to be done about it, nothing to sentimentalize, nothing to ignore or diminish. The emptiness is there. Rooms are alive when people are there, but when they die, the rooms stop. For several weeks the secondhand bookshop was dead. Then life slowly returned, like an embarrassed customer who has to buy a book on tick. You appeared, with the scent of spring.

47 In the Old Classroom

Into the old classroom the cold wind penetrates while the boys and girls are outside at recess. Outside? There is a distant din of voices, there were only boys then, the old desks have been replaced by new ones, but old shadows sit invisible on the benches and lean forward, flick paper pellets with yellow nicotine-fingers straight at the back of my neck, it feels as though a fly were crawling there, I slap it with my hand, I can still feel the slap, but only in here. The boy with the red hair gets up, stammers slightly, is it Stig? He blinks his eyes. Eight years have been pressed in and drawn out, like chewing gum, like glue, into the blackboard, the eight white lamp-globes on the ceiling, into the echoing corridors. Post-war era, era of hard, dreamless work. Plaster heads of Homer and Plato, Caesar and Augustus still gaze blindly from their pedestals, even if they were to open their closed mouths and attempt to shout to one another from one end of the corridor to the other they would not be heard, into their open mouths someone would sneak a cigarette end or a crumpled Coke can, that is the price of a two-thousand-year-old suffering, Gallic wars and Nordic ones, overthrown usurpers, and new, vigorous ones, resistant to everything, like rampant new viruses. How did I find my way back here, I who only meant to buy some food, go the post office, the bank? Is emptiness a road I am compelled to follow, all the way to the high door, the classroom that is concealed in my house, somewhere behind years of rubbish? In there an almost acrid smell of damp clothes, November mud and sweat rises, you encounter it as soon as the door opens. Here dreams are lined up in rows and marched in to morning prayers, if you hold your breath you faint and may be sent home, it is rare. In the recess the wind cuts like a scythe. Örfan's spectacles gleam as he stands by the window, he hardly turns round. Since he is late, would Daniel be so good as to step out in front of the class immediately and explain Prothagoras' second fallacy.

Prothagoras' second fallacy? Clawlike, black trees move indignantly outside the windows. The class grins, it rises amphitheatrically and darkens towards the ceiling, there sit those who are trying to hide, the big, coarse ones, they send messages to one another as I stand transfixed by cold light at a blackboard, if you stick your hand into it it never ends, it is only a black wall, almost a curtain behind which all wisdom is gathered: old men and old women who sit in there with the secret of life, observing you, weighing you, measuring you, turning away. Here there is no pattern, here there is a rotation, you are hurled out towards the periphery if you do not exert yourself. And the morning that is so cold that only daydreams can warm you. Örfan has a rigid face, he moves with effort, he has a stick, he understands the young, their rebellions, their capers, he teaches even the biggest idiot the sense and discipline of language, he has a rich fund of humour, or rather jokiness, he has countless stories about failures and misadventures, he laughs curtly and effectively, he does it on this occasion, too. On the teacher's desk lie the essay jotters, they emanate a gentle despair. Prothagoras was a joke, let it go with the ur-wind, instead read the top essay, a dainty morsel for dark November days, listen and learn! Why must I read aloud Stig Stilén's thoughts about war and peace, reparations and power? Helpless letters gather themselves into a desperate grammar. Over dizzying bridges we move, Stig and I, he has no dizziness, he laughs inwardly at Örfan, he becomes an airman, calm, cold, and purposeful, who would have thought it? Not Örfan. Eyes gleam out in the classroom, there in the corridors during recesses is the noise and din of the other world, the voices of the teachers, the givers of orders, the supervisors, the school councillors, the secretaries, the gentle observers, all is uncertainty and chafing skin, there is the echo of the coercion that Herman Stilén spread about him and Stig made himself free of, that Beda scraped away with short pantings, scoured the linoleum free of. This odour of purity and order maintained with effort, this struggle against chaos: the same striving at the Stiléns' as at the school. Childhood rooms glide into one another, the school leaves its windows and walls as imprints of the whole building, in the courtyard wet snow falls on Herman Stilén's dream car, soon it will vanish in the white silence.

The thoughts wander between the desks, from somewhere there is a smell of cabbage, from Beda's kitchen or the school's, everything is so small and insignificant, that is the nub and the truth of it day after day, year after year, until Stig flies out of the school with the others, until we run shouting into a big, dark and harsh world. Eight years are quickly forgotten, with Maria I watch Lena and Jan as they get their white students' caps, now comes the time beloved, yes, and summer sweet, and November is so far away. They smile at us, they vanish in their turn, some of them will never come back. They live at home, they are happy or shut themselves in, they sit silent at the table or talk to one another about a music we cannot follow, we are old, at last I sit like Professor Unrath at the teacher's desk and wait to be given detention, on the green board behind me someone has drawn incomprehensible signs. Daniel can go to his place. Daniel has grasped nothing of today's lesson, and nothing of previous lessons either. Daniel must stay behind in life and sort it out.

I steal my way out of my old classroom, did not know it was next door to here. But where do all those pushing, shouting children come from? Does the building have an extra floor I know nothing about? The whole stairwell quivers with their rampagings. And the old folk who are groaningly making their way upstairs, towards the torrent of children, where are they going? Ought they not to be making their way downstairs, and the children up? What kind of system do they employ? Perhaps as a physicist you could sort it all out? Problems should always, as you usually say, be examined with humour and seriousness in equal parts. But catch at a shadow. Which reminds me of Professor Shadow from Yale who came here once prying about for Nordic mythology, he crept around like a little badger with a fox's grin, I thought of Andersen's fantastic tale about the shadow. Perhaps Professor Shadow was only his own shadow? Perhaps some of us only live as shadows all our lives and become real only in someone else's memory and – heart? Then they receive their own life as a gift. Like shadows we sit at our desks, or move, like the Stilén family, in a cabbage-smelling fluid, in a world of secret catastrophes, grey habits and inner poverty, a stubborn petty bourgeois world bordering on madness. I know it.

48 The Book That Writes You

The museum is icy cold for want of funding. The steel sculpture with the blood-red wings has twisted itself round at a right angle in order to be able to see the museum committee's meeting. I remember the antiquarian booksellers, the basement and the dancing green table, remember the dark passageways and Viktoria's voice: Be careful! Deep inside I have moved in a circle, my body is a pale moon among drifting clouds, I see the dance of snowflakes and the early morning cold, when each tree-branch outside the window is hammered to silver, and the low-moving sun sends a golden reflection through the roof streamer of the house next door. From a broken studio window comes a squeaky voice, cursing the elements, water, wind, earth and fire, and above all the central heating radiator that has given up the ghost. I'm being pursued! he shouts, by his voice one can hear that his straggling beard has grown again and his eyes have narrowed in his black face, he is wading in thrown-away drawings, some of his desperation echoes in me. I have tried to assemble the week's birthday children, in a way they are all sitting in knitted jumpers, expectant as children at a children's party, Celan and Spinoza, Ionesco and Blake, Moravia and Louisa M. Alcott, it is all turning into a comic tragedy, a gaping laugh in the utmost distress, watching over it all are Juutas Käkriäinen and Toby Shandy, arm in arm. Farewell then, cool reflection and rational discrimination! Begone, tidal wave of vexations! Come tranquil winter's day with fingers of redness lightly touching bashful roof-tops, quiet windows, cool flights of stairs, inhabitants smiling in my dreams! From my devoutly resting room I enter a world of silent shelves. Will I also one day take from my shrunken inner self my laboriously dreamed-together life's work and set it beside these tales of brilliant achievements and bitter defeats? Will I tell of the morning's coffee-making or the basics of accountancy, the magic of the washing machine or the advantage of having one's socks divided into long and short? Will this immortal tome one day adorn the library's shelves, the library where all is changed, where jeans and Iceland sweaters go storming up the stairs and the chirping from the issuing desk does not come from birds? We must live through it all! The bread that must be bought, the contract that must be followed, the everyday that must be borne! In every book a life is hidden. The book that writes you and is one day put away, never to be read again. The thought makes you want to stand on your head in order to see more clearly. Progress? How does the Steppenwolf put it: 'Der Fortschritt ist zwar eine Treppe, /Doch führt sie, statt hinauf, hinab.'

In other words, I have no great balancing of the books to leave behind, what you get is a life. It is quiet, now before the winter gales. Thousands of miles from here you walk in the streets of Boston. Here we live in the expectancy of snow. The city expands in the cold, the sky is strangely light, the people talk about depression, misery, taxes, poverty, survival, unemployment, perhaps sometimes about friendship, warmth, love, what do I know. Here a few days ago I was at a class reunion. The Beatles flowed out in the background. Towards nightfall the atmosphere rose, old memories were dusted down, in the toilet I looked at my fiery red, heavy face, stood there with the water running and made an ugly face at this stooping, stocky, round, alien man with his watery eyes and his lank hair that is starting to get grey streaks in it. What have I become? When I came out I couldn't find our table. I saw it far away, but kept colliding with mirrors, then sat down drunk at an unfamiliar table with an unfamiliar solitary man, heavy velvet curtains bulged like sails into the pub from tall French windows, behind which the cold was sparkling above the familiar rear courtyard. What I talked to him about I can't remember, a little child ran past, my red hand closed around a glass, until Stig – the same red hair – and Klas – the same gap in his teeth – came and took me back.

You see: I am alive. Only just, but alive.

49 Viktoria Speaks

Each person's face reveals the human, most deeply suffering or sacredly alive, or both: there is no gaze, no movement of the mouth that is not connected with birth, happiness, pain, and the shadow of death. The newborn child, the old person in bed, the lonely man in his hotel room, the puffed-up speaker wiping the sweat from his forehead, the lover, the hater: they are all hurled out from the centre of the same birth, crying or mute, constructing or demolishing their own fate. You muster the last strength you possess in order to touch a beloved hand. You muster the last strength you possess in order to open a wound in the one you hate, within you. We move through ourselves as though we were in flight, accused of something we are not acquainted with; we stop and look at the beauty around us, human goodness and wisdom, human goodness and wisdom smashed, we are filled with happiness that grows dim and evaporates; the dark night surrounds us, and we try to light a candle in order to find a defence. What drives us unseeing through life? What prevents us from stopping, looking at the cold stars in the winter sky, finding our way to the warmth of human beings, being enriched and enriching? When I was young I lived a wild life, says Viktoria, I saw nothing clearly, and much is still wrapped in obscurity. I sit here and wish I were gone. I am eighty now, is that not enough? My fate is to have survived both Anna and Fredrik, Fredrik's fate was to survive Anna. Fate is chance and that mysterious order that gives us so much pain, each one of us, and in rare instances a great fortune. Perhaps it was a fortune that your Mamma never did climb Mont Sainte-Victoire, she gathered herself around an image, a vision, and moreover that of someone else, Cézanne. Not a bad way to calm and understanding. I try to sit perfectly still among those few objects I still have around me, objects are important, they anchor us in the simplest and most essential. I see myself in the mirror and what do I see? An old wrinkled face, a moon with birthmarks, a scooped-out cheese that no one wants to taste any more. I want to go away, like your Papa. I loved him once, for a short time; he suffered from it for the rest of his days, and over him and Anna there rested an invisible cloud, a shadow on the mountainside that would not go away. He accused me of not having given Anna enough warmth. She was so frigid, do you remember? Did you not know about that? Then it's about time you grew up. What are you now? Forty-nine? An age when one no longer returns, can no longer return to anything, is merely driven onwards, tries to find an anchorage, has a go with the drift anchor. You are quite big and clumsy, even as a child you were, but your gaze was always looking for something else, you had your fantasies, you kept quiet about them, hiding behind the books in Fredrik's second-hand bookshop, and now it is yours, and now you have Maria and Lena and Jan, and don't know who you belong to, the family, solitude or God. You'll have to pour your drink yourself, spill a bit for me, too, my hands are so trembly nowadays that the whole table shakes. Can you distinguish between the living and the dead? Do you think it's necessary? Many of those who shuffle in stairways and entrances seem more or less dead, while I still have long conversations with both Anna and Fredrik, they always answer so softly, so feelingly. Then Stig Stilén usually comes to visit, he is a lone wolf in his airman's uniform, soon he will be retired, he tells me about his flying, about the aether he goes racing through, it wouldn't surprise if his light blue eyes – blue, blue is my colour, do you remember my cathedral? – darkened with the sky towards evening and became black at night. Perhaps you think it's a strange contact, given the difference in our ages? Your old playmate, school chum, Papa Stilén's browbeaten boy! Unlike you, Daniel, he is very firm, straightforward and consistent, a bit frightening I must admit, but he awakens in me the last sense of a kind of love I keep a supply of, one that also includes you, you old hack. People think he's my son when we go out and he takes my arm. It dispels my customary resignation that surrounds me like invisible glue, making all my movements so slow. Soon the blue colour will not be visible on my table for all the bottles of pills, I've rented out my other room, you know that, one must take humiliations with the pride that an old hag's wisdom ought to give: I stand above the encroachments of society, my encroachments are even stronger, I have death on my side.

I so often think of Anna, all the things she never spoke about. Gently but consistently she excluded us. No, one can't make up for anything. But we have always had firm ground beneath our feet, we Cedermarks. You remember grandmother's room. So in a way we have always known where we belong. But you Urwinds, from what corner of the globe do you originate, where does your restlessness come from? To be sure, your breeze is great and fresh as the sea, but sometimes too cold. Yet: there is no hatred in you, so Anna must have immediately recognized something in your Papa. Nothing like: 'for they have sown the wind, and they shall reap the whirlwind.' If I remember rightly, those lines are to be found in the Book of Hosea, the one after the Book of Daniel. What does your Book of Daniel look like? You hesitate to tell me, as you have always done. What does Maria say about that? She has such wise, reflective eyes, she mustn't stay over there too long, or else you will lose her gaze. Are you happy? Have you given anything to those nearest you, grandmother used to ask, saucily. She didn't mean presents. Perhaps you think that fifty is a watershed in life? There are no watersheds in our lives. It is all the same wide water from the beginning, go there and draw limits. It is the navigation markers and the beacons that are important. You see: my mother's father was a sea captain. Yesterday I went and sat in a church, there was no one there except me. It was bright and cold, and white was the dominant colour. As it should be in winter. I felt abandoned. It felt as though it was enough now, the loss, and the loneliness. Then I thought: it is probably fixed and measured that way. And all the days and the years that have passed, and all of us who do not leave behind any traces at all. And yet perhaps, nevertheless. I closed my eyes, at last it all became completely empty and silent, the church, the world, my head. And after a moment, as when one has come over the crest of a road, I was filled with something. With what? With a kind of grace? I have brooded so much on the word grace. No one will take your word unto him if he doth not receive thy grace, I think it says in an old psalm I remember from my childood. Grayce, it was spelled then. Grace, it can be diluted into blessing and mercy, but I see it more strictly, as a face grows stricter when it grows old. And strictest in death. Even though the heights may totter, my grace will not leave you. Calling and rebirth, not even those words say to me what the word grace says to me. And all those worldly meanings, living on charity, taking advantage of generosity, all those proofs of favour, no. Forgiveness of sins? Marks of favour? No. Perhaps mercy is closest, after all. But there is in the word grace a lightning-like power, a light-saturated moment, a vision that fills you and stays with you even when you have apparently forgotten it. I sat murmuring to myself, looked up at the wintry cupola, later in the evening looked at the sky, how unfathomable and limitless it is. Memories from grandmother's Bible appeared and shone strangely, even when I had gone to bed. I thought about whether they were right, the words in the Book of Moses about 'I have been a stranger in a strange land', and the Book of Chronicles' 'our days in the earth are like a shadow', and something rose up against this: my days have been filled with darkness and light and all the colours of the rainbow, I have felt at home in many places, but not truly at home, except sometimes in myself; but in the room I now sit in I am no longer at home. Just as well that I leave it. Don't you think?

Was it an appeal, a rhetorical question, an assertion of fact? She looked at me with a smile. In the silence the room was crossed by a tremor. The wind had begun to blow. I expect it was a windless day when I was born, I said, those who are born on a windless day become blockheads. And the other winds, asked Viktoria, nervously lighting a cigarette, the now quite pale eyes blinked, I held her hand with the match and brought the flame to her face, that old, strangely disturbing map of the world, she wanted to blow out the flame herself. The children of the west wind, I said, they shall have food and clothes. The children of the north wind receive wounds and give wounds. The children of the south wind receive honey and fruits, in their house they will entertain bishops and good musicians, but the east wind is the best, those who are born in it will never suffer want. Then I suppose you are both west and north, and southerly wind, but as for the east wind, then it all depends on what you mean by want. Outer or inner. If it is inner, then I am not a child of the east wind, I said.

We sat again in the familiar silence that was our common estate. We listened and heard the city. There were the metro, the harbour, the trams, the wind from the sea, the odour of fish, the smell of mash, the snow's immense water-scent, the howling of the ambulance, the tango from the radio, the creaking of the dying trees, the voices from city districts like ice floes colliding in the circulation of my blood, voices from long ago, in summer rooms:

'When I die I'll be a tree.'

'When I die I'll be a bird in that tree.'

'When I die I'll be earth, and nothing else.'

50 The December Festival

The December day dawned with a clear, sparkling sky. The north wind came, first as a scarcely visible turbulence sweeping up the light snow from the ground like a veil among the motionless trees. It slowly gathered strength, making the houses move closer together, without giving one another a look. With black window eyes, with tar-combed metal roofs, with uneasily swaying chimney-pots they rose beneath a moon that had been lashed white by the snow to the point of invisibility. It was time for the annually recurring December festival. I had just turned fifty. I walked into a new decade with no ideas.

The festive procession, the procession of fools assembled in the darkness of the gateway and walked slowly along with grey billowing veils, indistinct forms on high stilts, lanterns shining above mask-like faces, snow-powdered and bleeding red. Bundles in disguises staggered along. I hurried down the murmuring flight of stairs and positioned myself by the door. The wind was steadily increasing, beating with drunken contempt on roofs and doors. Pale faces came and went in the windows, while children, stuffed and wadded like bales of hay, ran shouting between the lit torches and their parents blew on their blue-frozen hands, stamped their feet and shouted inaudible words to one another. Struggling against the wind the procession fluttered along like a grotesque full-rigged vessel in a gale. It approached the door of the Old Theatre which once a year came to life for this invocation of darkness in which both living and dead took part. No one knew the age of the blood-red theatre, as it waited, squeezed between younger edifices, waiting for December's tidings: the crest of the darkness and the light's slow return, the imminent presence of the summer solstice. From all the staircases, all the flats, through all the creaking and thundering doors, illumined by the roaming light from the building's own electricity transformer that shook as on the verge of collapse, the inhabitants came streaming, joined together in an obscure mass, turned back, shouldered their way through again, following the lunging and shouting of the procession. Did I glimpse Prologos there in his black cloak, were those Olof Urwind's yellow teeth exposed there in a corpse-stiff face, was that Granny shuffling along, bent to the ground but with her eyes gleaming with the fire of the underworld? Was that her hauling at coarse ropes, was that an old waggon passing there with the love of my youth, Lena with her flying brown hair, Fanny, clung round by a fat Petri in striped pyjamas, prison dress, almost? His wife the Bergsrådinna kept rapping him on the head with an umbrella without cease, but not a sound was heard. Together, hip against hip, Mr and Mrs Dahlgren clung firmly to the doors of an old, snow-filled Oldsmobile, shielded only by Emerentia Busch's red parasol. Behind the floats came a lemming migration of children, swinging their lanterns and dressed by Aunt Inna in yellow carnival costumes with breasts and bottoms shamelessly bare, powdered white with snow. And after them in a tar-smelling sleigh Grandmother and the rest of the Cedermarks came gliding, mildly gazing, smiling and dead. And there, in the throng, I glimpsed the boy in the woollen sweater and the knitted cap, beating a rusty old drum; in a flash he was gone again.

Perhaps you remember that I put an arm around you in order to borrow some of your warmth? With an empty gaze the Leather Jacket went past, chewing gum, stopped in front of us, drew a revolver, fired, and from the barrel, aimed at my heart, a little blue balloon flew out and rose like a smile into the sky. Wildly pedalling a bicycle, rigged up on a platform drawn by two piebald ponies, sat Herman Stilén with Beda bulging over the back carrier, a gigantic bearskin cap rested on his misty spectacles while Beda clung to him like an octopus in pink tights. A long row of rigidly staring placard-bearers in narrow pointed caps moved past, there were Pierrot and Columbine, I thought I glimpsed Bernt's blinking eyes as he tottered past on his childishly short stilts. Calmly, by herself, walked Hedvig Rosendal supporting Roald Berg, we thought they had moved abroad long ago, I shouted to them but they did not hear me. The role of Epilogos had been given to Viktoria. Supported by two young men in tutus she strode along with dignity in the blue-turning snow in her black fur coat and vanished with the others into the gloom of the theatre.

Now the inhabitants jostled forwards and in towards the velvet darkness, into the powder-scented seashell where we sank down into our chairs in blind expectancy. The enormous curtain billowed slowly into the auditorium as the wind blew outside, it had sneaked its way between props and ropes, hung about in the winding-loft, and was now blowing at the curtain as into a sail, so that the whole of the Old Theatre tugged at its moorings like an old ship, trying to put to sea, in clear contravention of the harbour authorities' stipulations. Dreamers and scoffers sat together cold-eyed and burning in the dark auditorium, and everyone's breath rose like smoke and became a single breath in the compact, whirling spotlight, so sharp that some children tried to walk on it. Up towards the ceiling with its painted flying clouds chalk-white faces leaned from the rows, moon-pale teeth were exposed, skulls lined up along the velvet barriers and black mouths were opened in surprise or horror: out came the Skeleton Man, studying as he rubbed his long hands the entrails in the enormous pot that Beda had groaningly dragged out in an old rattan perambulator. From its intestines, shrouded in vapours, rose the three witches, in shrill voices singing an innocent folk-song whose words were drowned in the audience's applause and whistling. Above us now the gigantic chandelier began to slowly sway, or was it the theatre itself, shaking to its foundations, so that the scenery on the stage pounded up clouds of dust, strangely traversed by snowflakes? Tableaux, glowing with inner tension or icily rigid, moved forward, there were the spring's pure green and the summer's forest of grass, there were the rooms of burning autumn and December's fires, there were ovation upon ovation like a rainstorm on resonant sheet metal.

Now the light became muted, all grew still and Gabriel appeared. We could not see his eyes but heard his voice: It is time to end. What we have seen and experienced is inexplicable, kaleidoscopic, like life itself. We seek and ask: What are we? 'Already at dawn the air is filled with countless pictures, and the eye is their lover' says the great Leonardo. He also says: 'The coloured patches on walls or the clouds in the sky are like the ringing of bells that contains all the sounds and shapes that can be imagined.' And what does the great Shakespeare say about our rooms and habitations? 'The poet's eye, in a fine frenzy rolling,/ Doth glance from heaven to earth, from earth to heaven,/ And, as imagination bodies forth/ The forms of things unknown, the poet's pen/ Turns them to shapes, and gives to airy nothing/ A local habitation and a name.' In these habitations we live. Of airy nothing are we made, to airy nothing do we return. See, above us opens the sky, cold and clear, strewn with stars, but we are here, earthbound for a moment in eternity, evil and good in bitter blending, and it is our task to tell them apart, evil and good, false and genuine, play and seriousness, dream and reality. Courage exists, I know it, mercy exists, and sharp perception. Feel with the eye, see the heart! I bid you good night and pass the conductor's baton to Daniel Urwind, he has the power to switch off our world revue, our life-music, and conjure forth a longed-for silence. Daniel, be so good!

A feverish horror washes through me, I get up, I would like to shout that such a power belongs to no one but God, I open my mouth but can't get a sound out, nothing is audible, the silence fills the auditorium to bursting point, the white faces whirl away, the rows fall empty, the scenery splits, the theatre opens, the darkness floods in and carries me away.

51 The Grateful Eye

It gets dark early, and the blackness finds its way in behind the eyes. The house suffers from rheumatism and cracks appear in the staircase. A smell of fried onions blows like a fatty breathing from the Arvidssons' door. Has Berg acquired a new grandfather? Or has he shrunk? He opens the door slightly, glides a little way out, grey-soiled and badly put together, with those pale eyes like buttons sewed firmly into their sockets. But with a rapid jerk he draws back inside again, and the door slams shut. In the white snow of the courtyard that is glowing with its own light through the landing window glides a car, a magpie flies up chattering into the nearest tree. I look up at Viktoria's window, but it is doused and dead. I unlock the door to the back room, no one has been there for a while, I light the lamp, put your letter on the table, sit down and lean my head in my hands. Do you think I welcome every ghost-like image that comes along? They pull and tear at me, they construct my unsuccessful life, they say something about me but I am no longer here. What I am looking for lies outside what I have jotted down. The text that is closest to me is silence, it exists there behind the words, not the shadow of the words but the perhaps a shadow of that silence. The important thing is not to give explanations but to point to the inexplicable that gives our existence its important antipole: so that our lives can preserve their balance. In your science, too, the irrational exists. The dream makes reality tangible, the myth makes it possible to understand, the fairytale makes it possible to be lived. Without the light from dreams the clearest facts are incomplete, lifeless.

It is cold now, and clear, as once in Viktoria's cathedral where birds found a refuge from the cold, but it is a clarity that jars on the eye. I long for days of mildness and mist, in them I thrive. Even the business of the secondhand bookshop goes better on mild days when the lamps can be lit all day and the shadows are not too harsh. Then the demands are less, the atmosphere for work is better, and the mind is calm. If one reads a book on a day like that the text speaks more softly and penetratingly than on a day like this. On soft days I can, like Antipova in Varykino's library, read 'not as though reading were the loftiest and most remarkable activity, but the only possible one, something which even the animals could do. As though she were bearing water from a spring, or peeling potatoes.' Exactly. I think I have been peeling potatoes all my life, especially when you are gone. I wonder if Hamlet ever held a potato in his hand?

I sit at your writing-desk, see the book lying open, smell your fragrance, see your hand-mirror, the nearer your things are, the more mysterious. The coffee cup in the kitchen, the bread-knife, the pushed-back chair, the pad of drawings: between all these objects there is a silent understanding, often closer than the one between human beings. The older we get, the greater the risk that we cut ourselves off from ourselves. But on the other side: when I see myself at a certain distance, I am seized by a new alertness that makes me more comprehensible to myself, and somewhat comical.

To continue the private philosophizing (is there really any other?): How will all this look when we are gone? How is it that this thought makes me feel sadness and relief at the same time? Why do my thoughts go backwards when they ought to point forwards? Because the sky is high, clear and cold? It is a war sky, I was at most two years old, lay looking straight up into that high sky in which silent aeroplanes now draw their white parallel trails. Down in the courtyard an old man staggers through the snow. I try to remember your dear voice. I go through one change of skin after the other, old man that I am. What emerges is child's skin. Is that shameful? At any rate, nothing can remain unchanged. If I seek stillness I hear the tinkling of the piano from the flat upstairs, a screaming crow is thrown like a flake of soot from nowhere over the roof-tops, up the staircase come heavy steps as though someone were on the way here with a message that will topple everything over. I live on a low flame, but even it burns its way through sheets and bed-base to you who turn away. Why in my dreams do you turn your back to me? Your strong, supple back? I sit here with my heavy floating face, the stubble grows but the heart shrinks. The unafraid walk across the bridges without getting dizzy, but I go plunging down.

I try to recapitulate: I have given you what I could, not much, some dreams only, a little scaffolding around an inner structure, fear and happiness mingled together. What is the meaning of it all? The meaning of life? That it must be lived, lived through. I feel as though in a single year I had gone from being a child via the life of an adult back to the utterly simple, grateful eye and what it sees. Come, sit beside me, let us talk, let us sit silently.

52 Later

Let us talk, let us sit silently! My prayers have been granted beyond measure. You have talked, we have sat silently. Christmas is over, with its heavy silence. You are here, you are absent. I noticed that as soon as you arrived, a day earlier than expected. I was happy, I consciously ignored what was not said between us, your hipbone was so cool, you did not resist, did not take part, afterwards I noticed you were crying, I asked: What's happened? You replied: Later. Give me a little time.

'Later': it has lain hidden, in the emotions, in the walls, in the room, among the rubbish in the attic, in the darkness of the cellar: later. It settled like a silence over Christmas Eve, Lena who had come to stay noticed it, was exaggeratedly brisk, afterwards we sat, when she had gone to bed in her old room, and looked at the Christmas tree, we had gone through the rituals, they were dead, we had read Jan's long letter, he is going to come back and resume his medical studies, we were pleased about it, then we sat silent again. Later, I said, is that now? And you leaned forward, you said that I had been in your thoughts all year, that you had met a man who had changed your life, he had left you but come back, you don't know where he belongs, whether you should go or stay, at any rate you will travel back, you couldn't write about it, you had to get time to think it over. From whom, from whom? From him, the stranger, or from me? I could have torn down the heavens, my mouth is ashes, I wanted to stammer out that my reserves of patience are exhausted. Something sickening and bitter is rising in me. Where now are the resources of the imagination, the wild world of dreams, who will help me now, when I am truly alone? Where you're going, no one has been before you! Wasn't that how I persuaded myself? Thousands have been here before me, the ground has been trampled by the deceived, a swamp, the marsh water rises to my throat.

Christmas morning with darkness and faint dawn. I could scarcely hear your breathing. I quietly get up, go into the living-room and stand by the window. Down there a few lonely lights are burning. The earth turns, creaking, before my frozen eye. All that rubbish we gather around us, archives of wisdom, stolen and saved-up! It has all been aimed at this, this lonely hour. All is open and unexplained, inexplicable. If you are to reach him you must go through me, you must know that, you said: Wait. You looked at me as though I were something familiar you had only now discovered. Was my gaze the same? Is it when we are driven out of ourselves that we truly begin to see? That birthmark on your temple there, oughtn't you to have it operated away, I say. I stretch out my hand, you don't move away, lean your head in my hand.

Later: that word! The concert on Boxing Day was in the end, as you realized, intolerable for me. Music, at funerals and farewells: painful. The old, hackneyed Bach Air, of course, lucky I had an aisle seat and could get out, sat and looked at a poster of a tree, a trunk with two doors, a hovering globe, a house with a lighted window, what did it represent? Bach, played to pieces, and I too. This nameless and tormenting thing we have to go through. Eyes and tears. You mercifully let me sit there alone for a while. I thought of something you said, something your grandfather said, that the moon eats clouds and shakes wind. It just appeared before me, without meaning. Then you came out, we went home together. We sat with Lena at the kitchen table, outside wet snow was falling, it settles coolingly on hot skin. Out to sea a pale streak of light is visible, the ice has not yet formed, a new year is close.

53 In a Cold Gateway

The snow stopped falling when I came back from the airport, it brightened up. The wind is stronger, streets open in various directions. I have gone through myself, the unknown in myself, and come out into a cold gateway. I stand on ice and asphalt. So many dead people in the earth beneath me. This incomprehensible life, it cannot be explained, only built. I have nothing more to say. Before you left, I went up to the attic. There lay a few pathetic remnants of my wings, the bamboo ribs, the whole spectacle. When I lifted my gaze I saw a young lad there, on a ledge, ready to go plunging down and dare the impossible. For a moment our gazes met. Perhaps, when we lie broken, a wind will carry us? Each day is a little lighter than the last. In the air, in the wind I sign my name.